THE
HALLOWED
KNIGHT

WILDE JUSTICE, BOOK 3

JENN STARK

Books by Jenn Stark

Wilde Justice Series

The Red King
The Lost Queen
The Hallowed Knight

Immortal Vegas Series

Getting Wilde
Wilde Card
Born To Be Wilde
Wicked And Wilde
Aces Wilde
Forever Wilde
Wilde Child
Call of the Wilde
Running Wilde
Wilde Fire

One Wilde Night (prequel novella)

Demon Enforcers series

For Elewyn
Shine on.

KNIGHT OF PENTACLES.

Chapter One

The first rule of the hustle is — everyone's hustling something. And nobody hustles nothing like clairvoyants at a psychic fair.

"A reading with Mistress Malificorem?"

I blinked down at the young, towheaded boy in front of me. He wore loose leggings and a hand-sewn tunic with a prominent Celtic tree of life symbol embroidered into it, and like most of the people at the fair, he looked like a time traveler from an era predating plumbing. Unlike the other guests, he held up a postcard. I took it from him automatically, if only to lighten the enormous stack he gripped in his slender hand.

Mistress Malificorem was apparently in tent #370 at the far end of the space given over to the Las Vegas Joyful Spirit Psychic Festival. She promised to reveal more than I wanted to know for the low, low price of fifty dollars per half hour. The card was printed on plain black stock, with bright red and white lettering that felt almost wet to the touch, though it didn't smear. Still, there was something about the promo piece that legit creeped me out. So, way to go, Mistress Malificorem.

"She paying you to help her?" I asked the child, whose pale blue eyes and winsome smile seemed at odds with the fell tidings of his employer.

"*Fifty dollars*, just to hand these out," he said eagerly, his voice flush with pride. He even sounded Irish, and I'd already noticed that this particular psychic fair had drawn more than its share of Emerald Islanders. "If enough people show her the cards from this stack, she may have me help her tomorrow too."

I smiled at his enthusiasm, waving the card dry as I watched him scamper off. Then I scanned the grounds, which were packed. Late April in Vegas was still cool enough to host an outdoor festival without fear of people keeling over from heat exhaustion. Even better, the garden-like setting of the preserve, with its natural flora carefully roped off from the tents, carny barkers, and food stations, made the festival one of the premier non-Strip events in the city. I hadn't realized it had become so Celtic focused, but then again, I didn't usually stay in town long enough to visit any of the local sights. When the psychic festival flyer showed up in my office this morning, however, I figured I should check it out.

Because the flyer didn't show up in the morning mail — it arrived via pneumatic tube.

Which meant it wasn't an advertisement. It was a cry for help.

As Justice of the Arcana Council, I was both the 9-1-1 dispatcher and first responder for such cries, as well as the official archiver of every complaint ever leveled against the magic wielders of the world. The short version of my job description was that I helped folks who were victims of psychics behaving badly. The long version involved fireballs, self-generating handcuffs, extensive frequent flyer miles, and a deep and recurring need for more librarians.

Since there'd been no Justice in the position for two hundred years, there was a considerable backlog of cases, all lining the stacks at Justice Hall. Nevertheless, the freshest requests took precedence, since they usually involved either victims or assailants who still walked among the living. Much easier to conduct interviews that way.

So, here I was, along a path that took me deep into a tent city of Irish-themed vendors. Unfortunately, the number scrawled on the flyer—167—went to a tent that didn't exist in the middle of Celtlandia. Which wasn't a great beginning for my search-and-rescue mission.

"Yo! Dollface." In keeping with the cosplay vibe of the festival, Nikki Dawes strode toward me in the guise of Tolkien's Galadriel—all-white gown, long blonde wig, and ice-blue eyes. The effect was spoiled only a little by the giant cups of beer she was balancing on a cardboard box of churro strips. Nikki, my right-hand woman since my earliest days in Sin City, could always make a look work. Even a look dusted in cinnamon and sugar.

"This is your idea of dinner?" I asked, taking one of the beers from her.

"It'll dial you down a notch. You're not even dressed appropriately."

I glanced down at my jeans, light hoodie, and sneakers. "It's Throwback Thursday."

Nikki waved a churro stick at me. "That would mean you actually committed to leaving your wardrobe by Hot Topic behind. Justice of the Universe or not, you still suck in the superhero costume department."

I reached into the front pocket of my hoodie with the hand not clutching my beer and pulled out my deck of

Tarot cards. "When you can come up with an haute couture pullover with pockets, you let me know."

At that moment, two little girls shrieking with delight burst past us, surrounded by a puff of bubbles that popped like gossamer kisses on our cheeks before we could flinch away. I swung my beer hand high to avoid splattering their strawberry-blonde pigtails. That left my card hand exposed, and the deck went flying.

"Oh — sorry! Sorry!" To their credit, the little girls stopped immediately and gathered up the cards, shoving them back at me while Nikki gamely held my beer. I didn't miss that some of the cards were facing upright, of course. When the universe beats you over the head with a message involving a Tarot deck, it generally was wise to pay attention.

In this case, though, the cards were a decided drag: the Moon, Five of Wands, and Ten of Swords: Something you never expected is about to hit you square in the face, there's gonna be a fight, and someone will be betrayed. It was either a hint of things to come or the beginning of a country song. Either way, it didn't sound good.

"You missed a card." As I took my first sip of beer, a young woman sporting colorful fairy wings on her back popped out from her tent and plucked an errant card from the ground, grimacing at it before she handed it to me. "Ah, Death," she said sagely. "You should sit a spell with me. Have a reading."

"Thanks, no." I smiled my apology, then took the card from her and stuck it into my pocket. So Death too. That could mean...any number of things. Transformation. Actual death. Or even a visit from one of my new coworkers on the Arcana Council. Right now, I wasn't up for any of those options, at least not until I finished my beer.

I took another long draught and thought about said coworkers. The Arcana Council was a group of ridiculously strong seers, sorcerers, and damned-near demigods whose abilities were grounded in the Tarot. Their immortal life's work was to keep magic balanced in the world, and in the wake of the recent influx of magic, that work had become hella challenging. As the Council's aforementioned first Justice in two hundred years, I'd been brought on board to help with the overflow of magical cases. Unfortunately, like most things Council related, the job hadn't come with a manual.

I returned my focus to Nikki, who was eyeing the woman's gossamer wings with renewed appreciation. "What did you find out? And no. I'm not buying wings. Don't even think it."

She sighed. "You would look *amazing* in wings. But we weren't imagining the weird energy of this show. This year's the biggest psychic fair they've run. Connecteds and con artists alike filled the vendor slots in record time, starting back in late November when they officially announced the dates."

"Late November…" I grimaced. It'd been a doozy of a holiday season this past year for the psychics of the world, psychics whose skills ran from fifty-cent card tricks to astral-traveling futurism. Collectively, they were known as the Connected. While every living thing possessed a certain connection to the world around it, Connecteds possessed a higher level of psychic abilities. They made up an international psychic community of individuals who operated largely in ignorance of each other, but who together had been a slowly growing force for centuries.

And as of late November, they'd gotten a woo booster like no other in the aftermath of an epic clash of spectral forces, as a small group of the most powerful magicians on the planet had successfully prevented the gods of yore from coming back to Earth. We'd won, but there'd been some fallout. Some decidedly magical fallout.

Basically, unbeknownst to most of the planet, psychic Earth was now rocking it old style.

"Yep," Nikki continued. "Normally, the mix at this festival is your standard slate of Tarot readers, aura photographers, channelers to help you connect to loved ones, that sort of thing. This year, they have all that and more—hypnotists, healers, animal communicators, wizards, warlocks, and a whole new subclass of spectral opposition warriors. Basically, everything you need to arm yourself against all things magical."

My brows went up. "Arm—you mean like the chain-mail-and-hatchet guy we saw near the gates?"

Nikki fended off my concern with a wave of her churro stick. "Not like him—or at least, not exactly, though let me tell you, that was some mighty fine chain mail. These are folk who offer spelled charms to protect people from magical attacks. Charms, not traditional weapons. No guns, no super-sharp pointy things, no mallets. Easily fifteen tents in this place are spectral opposition warrior tents, though, and apparently, this year, they're hotter than the tantric love healers."

"I don't want to know."

"Which is a personality flaw, you ask me." Nikki grinned. "Attendance is up too—record numbers by a long shot, maybe twenty thousand coming through the gate today alone. The organizers, George and Melinda Carlton, are over the crescent moon."

"And they haven't had any trouble?" I glanced down the row of tents, my gaze catching on two young women in long white gowns and tiaras, giggling over one of the stands of jewelry.

"They have not." Nikki took a long drink of her beer. "They've actually never had trouble here, surprisingly enough, even though it's a little bit of a hike from their usual hunting grounds. They own the Light Spirit Metaphysical Wellness Center over in Summerlin."

I considered that. "Kind of a fancy location for a psychic shop."

"Not a psychic shop, a *Metaphysical Wellness Center*," Nikki corrected me. "And business is booming, in case you were wondering. Best ever holiday season, and they've been hopping since the New Year. It seems like everyone's wanting to discover if they've got any woo in their blood, and the Carltons are more than happy to assure them that yes, in fact, they do."

"Nothing wrong with that." I voiced another concern that'd been building in the back of my mind since we'd arrived at the festival. "There's an awful lot of Celtic-themed tents here. There a reason for that?"

"Not that anyone can figure out, no," Nikki said, surprising me. "The Carltons are pure New Agers, not adhering to any particular bent for their woo, but they would agree with you on the influx of the Neo-Celt presence."

"Neo-Celts?"

"Yup, that's what they're calling themselves. After the spectral opposition warriors, it's the second biggest uptick in vendor type. We got Beltane coming up in a few days, but the festival will be over before then. So maybe they're just in the mood for a party."

Nikki glanced ahead, and narrowed her eyes. "Yo, we've got spectral opposition warrior land dead ahead. Be casual."

I glanced up, blinking as I took in two massive thugs in desert camo gear flanking the entrance to a row of tents. We were treated to a soft mist of cooling water as we crossed the threshold into the section, though fortunately it wasn't hot enough to make such precautions necessary. Still, it felt nice.

I glanced around the tidy formation of tents. "Well, this is kind of impressive. They've got their own warrior 'hood."

She nodded. "This where the problem is, you think? Not the tree-of-life huggers?"

"Gotta be." I gestured ahead. "X marks the spot." Before us was a tent fronted by a small, temporary placard stuck into the ground: 167.

"Lemme finish this up," Nikki said, downing the last of her beer and fried bread as I dropped my own half-finished ale in a trash can set off to the side. I didn't think I'd need to have both hands free to inspect a business that called itself "Spectral Opposition Warrior Services," but a girl couldn't be too careful.

The door flaps to the tent were staked open wide, and the place was overflowing with trinkets, jewelry, wall hangings, and chimes, as well as an entire side given over to pots of herbs and stacks of little plastic sleeves for your own personal holistic go-bag. I counted three bright-eyed attendants, none of whom seemed all that prepossessing, but no obvious owner. There were a dozen or so festivalgoers milling along the U-shaped pathway pawing all the junk, so we joined their number.

"Look at this." Nikki pointed at a small, highly polished amulet on a spongy cushion. "Mind Blocker—prevents someone from reading your thoughts."

"I'm more interested in the fireguard," I murmured, squinting at my own find—a small pot of slimy-looking unguent, looking suspiciously like Vicks VapoRub.

"Protects you from the damaging effects of spectral fire."

Nikki looked over. "Only spectral? Or all fire?"

"Only spectral, but who knew it was that common a threat?" I used fire on a near-daily basis as part of my job, blue fire perfectly sized for throwing, good for just about anything that ailed me. Apparently, I wasn't the only one.

"You *came*." A compact man suddenly appeared on the other side of the table. His eyes were a bright and piercing green, his skin pale and dusted with freckles, and his hair a thatch of pale orange and bright white curls. The perfect Irish grandpa. "You came, you surely did."

"You know who I am?"

"Who? Who, I can't say, exactly. But I know *what* you are. And what you are is enough, because we don't have much time." He shifted his glance to the left and right, then leaned forward.

I leaned back. "And you are?"

"Seamus McCarthy, leastwise that's what I'm usually called in the open." He flashed a grin, his tone light despite the seriousness of his next words. "But they're coming. Tonight, we think. We'd hoped they'd hold off until the festival closed for the evening, but we worry they'll come earlier while the world holds fast to sleep."

"They who?" I asked, trying to follow his words without getting caught up in the lyrical cadence of his speech. It was harder than I would have expected.

"The ancient ones," he said, with a reverence bordering on awe. "Even more powerful than I would've believed. It's a fae wind that blows no good, I tell you that plain."

"Ahhh...you contacted me about a fairy problem?" Despite the man's sense of urgency, I deflated a little. I had precious little time as it was; I couldn't waste it on pixie dust. "Explain. Are you planning a turf war with the Neo-Celts on the other side of the fairgrounds, is that what this is? Because, no offense, but from your appearance, I'd think you were one of them."

To my surprise, the man's gravity only deepened. "And I was one of them, exactly so, until the Green Knight started acting the maggot. He's dangerous. He truly is."

The Green Knight? I kept my expression neutral as I tried for casual. I hated not knowing what was going on in the Connected community, especially now that I was supposed to be policing it. The Green Knight sounded like something I should've been on top of. "Oh, him."

"Yes, *him*. A druid who should know better, given all his training. But no. Instead of fearing the gods and protecting those of us who've already defeated them once, he welcomes the Tuatha dé Danann back to Earth with open arms."

Whoa, whoa, whoa. So not fairies, then. Actual straight-up gods. Beside me, Nikki straightened.

"He's already reached out to them?" I asked. Given the full-on Celtic love fest going on around me, I could see how a summons of the ancient gods of the Irish might happen. We'd already pushed back a legit run from the gods last winter, so the only way new ones could wander in was if a human invited them. Which humans rarely seemed to tire of doing. Never mind that gods were bad news, especially the super pretty sparkling ones. Always. Full stop.

"He's done worse." Seamus grimaced. "He summoned their ancient enemies as well, the Fomorians. Which is why it's good you've come, it is.

16

My fellow spectral opposition warriors have been talking since we all arrived, long into the night, and we're not wrong. There's already a *movement* of the ancient ones underway, facilitated by the Green Knight and his zealots. The old gods from the lost ages are coming back into the light. They're seeing what we've done to the planet that was their gift to us. They're not happy, not at all. And they're plotting to take it back, by any means possible."

"You know, maybe we should start over at the beginning."

"I'm telling you, there's no time," Seamus said. "You're strong, I can feel it in you. From what I hear, you're the strongest member of the Council after the Magician, and he's nervous you're going to become even more powerful than he is, mark my words."

"Where exactly did you hear that?" I asked sharply, while Nikki kicked my ankle. Even through my socks, the pain made me blink. The elven boots she was rocking did not mess around.

"That's of no consequence. What you need to understand is this, Justice Wilde. No matter how strong you are, the spectral opposition warriors can make you stronger," Seamus continued, leaning forward again. "We can spread your word to all who would hear, extend your reach throughout the world, and defend the weak against the strong. And well we should. Because we've run out of time. The Green Knight is ready to strike."

Nikki fixed her gaze on the man. "Lookit, buddy, you want us to knock some heads, you need to start talking and fast. *Who's* coming, exactly, what do they look like, who are they affiliated with, and what's their dice roll on strength?"

He swung his gaze to her. "You think I'm lying."

She shrugged. "Honestly? No. Your little calling card showed up in Justice Wilde's in-box today, so I'm willing to believe you're telling the truth. But there's something about this place that's making me twitch, and I want to know what it is."

"Fine." Seamus thrust out his hand, and I jolted in surprise. How had he known what Nikki's unique talent was?

Still, she didn't hesitate. She reached out and grabbed his wrist, her eyes going sharp. Nikki had the ability to read anyone's memories. Not their thoughts, not their plans, simply the way a particular individual had seen the world up to this point—all their collected memories, with an emphasis on any traumatic experiences. This skill set had helped tremendously when she'd been a cop, but it'd also come in handy in the years since as well. And now she dropped the Irishman's arm like it was crawling with bugs.

"*How* did you let this happen?" she demanded of him. "You had *one* job."

"I know," Seamus groaned as I swung my gaze between them. "I'm the Green Knight's sponsor, his mentor. And, most damning of all, his father. But when he started down this path, I didn't realize what he planned to do. I've failed, I know I have."

"Yeah, and you need to un-fail, right quick," Nikki said. "There's not going to be a fairy war in Vegas, boyo. We're totally not zoned for that."

I jolted. "Wait, what?"

"It's already started, don't you see?" the old man keened. "Why do you think I'm here? The most powerful druid in Christendom has summoned the ancient ones with rites far darker than he understands, and you have to stop him before it's too late."

An earsplitting howl erupted directly behind us. Nikki and I whirled, both of us instinctively clapping our hands over our ears.

"*Banshee*," the old man gasped. "Someone will die this night!

CHAPTER TWO

The sound abruptly cut off, but our tent emptied anyway, everyone screaming and running in opposite directions. Nikki and I fought our way through the small crowd to find an old woman on the ground, her hands up, her head bowed, her entire body shaking like a dandelion in a hurricane. Standing over her were two bulky men in long robes, menacingly holding small rods that glowed at the end…as if there was any other way you could hold a small rod that glowed at the end.

"Is that a cattle prod?" I demanded, striding forward. To my surprise, the men fell back with immediate and obvious deference. That was weird.

The woman on the ground, barely more than a huddle of blankets, didn't attempt to crawl away. She didn't attempt to do anything but shiver. "What's going on here?" I pressed.

"She sought to bring the blighted fae upon us," the man to the right said, his voice awed. "We won't allow it. We're warded."

I nodded, glancing to Nikki. As big as these yahoos were, the fact that they backed down so quickly from me didn't sit quite right. It almost made me think...

Cosplay? I mouthed to her, and her eyes lit up. This could be all an act, a show for the paying guests. Lord knew there were enough of them standing in a circle around us, staring in wonder.

"Okay, well, ah, go easy on her," I hazarded, though my hands had started tingling. Tingling hands weren't a good sign, but it was probably because the woman remained curled up on the ground, trembling like it was her job. "She may have wandered into the wrong place, a harmless old woman trying to get to the food carts."

I expected the men to look mutinous, but instead, they crossed their glow sticks over their chests. "Justice," they said, almost reverently.

Err...also weird.

"Right," I confirmed to no one in particular, and I nudged the woman's foot. "As for you, stop screaming bloody murder in the middle of psychic fairs. You stress people out with that kind of thing."

"Nooooo," she moaned beneath me, and I looked down at her more sharply. Had the glow thugs done more damage than I'd realized?

I crouched down, leaning close, but hesitated to put my hands on the old woman. For one thing, my fingers were positively sparking at this point, and she'd been traumatized enough. Getting shocked by my overeager fists of flame wouldn't help anyone. For another, there was something still super odd about all this.

As if reading my thoughts, Nikki approached from the other side, squatting next to the woman as well. The woman's hair was a tangled mass of gray spilling over her shoulders, but all Nikki needed to do was connect with her actual skin for a moment, and she'd get the information she needed.

"Let me help you up," Nikki said.

"No!" The woman moved so fast, I nearly stumbled back, turning to me with a face that — well, it wasn't a face at all. It was ice and shadow and a mouth that took up most of the real estate where her nose and cheeks should have been. Nikki still managed to get a grip on her.

"Bomb!" Nikki shouted as the woman wrenched her robe open.

I didn't wait around for the details. I lurched forward, wrapping up the woman in my arms and enveloping us both in my trademark fire burst that would simultaneously distract everyone nearby and allow me to blast this bitch straight to Judgment —

"You dare!" She screeched again, and to my shock, she twisted and writhed in my grip, my hands passing right through her. As my blue fire leapt around us, creating a shield that blocked us from the outside world, I tried once, twice to get a fix on her wriggling form. I got nothing but a handful of robes for my trouble, and even that was difficult to manage. Then the woman's unearthly howl rose up, up, up to the heavens a second time…and, poof. It blanked out. I was left with the smoking ruins of a shawl.

The fire fell away, burning out as quickly as it had surged —

And the crowd surrounding me burst into wild applause.

I whirled around, trying to make sense of what I was seeing. Nikki stood next to me, a protective arm stretched out in front of me while her body blocked the crowd in a menacing pose, while the two men with glow sticks formed similar poses, boxing everyone out. They needn't have bothered. The onlookers immediately started breaking up, and the chatter that reached me was excited, satisfied—and off-putting.

"Oh my *God*, was that even in the schedule?" one girl with spiked pink hair sticking out from her head in all directions demanded of her friends. "That should totally have been in the schedule."

"That was so much better than the guy with the saw," somebody else agreed from the other side.

"Did she kill that old lady?" These hiccupping, slurred words were nearly drowned out by the ones that came after in a far more authoritative tone.

"Dude, it was totally faked. That was some sort of doll that broke apart—you remember seeing anything until she started screaming and got knocked to the ground? No. She showed up out of nowhere. Total crash dummy."

I grimaced, not sure if I was happy that people were so clueless, or concerned at how willing people were to see only what they wanted to see. I patted Nikki's shoulder to let her know I was okay, not yet trusting myself to talk. I winced as the smell of burnt hair hit my nostrils. Oh well. I was due for a haircut anyway.

She straightened, then took the shawl away from me. "You sent her to Gamon?"

Gamon was Judgment of the Arcana Council—sort of my meaner, tougher, older cousin who'd just gotten out of juvie. Once I was called to intervene where some member of the Connected community was wreaking havoc, my job was to deliver the perp to Judgment. In her newfound role, Gamon tended to favor punishing first, asking questions later. I usually had no problem with that. Most of the asshats I'd delivered to her were more than deserving of her wrath.

Only, I hadn't sent the wailing witch to Gamon. Instead, the woman had ghosted. Literally.

"I tried to." I coughed. My ears still rang from the woman's screech. "There wasn't enough of her to send. And sweet Christmas, that scream at the end."

Nikki quirked a glance at me. "What scream at the end?"

"You're safe?" asked a big guy as he and his buddy moved toward us.

I looked down at my hoodie and jeans. Not so much as an ember burn on them. I was getting better at this all the time.

"I'm safe," I acknowledged, not missing the sigh of relief that went through the warrior detail. Who were these guys?

"And so the gauntlet has been thrown." Seamus McCarthy emerged from his hidey-hole and pulled what was left of the old woman's shawl from Nikki, turning it over in his hands. "A banshee, who stared Justice full in the face before you killed her dead."

I flinched. "Pretty sure I didn't kill her, I sent her to Judgment. Then again, I was kind of distracted by the bomb, so no promises."

"Hold up there, Sparky," Nikki said, her hands going up. "Who said anything about a bomb?"

Real anger didn't steal upon me unawares; it lit me up, from my crown to my now-sparking fingers. "*You* did," I snapped. "That there was a bomb, that the woman was carrying a bomb."

I shot an irritated glance to the nearest thug with the glow stick. "You heard her say it, didn't you?"

He shook his head. "I heard her cry out, but I thought she said 'gun.' I rushed forward to help, and then was pushed back by your mighty wall of flame."

His voice was filled with awe. I felt a migraine coming on.

"Right. And you?" I asked the other guy.

"I thought she yelled 'stop,' but I didn't know who to stop, so I turned to hold back the crowd. But then there was the screaming."

"So you *did* hear that. The screaming part." My ears still rang from it, so it was good I hadn't completely lost my mind.

"I did." The second man nodded, even as his friend frowned. Clearly, he hadn't.

"Of course you heard it, Theo." Seamus said quietly, stepping up beside me. "You've got the druid blood in you, that you do. There's probably a lot of fairy folk you've heard over the years."

While Theo blushed, I turned to Seamus. "You sent that flyer to me, and I came. Then this old lady or illusion or whatever she was shows up and starts wailing her fool head off, and when I come out to deal with the situation, she explodes in my hands. Please tell me, I *beg* you to tell me, this was the reason you called me out here. This was your big Neo-Celt threat."

"Not exactly." He shook his head. "She's but a warning of what's to come. I called you because my own son has made clear his intention to bring forth the ancient gods of the Celts, both the dark- and the light-bringers, by whatever means he can. He believes he is the Green Knight, and that it is his duty to lead the ancient ones back into the world of the living. We can't allow that. *You* can't allow that. The battle of our distant forebears to defeat the fae cannot be undone to satisfy the whims of fools who do not understand the gravity of what they think they want."

"I…" I stood for a moment, staring, unwilling or unable to believe my ears. As much as I wanted to write

Seamus McCarthy off as a lunatic, the old man wasn't joking. Every fiber of his being was vibrating with earnest truth, and a quick glance from Nikki confirmed it. Around us, the proprietors of the tents of the other, ah, spectral opposition warriors were now standing in front of their doorways, ignoring the curious crowds of trinket buyers and potion hounds. Instead, they were looking at me. I'd seen this look in the eyes of acolytes before, whether or not I wanted them. They not only believed, they *wanted* to believe.

Super-dangerous combination.

"How many of these folks are actual Connecteds?" I mused aloud, mostly for Nikki's benefit.

It was Seamus who responded. "It's not the spectral opposition warriors you should be worried about," he said. "They will serve you, and proudly at that. It's the damned Neo-Celts that are the problem."

"The Neo-Celts?" I squinted across the tent line to where a huge temporary sculpture of the tree of life had been erected, apparently signifying the opening to Celtlandia. "Seriously?"

"They're lulling the world to sleep, they are, with their cheap jewelry and terrible harp playing and divine trinity hocus-pocus," he growled ominously. "Don't even get me started on the druidic resurgence they're co-opting. They're cornering the market on all things supernatural and drawing a base that grows every day. It's one thing to get a Celtic cross tattooed on your ankle, it's another to actually believe that the ancient ways are better than the life we've forged for ourselves with our own hands and hearts. The ancient foes of mortals are *not* the impossibly beautiful, oversexed demigods that people imagine them to be."

"Wait—what?" Nikki asked, looking over at him with real interest for the first time. "No one said anything about oversexed."

The old man glared at her. "You make light, but you of all people know that glamour is one of the easiest ways to misdirect your foes, to make them believe you're not as deadly as you truly are. If the Green Knight gets his wish, however, you'll be on the front lines of experiencing exactly how dangerous the ancient ones truly were—again, not the glittery pinup models people have made them into, but the deadly, deceiving, and merciless magician assassins of the ancient world."

"Ummm, they still sound kind of hot," Nikki muttered.

I shifted, keenly sensing the attention of the small tribe assembled around me, then farther, the sprawling mass of people spinning through the psychic fair. Drawing in a deep breath, I flicked my third eye open to see what I could see about the energy dancing across the open park.

And flinched.

Thing one, there was a lot of energy. The entire park was hitting on all cylinders this afternoon. Whether it was due to the excitement being drummed up by the alcohol and stimulants flowing through people's systems, the thrumming music striking up at the far bandstand, or real magic snaking through the crowd, it didn't really matter. The bottom line was this festival was a tinder keg waiting to blow, not unlike most sporting or musical events. The difference here, though, was that these particular attendees could get into more than a fistfight.

"Tonight's not the last night of the festival, is it?"

"It is, though there's still a half-day left of events tomorrow," Seamus said. "But more importantly, it's the last full moon before Beltane, the pink moon, and there is magic in that moon, Justice. It's a call for new birth and life. To many of these foolish Neo-Celts, it's a symbol of the return of the ancient peoples they so revere. Or so say the adherents of the Green Knight."

"Okay, I'm done. You broke me." I sighed, spreading my hands. "I haven't even heard of your kid, and you'd think I would have if he was all that impressive. So give me the whole scoop. Does he have a dragon, too?"

Seamus shook his head, keeping his tone serious. "No. He's only recently taken on the full mantle of druid and drawn adherents to him like moths to a flame. We also sought to pass him off as a joke, none more so than I, but — he is no joke."

"We…" I looked at the old man more closely, but there was nothing obvious in his demeanor to mark him as anything but a Connected of middling ability. "Ah…you're a druid too? It's a family thing?"

"For centuries untold." he nodded. "But I'd be worried even if I didn't believe in magic, I tell you plain. We've good reason to believe my son will start his campaign in earnest tonight, to draw out the Tuatha dé Danann out by first summoning their avowed enemies, the Fomorians."

"You mentioned them before. They don't sound like a barrel of laughs."

"They are not," he agreed. "If the Fomorians walk again in the light, you can be sure the Tuath Dé will follow. Conal's going to get a lot of people killed before all this is done, and that's not the worst of it."

"Conal," I echoed, frustration lighting along my nerves. "Conal McCarthy. That name rings absolutely zero bells, and if he's this big a problem, I should've heard of him before now."

"Heads up, everyone. They're moving."

The words flowed across the open space of the spectral warrior tent city with a hiss and a crackle, and I scowled past the old man to the bush beside him—where I realized a small speaker had been set up. Similar speakers piped the alert up and down the narrow lane.

"Wait, who's moving?" I asked, trying to peer through the tents.

"The Neo-Celts," Seamus said with satisfaction. "They don't know who they're dealing with, though, if they think they can attack us with Justice among our ranks."

I shoot him an exasperated look. "Are you seriously hearing yourself right now?"

"We do have movement, dollface." Nikki pointed to a break in the tents, and sure enough, a procession of people in long green robes were holding electric torches aloft, and the sound of Celtic music was growing stronger. It was slow and melodic, almost mournful, but there was a magical quality to it that whispered through my bones.

This couldn't be good. I eyed the approaching group more nervously. "Why does this feel like Enya's version of the dance scene from *West Side Story*?"

"I don't like it," Nikki agreed. "There's nowhere to move in this lane. We need to take this—"

"Hey!" A good fifty feet away from our location, a shout rose up that was loud, irritated, and decidedly drunk. "You can't come walking through here when I'm doing a reading, man! That's totally rude!"

"Uh-oh," Nikki muttered.

The angry-drunk voice continued. "And who the hell do you think you are with that—yo! That's my kettle you're knocking over. It's time for you to back off, bruh. *Hey.* Stop that. What in the actual *fu*—"

29

Without any further warning, an explosion of birds, smoke, and fire ripped upward into the sky.

CHAPTER THREE

I burst past the line of spectral opposition warriors, or whatever the hell they were calling themselves, and, together with Nikki, ran into the melee. The central problem seemed to be with a group of men and women dressed as Roma traders who'd pulled their colorful wagon-style kiosks into a loose circle around a permanent fire pit that was clearly part of the park's foundational décor. The traders had set up all manner of kettles and bowls around the fire, all of which were for sale at festival pricing, and the advancing Neo-Celts or whatever the hell *they* were calling themselves had knocked over several of their wares. Ordinarily, this wouldn't be a big deal. The kettles and pots were made of metal, from what I could tell, and nothing had been broken—but the insult appeared to be all the spark needed to ignite the already smoking fuse.

To make matters worse, everyone around the commotion seemed to be paying attention to it, so I was definitely not making good time through the throng.

"Get security!" I shouted to no one in particular, least of all Nikki, who'd be far more useful to me in the middle of a fight than running through the crowd looking for guys in khakis. Still, it felt like someone needed to say it. I swept the line of assailants with my third eye, breathing a sigh of relief. The Neo-Celts were Connected, somewhat, but they weren't amassing any electrical load worth worrying about. The men and women of the traders' village were all shapes and sizes, but their electrical signatures had no Connected spark whatsoever. That meant this fight should be—

A fireball landed to the right of the clearing, a direct hit for one of the colorful wagons.

Not just any fireball either. The conflagration that immediately erupted in its wake parted like a doorway, and three dancing tongues of flame leapt out, each of them crackling and popping with energy. They weren't sentient—this was all an illusion—but it was an *impressive* illusion. People screamed, apparently scared for the first time, and I wondered for a split second what effect their reaction would have on the firebomber. Quell him into submission or jack him up?

I didn't have to wait long for an answer. Another bomb exploded next to me, near enough that I jumped back.

Crap! Not an illusion—this was real-ass *fire*!

"Who's throwing that?" I demanded, whipping around to identify the source of the flames. To my shock, it was a girl no more than ten years old, her mouth open in a silent scream as she stood in the center of the clearing, surrounded by larger girls and boys, all of them wielding long, gnarled staffs. I couldn't tell who were the Neo-Celts and who were the Roma in this scenario, but it didn't matter. This little girl wasn't intending to throw fire, she was simply scared. A very scared, very powerful little girl. I looked around self-consciously for Drew Barrymore standing in the crowd, then opened my own palms, feeling the sparking electricity that was always skittering at a low ebb inside me spring to life.

Near the young girl, an older woman was on her knees, her face a mask of terror as she implored the girl to think, to pause, to breathe. Terror, but not surprise. She'd seen this before. Seen it and understood it for what it was.

Unfortunately, the kids with the sticks weren't reacting with terror—but with glee. "To light, to light," they chanted in a language I could instantly translate for all that I couldn't place its origins right away. An onboard Google Translate function was one of the perks of my job as Justice, but I didn't have time to research conjugations. The language was old, it was powerful, and it'd been co-opted by spell-casters since the dawn of time.

The tops of the twisted saplings being held by the older kids burst into flame, and a game of fried chicken was instantly in play.

"*Mommy,*" the little girl wailed, and I didn't wait. Regardless of who started this fight, none of these asshats should be playing with fire until they learned how to control it better. I thrust my hands forward, and my own wave of spectral flame shot out, toppling the kids like bowling pins. With their connection to their magic momentarily disrupted, the fire winked out—

And not a moment too soon.

"Sara!" Nikki's shout was my only warning as I felt a dark presence rush up beside me, not a shadow so much as an absence of light. I whirled in time, but I couldn't evade the creature, not with so many humans around. I didn't know which side summoned it. I didn't care. It didn't belong here. I thrust my hands out again, and light poured from my fingers, exploding it into dust.

Then I looked up and saw the real problem.

The Roma had fled. In their wake, two lines of adversaries squared off against each other, the Neo-Celts and the spectral opposition warriors. Even as I raced forward, I flicked my third eye open, studying the lines of energy —

"Son of a *bitch*!" Nikki's bawl of fury redirected my attention, and I whipped around to see her swinging an enormous spiked club at the chain-mail craftsman we'd noticed earlier near the front gates of the fair. She was grinning — but so was he. Dressed head to toe in metal, the hulking bodybuilder went after Nikki with a hatchet that looked like it could actually split skulls. Meanwhile, the spectral opposition warriors were closing in on a knot of conjuring Neo-Celts who were exhorting green mist to spurt up from a cauldron they'd apparently hauled along for the party. Around them fluttered a half-dozen butterflies that seemed to be...clapping?

"God save the Queen!"

I whirled to my left. In front of me an entire company of Elizabethan soldiers — and three honest-to-God horses — came barreling in from the side, one of them executing a damned near perfect jump over several kegs of beer. From the other edge of the clearing, a group of kids lofting real-enough-looking spikes and staves roared forward, some of them dressed in robes, some in armor, and some pulling longbows from their backs.

"Leeeeeerrroyyyyyy Jenkinnnnns!" another voice shouted, and I spun a third time as a group of twenty-somethings in full-on Wizards of Warcraft gear pounced on what looked like a miniature army of dwarves, only the dwarves were shooting fireballs against them, catching their opponents' clothes ablaze. All this would have been really cool in a video game —

but this wasn't a video game. This was a knot of chaos in the middle of Las Vegas, Nevada, and somebody was bound to notice.

As if thinking of him made it so, an all too familiar voice cut across the clearing.

"Ah, *shit*. Sara! I knew I would find you here! Jesus, Mary, and Joseph—"

I grinned even as I knocked the dwarves nearest to me senseless with a puff of blue fire, rounding up the assassins' guild for good measure. Meanwhile, racing through the Elizabethan knights and all their stamping hooves was a man in a suit too nondescript for him to be anything other than a cop. A cop with a particular aptitude for knowing when I was going to be in trouble, anyway.

"LVMPD!" Detective Brody Rooks roared as he pounded up to me, barely able to be heard above the chaos. His gaze pinned me. "A little help here, Sara?"

I lifted my hands, then cut them wide—

And everybody froze.

Solid. Unmoving.

"Ummmm...." I looked around, startled, as I shook out my hands. Brody was caught midsnarl, while Nikki's delighted grin stretched wide as she heaved her club over her head in preparation for the mother of all strikes against Captain Chain Mail. All the various knights errant and their infidel opponents looked like players stuck on an invisible chessboard, and last but not least, the spectral opposition warriors and the Neo-Celts remained poised in intractable opposition. Everything was frozen in place in the city, time held out of time.

Had I done this? I hadn't done this. I couldn't have done this.

Then, time started moving backward.

35

Nope, I totally wasn't doing this.

"Miss Wilde."

I straightened carefully, and a moment later, Armaeus Bertrand stepped up beside me. As always, my pulse jacked as I shot a sideways glance at the demigod who'd claimed me, heart and soul. Tall and sleekly muscular, his features made the most of his French-Egyptian heritage, as the son of a pile-driving crusader knight and the Egyptian priestess he'd met and fallen in love with while fighting for his king. Thick, glossy, raven-black hair winged back from his forehead, and his leonine golden-black eyes were the strongest feature in a face chiseled in bronze. Those eyes looked at me now in patent amusement.

I blew out a long breath. "Oh, good. I was hoping it was you." My ever-evolving abilities were super impressive, but not *that* impressive. Which I was okay with, since what was going on in front of me was off the chain.

"You gave me no choice. You didn't step in quickly enough," chided Armaeus. "You won't always have the power to interrupt a crisis, Miss Wilde. But you can still change the course of events to preserve those who should remain hidden."

"But that's the problem. These guys don't realize they should be hiding," I said. "They're using their powers, in the open. They don't know what they're about to invite down upon themselves."

"Agreed. So I think, perhaps..." the Magician's voice softened as time slowed then finally stopped once more. "I believe this is your cue."

He didn't have to tell me twice.

The little girl screamed, fire erupting around her in little breathy pops, catching tents on fire. Her mother reached for her—but this time, I got to her first. I swept the little girl up into my arms and turned toward the older children advancing on her with sticks, casting out my own blue fire in a wide arc to silence the angry spattering of the weapons. And all the while, I didn't stop talking.

"There will come a time when you will be stronger than anyone around you, little one," I said. "There will come a time when you will go up against a force that is your equal. There will finally come a time when you will recognize that, despite all your many strengths, you are not the strongest person on the battlefield. In all those times, your response with your powers should be the same: do what is just. Choose your friend wisely and your enemy nobly. Do not make victims of those you defeat, lest you make enemies of them in the same breath."

By now, the girl gaped at me, whether because the message was going over her head or because she couldn't believe I spoke her language. But the result was the same. She stopped crying, and she stopped making spontaneous fireballs.

The distraction of the child gone, I shoved her back to her mother and turned to the rest of the crazy people. One by one, I blanked their memories, scrambling their minds with a current of power until they didn't know what had brought them to this place, bearing weapons for no good reason. The cops still came, Brody still showed up, but by the time both events happened, the erstwhile fighters were all standing around staring at each other, looking somewhat bemused.

Except Nikki and her chain-mail master. Those two continued fighting.

Ignoring their clanking and swearing in the background, I tried to focus on Brody.

"—and I would like just once to enjoy a day off without having to untangle some mess you've found yourself in the middle of," he finished, clearly at the tail end of an impressive rant. He looked at me pointedly, and I nodded with as much understanding as I could muster.

"I'd like that for you too," I said, already trying to edge away. "I'd hate to get you into trouble. Maybe I should make myself scarce." The crowd who'd assembled to watch the "mock battle" was already beginning to drift off, and Nikki and her sparring partner would eventually come to terms. Old Seamus McCarthy had disappeared back toward spectral warrior-ville, and the Neo-Celts were slinking away as well. Only the Roma, knights errant, and cosplay groupies seemed at a loss where to go, and they'd been dragged into this through no fault of their own.

Brody was watching the approaching police cars. "So—I'll go ahead and move on, then," I said helpfully. I needed to find Seamus McCarthy and nail him to the wall until he gave me the full scoop on the guy behind all this. The Green Knight or whatever.

The detective swung his gaze back to me, flinching when Nikki delivered one last, clanking blow to her opponent, the man going down with a grunt. He glowered at me. "You already see Sariah here?"

That stopped my retreat. I ignored the high-pitched laughter of children off to the side as I focused on Brody.

"Uh, no…" I allowed. Sariah Pelter and I went way back. *Way*, way back. All the way back to when I was seventeen years old and faced with a trauma so intense that my psyche sort of…split. The woman who eventually became me, Sara Wilde, ran away from the fiery explosion of the only home I'd ever known like my life depended on it. The essence of my spirit that rebelled against running away from anything, that wanted nothing more than to scream in outraged indignation and pile back into the flames, beating the crap out of whoever or whatever had done this to me — had broken free. I'd run forward and became a Tarot-reading adventurer dedicated to protecting the most vulnerable of Connecteds, while Sariah had gone straight to Hell. And she'd remained there for more than ten years, until a job had brought me face-to-face with her again.

Now she had returned to the world above, struggling to find her place. Well, maybe not struggling. Maybe I was the only one who was struggling with it.

Either way, our relationship was...complicated.

"Sariah's here? As a tourist, I hope?"

Brody snorted. He and Sariah had a complicated relationship of their own. "Sariah goes nowhere as a tourist. She's set herself up as a reader."

Suddenly. the postcard from the boy felt like it weighed twenty pounds in my pocket. "Let me guess. Mistress Malificorem?"

He smiled grimly. "Be sure to ask for the friends-and-family discount. And get a stiff drink while you're at it."

CHAPTER FOUR

I collected Nikki and pulled out the postcard the kid had given me. Mistress Malificorem was due east, a path that would take us straight through Neo-Celt land. Probably a good idea for me to check that out anyway.

Beside me, Nikki was rearranging her outfit, surprisingly unharmed by her altercation with the chain-mail craftsman. When I offered her the card, she took it, making a face as she shook it. "Mega gross. It's still wet," she muttered.

"I think it's got some sort of weird finish on it." I peered over to the chain-mail guy, already struggling to his feet. "We should've had Brody arrest him," I said for the third time.

Nikki snorted as she adjusted her wig. "For what? A half-assed hatchet job? That guy was a softy."

"That guy weighed nearly two hundred and fifty pounds. I'm thinking most of it was muscle."

"And you would be right." Nikki sighed dreamily.

We breached the collection of green tents that marked our return to Celtlandia, everything looking remarkably normal for a group who'd just been on the warpath, and I glanced back over my shoulder, measuring the distance to the spectral warrior tent city. For supposedly avowed enemies, these two were awfully close to each other. "So what do you think about—"

"Oh, blessed be. You're back."

The woman who ducked out of the tent in front of us bounced up and down with excitement, her wings bobbing behind her, bringing Nikki and me to an abrupt halt.

"You must step in for a reading," she said, clapping her hands. "You stopped the conflict, and the time is quickly coming to an end for anyone to be able to do that."

"What do you mean by that last part, sweet thing?" Nikki drawled, and the woman beamed at the attention. I didn't remember seeing her on the front lines between the Neo-Celts and the spectral opposition warriors, so that made her, what? A hanger-on? A pacifist? Or just smarter than the average fairy?

Not that she was an actual fairy, of course...

"Come in, come in. Truly, I've been waiting for you for so long."

Nikki and I exchanged a look, but obligingly, we entered the woman's tent. It was surprisingly spacious inside, with room for a small reading table and a couple of chairs, a low set of cushions around a central altar, and a stand filled with little crystals and bowls, most of which were filled with water and yet more floating crystals.

"Nice place," I observed as she gestured us to the chairs. We both took seats carefully, perching on the edge.

"This tent is heavily warded," the woman preened, smiling at the crystals. "No one who means me harm

41

can enter, nor any who would do our order harm. You would have been turned away at the door had you wished us ill."

"Ah—well, that's outstanding," I said as diplomatically as possible. I casually flicked my third eye open, and my sixth sense only confirmed what the rest of my senses were telling me. There was no magic here. The young woman might possess some modicum of reading talent, but she was not profoundly Connected. The energy vibrations from the tents surrounding her were remarkably strong, but her own location seemed almost eerily devoid of Connected energy. I frowned, tightening my hands into reflexive fists. Was there some sort of energy suck going on here? Or was this woman legitimately that deluded? I didn't know which answer would be worse, but the latter would certainly be less dangerous.

"So, do you read with cards?" Nikki asked. "Or are you a pendulum kind of girl?"

"Neither." The young woman dimpled. "I channel the dead."

"The dead," I repeated flatly. "I'm not real big on séances, and I pretty much think the dead do a good job staying where they are. So I appreciate your time, and I'm happy to pay you some small gratuity for it, but I don't think this is a reading that I'm going to be taking—"

"Sara, sweetie. Stay. For just a minute."

Even more so than the name she uttered, the sound that came out of the woman's mouth was so alarming, so disturbing, that I sat back in my metal folding chair, my skin breaking into an immediate cold sweat. I knew that voice, the scratch-gravel tones of a woman who sounded far older then the forty-odd years she'd lived. The coy, insinuating pout that had allowed her to get whatever she wanted in life except for, arguably, that which she most craved.

The young woman with the fairy wings sat before me in the perfect blush of health, while the woman whose voice she spoke with had been dead in the ground for more than a decade now.

"Sara," my foster mother said again. "There is danger here. You have to be careful. You have to listen."

I felt the eerie chill crawl up my arms, but I sat rooted in place. "What do you mean I have to listen? To you?"

The young redhead's plump mouth curved into a bitter smile, and Sheila Rose Pelter kept speaking. "Not me. I know better than to ask you to listen to me. When did you ever?"

Well, that wasn't really fair. During the years the woman I'd believed to be my mother, Sheila Rose Pelter, had cared for me, she'd spent most of her time passing me off to other babysitters while she partied with her friends. When I was a child, I'd never understood how we always had enough money to survive despite the fact that she never seemed to work and that she'd always seemed right on the edge of being drunk. As I got older, I began to truly fear what the answer to that question would be. It was only years after her death that I learned the truth, that my father had left me with this woman to care for me, hiding me away as best as he could from my birth mother who'd been far more frightening to him than the prospect of leaving me with a stranger. It didn't help that my father was a member of the Arcana Council himself, and that my birth mother was, well, a goddess known for encouraging bloody human sacrifices.

Needless to say, I wasn't going to be buying a 23andMe DNA kit anytime soon.

"I'm listening now," I said, while Nikki remained silent beside me. The urge to leave grew even stronger, but I also felt a weird compulsion to stay, not one that was magically cast, but born of my own insatiable need to know more. More about this woman I'd thought was my mother, more about what had happened the day I'd fled Memphis, Tennessee, the day my mother had been killed. I'd never gotten to say goodbye that morning. I wondered if I would here.

"Don't let anyone feed you lies about the conflict that is coming," the young reader spoke in my foster mother's voice. "It cannot be stopped, and in truth, it has been brought about in great part by your own hand."

I leaned forward. It'd been a long time since I'd had a mother-daughter conversation, but this was definitely not right. Sheila had never spoken so formally in her entire life. What was going on here?

"Okaaay…" I said, as beside me, Nikki finally shifted slightly in her chair. Either she was picking up on my energy, or something felt strange to her too. "So what's the truth that I should know?"

"That you should leave the path clear for those who would take greater care of the planet. That you should help them, not stop them in your pride and foolishness."

I glanced around again, employing my third eye. No doubt about it, while the energy in this tent felt like it was being smothered with a lead blanket, the energy in the surrounding tents was flaring brightly, like beacons in the gathering evening. I made no move to flare my own energy into life, but was that these people's plan? Did they think they had dropped me into some sort of dead zone? Did they not know who I was?

"Who is 'them'?" I asked. "Who should I be looking out for as the face of this new beginning?"

"The Green Knight, of course," the young woman continued in the same gravelly tone. "He will tell you all you need to know soon. So soon. The doors are even now opening, but what you most need to do now…is rest."

The spell dropped on me with such impressive speed that it took me a second to realize what was happening. Nikki collapsed beside me in a boneless heap, and as I glanced her way, the blanket of lead I'd felt depressing the magic in this space now felt like it had been dumped directly on top of me. My entire body lit up with alarm and urgency, but I had no immediate fear for myself. Nikki, on the other hand…

I turned toward her, my third eye narrowing, and saw the truth. I wasn't the target here. She was.

I whipped my head back toward the woman, whose mouth still moved, dropping her poison in the voice of a woman whose love I'd wanted more than anything in the world, and whose love I'd never fully received. Because in the end, I'd been merely a transaction to Sheila Rose Pelter, even competition in a weird way when she had striven to convince the world that she was as Connected as I was. But that didn't matter now.

What mattered was that she would never have called me Sara. When I'd been a child back in Memphis, a child who'd run so desperately from the burning conflagration of her home that it was like my very feet were on fire, my name hadn't been Sara Wilde. When I'd endured trauma so intense that my young Connected mind couldn't break me cleanly from the terror of my past or the fear of my future such that two children were born—one that fled forward and one that dived back into the flames—it wasn't Sara Wilde who'd made that split. Sheila Rose Pelter wouldn't know that name.

I leaned forward. "You've got exactly thirty seconds to stop whatever spell you've dropped on my friend, or I will kill you so dead, no one will *ever* be able to channel you back to this plane."

The young woman's eyes widened and her voice faltered as behind me, another voice spoke. "I wondered when you'd figure it out."

The woman squeaked and wheeled back, but Sariah was too fast for her. My fiercer half, who looked almost exactly like me, lunged forward as I turned to Nikki, dropping my hands to her neck, straining toward her pulse, which fluttered as wildly as a bird in a cage. Instantly, my third eye fixed on Nikki, and I reached deep into her psyche, intending to heal, but I felt a veil between us, my own abilities oddly blocked. I had to focus so deeply on breaking through that veil that I only came out of my fugue when I heard the unmistakable sound of bones cracking. I looked up in shock to see Sariah standing over the still form of the woman with butterfly wings—wings she'd ripped clean off.

"Sariah," I gasped as Nikki coughed woozily beside me. "What did you just do?"

"What needed doing." She jabbed a finger at the crumpled figure on the floor. "Look familiar?"

"What are you—?"

Then I saw it. Sure enough, the woman on the floor was no longer the angelic redhead with the butterfly wings, but the shattered, faceless crone who'd wailed the banshee cry. "What is going *on* here?"

"A fantastic question, but one I have no clue how to answer," Sariah snarled. "I've been getting attacked by every manner of crazy since I set up shop this morning and I only now realized you're to blame."

"Yeah, I got your card." I scowled from her to Nikki as Sariah squinted at me. "How'd you get in here without anyone noticing you?"

"They did notice me. So right now, it might be a good idea for us to poof the hell out of here. You know how to do that?"

Nikki moaned beneath me, still way too weak. My right hand ached, and I suddenly realized that the shard of Nul Magis I'd gotten stuck in my palm on a recent job was thrumming hard enough to make the bones quiver. The sorcerer who'd flung the Nul Magis had intended to drain a sorcerer of all his magic, but I'd intercepted it. And as it turned out, I had a little more power in my well than the average wizard. So instead of incapacitating me, the Nul Magis had stuck in my palm and set up house, serving as both an early warning system that magic was being cast around me...and a tool to quell that magic with a really solid handshake. But for it to be gyrating so intensely now...probably wasn't good. "I sure as hell can get us out of here," I said.

One of my newest and least-developed skills was a form of teleportation that involved me and anyone I touched becoming thinner than air. In that form of pure energy, we could move anywhere—as long as I'd been there before. Sadly, I hadn't been to the tent of Mistress Malificorem, and I had no particular desire to go there right now. Not yet. Not with Nikki still not fully conscious. I needed to get her somewhere she could recover in peace.

"Give me your hand," I said to Sariah as I reached for Nikki with my other hand. Even in her depleted state, Nikki had enough sense of self-preservation to groan.

"What?" Sariah demanded, narrowing her eyes. "Why'd she make that noise?"

"Relax." I smiled. "This will only hurt a little."

I poofed us out of the tent. A moment later, we flickered back into existence in my office at Justice Hall, with one small problem.

No Sariah.

CHAPTER FIVE

"Crap," I bit out, as I helped Nikki to the couch. "You good?"

She waved me off, sinking against the cushions. "Go," she managed. "I'll be here when you get back."

Again, the trouble with my ability to destabilize and reappear in a new place was that I needed to know the place I was looking for—ideally, I needed to have been there before. Nikki and I had toyed with the possibility that I could find someone by knowing the *person* but not the place, but we hadn't had the opportunity to test that theory. We suspected it would take a pretty thorough knowledge of the target in any event, but in this case, Sariah was the perfect test subject.

Some people spent their whole lives trying to find themselves, but I didn't think I'd need that kind of time.

Focusing really hard on my sister/alter-ego/crazier half, I poofed back into existence at the edge of a space that was already looking way too familiar—same enormous thugs sporting desert camo gear, same huddle of tents nearly overrun by enthusiastic tourists.

Same Spectral Opposition Warrior Services signs, with *Buy One, Get One Half Off* warding amulets.

I started forward but was almost immediately hauled back, a hand clapped over my mouth. My fingers instantly burst into blue flame, when my own voice — or close enough — hissed in my ear. "You want to give me your magic fireballs of power, go ahead, do it. But I'm trying *not* to draw attention to ourselves here. Something is seriously screwed up here."

Sariah's hand tightened on my mouth a second further, then she released me and we both stood back. We weren't smack in the center of the group of tents, but we were hardly hidden. Yet no one seemed to be paying any attention to us.

I glanced at her. "You mind telling me what the hell is going on? How'd you end up back here — without me?"

She shrugged. "Our abilities keep evolving, they're just not the same abilities. You get flame transpo, whereas I can now absorb whatever I most need from whoever I touch last. Kind of like an opportunistic Rogue, but nobody loses their shit over it, 'cause I only sort of borrow their skills for a minute."

"I think this conversation would go better if you weren't comparing yourself to an X-Man."

She rolled her eyes. "And part of *your* problem is you don't have a sense of humor. You're leveling up so fast, it makes my head spin, but you act like every new skill is some terrible burden you can't wait to unload, whereas I'm happy for any scraps I can find."

"Sariah..." I passed a hand over my brow. "The distinction you're failing to note is that I actually feel a responsibility to use these abilities in a way that doesn't screw anyone else up."

"Yet another character flaw. But shut it, we've got more important things to figure out here. That bitch witch with the floaty wings did a pretty damned good impression of Mommy Dearest, and I want to know why."

"You heard her?"

"Oh, yeah. Some things you don't forget, and that voice is one of them."

I nodded. I could relate. "Okay, you heard the woman speaking in Sheila's voice, you came to explore, you found me."

"Which was not part of their evil plan, I'm thinking," she said, nodding. "That entire setup was to take out Nikki, unless I miss my guess. Which was a pretty shit move, and stupid too. It takes a lot to piss you off, but hitting her would do it."

"You got that right," I muttered. I looked around and realized no one was looking at us. "Um...did you also steal my ability to hide in a crowd? Is that why no one sees us?"

Sariah fired her finger gun at me. "Just because you're not willing to use it doesn't mean I'm not."

I opened my mouth, then shut it again. "I haven't had time to test that ability."

"Congratulations. It works. But there's something shifty about the old Irish guy who's hanging out in the middle of a bunch of anti-magic warriors. And there's also something shifty about said anti-magic guys signing up to be your bodyguards."

"They're not anti-magic," I corrected. "They're anti-being-controlled-by-magic. There's a difference. And just because Seamus is Irish doesn't automatically make him a Neo-Celt. People change."

"Not as much as you'd like to think," Sariah retorted. "No way would a druid hook up with a bunch of anti-magic thugs, full stop. That's totally not their deal. Which means these guys have probably way more magic in them than they're letting on."

"Seamus is a druid. Right." I'd been so focused on the banshee's first attack, Seamus's little riff about druid blood hadn't fully registered. Now, however, it was starting to make a little more sense. Druids were the wise men of yore, the shamans, the warlocks, the old-school know-it-alls...and that knowledge included arcane magic. I'd always expected druids to wear cloaks embroidered with trees, sporting snappy antler hats on their heads, but it was the twenty-first century. Seamus's cargo pants and Jesus sandals were probably the go-to uniform.

So why *was* he leading a gang of spectral opposition warriors? Some of whom were semipowerful Connecteds in their own right? "Maybe he's scared?"

She shook her head. "I don't think so. More likely his order is getting ready to go to war, and he's some kind of advance scout, rounding up all available troops."

"You mean he wants *me* to go to war."

"If it makes you feel better to think of it that way, sure. But make no mistake, this morning's little demonstration was most likely a test of your skills. If you ended up as a greasy splatter, he was still moving forward. There's something off about him that I recognize from too many people down under. He's lit from within by a fire that will not be easily put out."

I shot her a wary glance. "And you care about this why?"

"Because ever since I got out of Hell free, I've been working on learning the cards again—not to find shit for other people like you, but just for straight-up reading. I remember being pretty good at it once upon a time.

Anyway, for the past week or so, the cards have been creeping me out like it's their job. We're talking serious, serious trauma. If you hadn't showed up on my doorstep today, I was going to seek you out."

"And you think it's this green man that Seamus was talking about who's the problem? You believe him?"

"Not the green man, the Green Knight. There's a difference."

"Yeah, I remember the same story you did. Seeing as how that was the last year we spent in school."

She smirked. "Who would've thought Mrs. Rice's class would have come in handy after all? But this guy doesn't have anything to do with King Arthur. He serves a far different master. The fae and all their creepy minions."

"Don't start with me, Sariah. I'm not real big on blaming brownies and pixie dust for what real people are actually doing."

Sariah rolled her eyes. "You know, I had an awful lot of time to explore my home away from home while I was cooling my heels for a decade. I found a *lot* of shit down in Hell that made no sense. That shouldn't have existed, that arguably *didn't* exist except in the minds of a few feverish people who believed in them with all their might. But what I learned too was that there were occasions where said feverish minds willed something into being that had no business existing. It happened more often than I would've given it credit for."

I curled my lip. "And that's what you think happened here, that fairies were created by us? If you imagine it, they will come?"

She shrugged. "Stranger things have happened. Like you, for example."

I opened my mouth, then shut it again. She had a point. Before I could come up with a reasonable reply, she straightened. "Here we go."

Seamus McCarthy came out of his tent and nodded to three other people across the small clearing. They all turned toward another tent, this one set back off the public pathway, clearly some sort of supply hut. Sariah grabbed me and started forward.

"We can't just follow them in there."

"Sure we can. Or more to the point, you can while looking exactly like one of their own, which means I can as long as I'm hanging out with you. Pretty neat, huh?"

We followed the group closely, slipping into the tent behind them. It wasn't a large tent, so we pressed ourselves up against the walls on either side of the opening, hanging in the shadows. Anyone looking might realize we weren't who we seemed to be, but as Sariah clearly had expected, no one looked.

Seamus started right in. "She'll be back."

"She may be too angry," another man spoke up, his voice gruff, accusing. "You let the Neo-Celts breach our wards to test her with that banshee. That could have gone very badly."

I glanced at Sariah, who smiled smugly.

Seamus only shook his head. "It didn't, though. And our cause here is true. Plus, she won't be able to resist the attack on her own."

"She killed the fairy witch," one of the women said, a thin, hard-eyed blonde. "I didn't think she had it in her."

I shot another look at Sariah, who shrugged. They thought I was Sariah and that I'd killed someone in cold blood. Then again, the woman had attacked Nikki, and if I hadn't had Sariah there to distract her while I attended to my friend, she might well have died. I could heal a lot of things, but I couldn't heal dead. Still, there was a certain casualness to Sariah's dispatching of the witch that unnerved me. Had a violent, pragmatic shard of my soul been stripped away that day more than ten years ago, a shard I never truly realized was gone? And what did that mean for that shard of a soul to have taken human form once more?

I couldn't focus on that right now, but I'd need to. Soon.

"Will she act by Beltane is the question," another man said. "If she doesn't, this is all for nothing anyway. We're dead."

"She will act," Seamus said. He looked up with ancient eyes, right at me. "Won't you, Justice Wilde?"

"Shit," Sariah muttered, and before I could move, she went up in fire and smoke, co-opting my traveling ability just that fast. I watched her go, but I didn't need to follow her this time. I was where I needed to be.

I stepped forward, letting the veneer of my disguise fall away. The other people in the room stiffened, their faces blanking in surprise and mistrust — and maybe a little awe. I was fine with that. A little awe could go a long way.

"What else aren't you telling me, Seamus?" I asked levelly. "This will be the last time I ask."

He stared at me a long moment, then seemed to shrink in on himself. "Fair enough, Justice Wilde. The truth is, Conal McCarthy isn't the only fool in my family. When I was much younger, I also prayed for the ancient gods to return. Unfortunately, I attracted not the Tuatha dé Danann, but their ancient foes, the Fomorians."

"Are they sparkly, too?"

"Not at all. They also hold a grudge. Things could have gone very badly. As it was, my druid order vanquished them and all was well. But if they return, when they return—I will be a homing target for them, a beacon amid humanity." He sighed heavily. "All that to say, I accept my responsibility here. And my sacrifice. Should you have need of bait…"

"No." I spoke a little more sharply than I intended, and the entire crowd jumped a little, Seamus most of all. "If they come back, then first, you hide. Second, you contact me. If that doesn't work, then you remember what it was you did to blast them back into their hole the first time, and do *that*. Screw being bait. I need you on the front lines, and I also need you to tell me everything you can about your kid."

As I continued, the old man straightened, his chin coming up, his eyes fierce. Finally, he spoke.

"Our family has long been a member of the ancient order of druids, generation upon generation, age upon age, our teachings and practices handed down by the spoken word, the cycle ever unbroken. In the generations where there were no sons, our daughters would carry on the line, but for the past several hundred years we've kept the druid families intact, working in the shadows, honing our craft. In my own line, I was blessed with not one but two boys, several years apart, both of whom grew up to be straight and true, but only one with the spark of the green man within him."

"Ahhh…the green man." I knew the symbol, of course. A man nearly hidden in a swath of foliage, representing the cycle of growth each spring. But I wasn't sure exactly how it pertained, here.

"Yes, indeed. The highest blessing a druid can aspire to. I rejoiced at first to see such a strong light and nurtured it as best as I was able, bearing in mind my own foolish mistakes. But that spark grew quickly out of control several years ago. Eventually, I was forced to defend myself against my own son and stop his murderous hand as he turned his mania on his own brother."

"Whoa, hold up. Brother?"

"Niall," Seamus said with a soft sigh. "Conal's older brother. A good, loyal boy, but he never had the spark. Eventually, Conal turned on him, too. Meanwhile, I've lived in exile from my own order ever since, unwilling and unable to take up arms against my own blood. But my position as father can no longer take precedence over my position as druid. Not when the fate of the world hangs in the balance."

"What is it exactly that you think your son is going to do?" *And whatever happened to son number two, while we were up?* I didn't waste my time disputing the man's belief. While so much of religion was based on an unfounded faith, I'd seen too much magic in the world to know from a distance what I was dealing with here. Until I saw Conal in person, I wouldn't have a clue as to his actual strength.

"First, let me answer that which remains unspoken," Seamus said, surprising me again. "Niall, Conal's brother, lives — more than lives. He's become Conal's right-hand man, helping him in all his pursuits."

"That seems…imprudent."

"I agree, but Niall is by far the weaker of the two, and what light he has, he hides." He squared his shoulders, gesturing to the room. "Very well, then. You naturally want to know what Conal will do, and you want to know what he has done to engender such fear within me, within all of us. That's a fair request, so I'll start with what he's done. In the space of the last two years, since he has begun his ministry in earnest, he's gathered to him an international following that now numbers in the hundreds of thousands. With that following has come gifts of money and ancient gold."

"Ancient gold?" That surprised me, and, curse my avaricious spirit, intrigued me as well. "What kind of ancient gold?"

"There was a very specific kind of gold mined in Ireland, a uniquely pale ore that was said to possess magical qualities. That gold was heavily sought after whenever it was sent outside of Ireland, which was often. Rome couldn't vanquish Ireland, but it could take its gold, and it did. Not only Rome either. This pale Irish gold found its way into the royal courts of Europe and as far away as China and Egypt. My son has asked for that gold back, and it is coming to him."

"Really." I wondered how much the Magician knew about this. He'd said nothing when I'd received the summons from Seamus, but that didn't mean he was unaware. His actions on this very festival today proved that.

"With this gold, my son has begun performing the rites that've been buried in our family to stir the people to him and give them what they need to believe. He has become the alchemist, determined to create a new conductive metal that can maintain a significantly high electrical current. High enough to change the vibration of anything around it. To hear him talk, it can shatter mountains into rubble, crystallize oceans into ice, and vaporize people into thin air."

"That does not sound good."

"It isn't good. And he has only tapped the barest potential of it. And as I've been trying to tell you, to bring this weapon to full flower, Conal says he will bring back the Tuatha dé Danann themselves, by first setting the Fomorians free. And I believe he can do it."

CHAPTER SIX

Seamus didn't have much else to say, but by then, he'd said plenty. A threat was coming, it would hit at Beltane, and...we needed to stop it. Between what he'd shared with me today and my up-close-and-personal vision of what newly empowered Connecteds could and would do without proper restraint, that was more than enough for me to get started. Our little powwow broke up shortly after that, and I emerged back out into the evening only slightly dazed. At least until I realized that Brody was standing there, waiting for me. Then I became fully dazed.

"Do *not* tell me there's been another psychic food fight," I said.

"No." He held up his phone. "You ever see one of these before? It's called a phone. You know what they're used for?"

I felt around my pockets, and frowned. "I might have lost mine. I was a little busy earlier today."

He sighed heavily. "That's what Nikki thought, but she wanted you to know. She's not doing so hot—"

Without hesitating, I lunged forward, wrapping my arms around Brody. We appeared a moment later in the lobby of Justice Hall, where there was no Nikki. Instead, there was only Mrs. French, wringing her hands and white as a ghost.

I whirled around as Brody spun away from me sputtering curses, batting furiously at his shoulders as flames licked along his cheap polyester suit jacket. "Don't you ever—and I mean *ever*—do that to me again—"

"Where is she?" I tried to modulate my voice, but I could practically hear the walls vibrate with my shouted question, and even Mrs. French took a step back.

"She's safe, she's completely safe, she told me that herself, that that would be the first thing you would worry about, the very first."

"Mrs. French—"

"But she said she'd be in tip-top shape in no time, those were her very words, and that you weren't to worry at all, just—"

"Mrs. *French*," I tried again. "Where is she?"

This time, it was Brody who spoke. "She's under observation at Dr. Sells's clinic, if you would've let me get a word in edgewise. Apparently, no sooner did you drop her off than she collapsed, and then she went poof."

That stopped me. "Went poof. Never mind. Where's her room? Have I been there?" I began to destabilize even as I spoke, but Brody held up his phone again.

"Sara! You need to take a breath. She's okay. She's got Dr. Sells watching over her, and the Council is on it. We can go there now, but we should go the ordinary way."

I blinked at him, hovering on the edge of corporeality. "What ordinary way?"

"By *car*. Which means you need to take us back to the goddamned festival so I can get mine."

"Well! That's no trouble at all, Detective," Mrs. French said brightly. "Justice Wilde has several vehicles at her disposal here. You can take any of them at all."

I glanced at her. "I do?"

"Indeed yes, ma'am. But please do keep me posted on Miss Dawes's condition, if you would? She's a bit cheeky, but it's all for show. Oh! And while you're here." She bustled out of the lobby and into my private office, but I was already shaking my head as she reemerged.

"No way," I said, lifting my hands. "I've got no time for new work, not now."

"Well, this isn't new, exactly," she said. "Before she collapsed, Nikki said something about the Green Knight of the Celts, and that name rang a bell, I mean, beyond the Arthurian legend, of course, which was all tosh and nonsense. I pulled what I had on past cases regarding the reference, and—" She offered up the file.

I took it from her, then skewered her with a look. "How bad was Nikki? And do *not* lie to me."

"Well, ah—" Mrs. French swallowed, shooting a look at Brody, who stared steadily back. My guts twisted as I watched the parade of emotions across her face.

"Spit it out, Mrs. French."

"She—well, you see, dear, she's in a coma—"

I didn't wait around for the rest. I'd been to Dr. Sells's clinic often enough in the past year, and though she had multiple locations around the city, the biggest and best equipped was also the one with which I was the most familiar. I showed up at the entrance to the clinic blowing sparks, startling a mother and her two kids as they hurried past me into the parking lot. I rushed through the front doors and looked around wildly, making a beeline for the woman at reception.

"Nikki Dawes," I snapped. Once again, there was a weird shimmy-shake to the walls, and the woman looked at me with wide, frightened eyes as I practically climbed over the desk to read her monitor.

"ICU!" she squeaked. "Third floor but you can't—"

I couldn't poof to the ICU because I couldn't remember if I'd been there, but I did race up the stairs with impressive speed. That was another skill I'd picked up along the way of my development, sort of like the miraculous power of healing, and apparently, it was still extant. *So why hadn't I been able to heal Nikki?*

I reached the third floor and burst out onto the main hallway, immediately catching sight of Armaeus Bertrand, Magician of the Arcana Council.

Same bronzed skin, same perfect hair. But unlike his more formal suit from the psychic fair, now he wore a typical summer-weight suit and gleaming laced loafers, platinum winking at his wrists and neck. He looked up at me as soon as I skidded into the corridor, and while I didn't expect a smile given the circumstances, I also didn't expect the panic in his gaze.

"*Sara,*" he whispered in my mind.

My heart skipped a beat as I broke stride, Armaeus now seeming too far away from me. I tripped, the lower half of my body losing all feeling, and then I looked at the floor to see what was impeding my feet. The floor was suddenly a lot *closer* than I remembered it being before, and my heart was hammering a lot harder, and—

Armaeus's strong arms wrapped around me before I face-planted in the linoleum.

I blacked out, which made it easier to accept the full energy of Armaeus flowing through my body, racing along my circuits. I couldn't speak, couldn't hear, but I could feel his presence even if nothing else made sense.

He was like a balm to circuits that I hadn't even been aware were scorched, but at the first pressure of his touch, I nearly collapsed all over again with pent-up pain. How had I not been aware I was so damaged? And when had this damage happened?

"*Sara,*" Armaeus said again, but everything he spoke after that was a blur of soft, melodic syllables I had no energy to follow, as much as I wanted to. I fell down into a deep, dark hole, and I was only aware of lights sparking on the fringes. I wasn't in pain, exactly. I wasn't even truly afraid. I was just—so…so tired.

Why was I so tired?

The crack against my sternum came so quickly, so abruptly, that my eyes flew open and my hands sprang wide, defensive blue fire immediately erupting at my fingertips. I lurched off the bed only to be shoved right back down again, and I stared from the beautiful, tortured face of Armaeus to the haggard face of Brody Rooks right behind him—to the face of a third person who I hadn't realized had entered the room, but whose smirk I'd still remember when I was ten years dead.

Aleksander Kreios. The Devil of the Arcana Council.

"I told you that would work," Kreios said smugly. Today, he'd adopted his most familiar glamour, that of the Mediterranean playboy, with a long flowing mane of hair, sun-kissed skin stretched over high cheekbones, a strong jaw, and achingly soft lips, brilliant green eyes, and a long, lean body that would have looked just as comfortable lounging on the beach as loitering at the side of a hospital bed, in an open-necked linen tunic and frayed khakis. I couldn't see his feet, but I assumed they were shod in thick-soled beach sandals. Because: Kreios.

"If I'd known there were going to be so many people in this room, I would have assigned you your own ward. Now move it." Dr. Sells's autocratic tones sounded from the doorway, and I blinked my gaze that way. The crisp, efficient, gym-teacher-with-a-stethoscope Dr. Sells, the Arcana Council's chief clinician for now going on eighty years, with her tightly banded chestnut hair and her no-nonsense glasses, stalked into the room. Brody and Kreios obligingly moved to the side, while Armaeus didn't stir. One of his hands remained planted on my leg, and his eyes were glued to the monitors beside the bed. That alone was so strange, I scowled at him.

"Um...since when do you need to check the monitors to see how well you're healing someone?"

"Since the poison blanketing your system made me blind to you as well, Miss Wilde," he said, his words soft, almost formal. "As it made you blind to yourself. If you hadn't the shard of Nul Magis embedded in your palm, eradicating the worst of the magic, you would likely already be dead. This is deep and unknown magic to me."

I blinked in shock, but Armaeus refused to look at me.

"He's right about the poison," Dr. Sells said, switching out my IV bag with an efficiency born of generations of experience. Originally human, she'd been conscripted into Armaeus's personal army in the 1940s, when he'd first come to Las Vegas. "We haven't seen anything like it before. The toxin was likely administered orally, but for something as strong as this, you should have tasted it or known it was entering your system. Before she dropped into a coma, Nikki confirmed you'd both consumed beer from the festival. Is that right?"

"Wait, she's *still* in a coma?" I demanded, sharply enough that Armaeus finally glanced at me. "Why aren't you with her?"

"She's recovering." Once again, it was Kreios who spoke. "She, like you, simply needed to be reminded of the dangers of going too deep into herself. Sometimes the body is smarter than the brain. Not often, granted, but sometimes."

"You shocked her awake." I cast a wild look around the room, my skin icing up when I saw the paddles. "You gave me an electrical shock."

"You had fallen so deep, so quickly," Armaeus said. "Too deep. My first instinct was to go deep as well to bring you back, and I did. And that helped, but I am healthy and whole. When you turned to Nikki to heal her, you compromised yourself further without realizing it."

"So I didn't help her," I said flatly. "But she'd responded, she came to, she seemed fine. I had no idea she was even still sick. Maybe a little dizzy…" A wave of queasiness swept over me, and I glanced to the side, biting my lip.

"You did help her. You saved her life, in fact. But she is not healed yet. Again, this toxin was working well below the level of discernible energy. You wouldn't even have noticed it lingering. I only found it this time because I knew what I was looking for, and even then…" He thinned his lips. "It should not have resisted my magic. It should not have blocked me so effectively."

"But it didn't matter in the end," I said, trying to understand. "You revived me with a set of shock paddles, like I was having a heart attack."

"My idea," Kreios put in again, with such obvious pride my lips quirked.

"It doesn't change the fact that we don't know who made the attempt on your life, poisoning your ale at an open-air festival," Armaeus said. "How was it slipped into the drink without you realizing it?"

"It wasn't the ale." I shook my head. "We would have noticed that. I bet it was the misters we walked under when we went into the spectral warrior section. Those bastards did that to us and then had the nerve to ask for help." My blood ran like ice through my veins. "I'm going to kill that old man."

"Both good guesses, and you're both wrong," Dr. Sells said. "For the toxin to work this thoroughly, it needed time to sink into the skin, particularly considering how little exposed skin you have available. Ingesting it with beer would work, but you absolutely would have tasted it at the concentration needed. Most likely, this toxin would've needed to be injected. Nikki had several cuts and abrasions on her—they could have served as the entry point for any of the toxins. You heal so quickly, I can't tell when you received any of your injuries, so I…" She sighed. "I'm simply not sure."

"So when could I have picked it up? When I was healing her?"

"Possibly." She swung her gaze to Armaeus. "What are your readings indicating?"

"The toxin entered my system exactly twelve seconds after I laid hands upon Miss Wilde's hands," he said. "Because I was waiting for it, I isolated it immediately and it did not spread. But the entry point was definitely skin-to-skin contact. I know you say that it could not have traveled so quickly through such basic contact, but that doesn't change the reality of the data."

"Okay, then, who else did you touch?" Dr. Sells asked me.

"I mean, God only knows," I protested. "I was in and out of easily a dozen trinket shops even before I headed to the spectral warrior section. And then there was that little kid with his stack of cards…"

"Cards?" Armaeus prompted.

I obligingly pulled out the card advertising the tent of Mistress Malificorem. As I offered it, Armaeus reeled back, his hands coming up automatically to ward me off.

Dr. Sells stepped forward and pulled the card from my hands. I notice that hers were encased in gloves. She dropped the card into a plastic bag and sealed it. "Was the boy Connected?"

"I…I have no idea. He said he was handing out cards for Sariah—well, for Mistress Malificorem. He said she had stacks of these back at her tent." I frowned. "Wait a minute. Sariah touched me too. Why wasn't she affected?"

Armaeus's brows shot up, and he scowled. "That is…curious," he allowed. "Did she touch your hands?"

"No. But Nikki touched the card too." I looked down at my fingers, which strangely didn't look like the appendages of evil. "Anyone got any bleach?"

"Let me take a look at that postcard," Brody said. He peered at the postcard, then shook his head. "Wrong tent for Sariah. And since when has Sariah ever needed help promoting herself? I don't know who sent that kid around, but he clearly thought you knew Sariah, and he clearly wanted to get this card in your hands."

I made a face. "I don't even know what that little boy's name is. What if he's also in a coma?"

"Let me check on that," Brody said, turning to the door. "There's too much about this that isn't making sense. It's way too organized…" He left the room, still muttering.

"Where's Nikki?" I asked.

To my surprise, it was Armaeus who answered with a short, bitter sigh. He seemed to be taking her ongoing fragility personally. "Resting, as you should be. But not for long, I'm afraid. This attack on the Council cannot go unanswered."

"Attack on the Council? That's maybe overstating it." I swung my gaze from his face to Kreios's, but they both looked equally grim. "It was just somebody taking a potshot at me. Or, I guess Nikki, since she's worse off." Someone was going to get blasted beyond the veil for that, I decided. There wouldn't be anything left of them but smoke.

Kreios's smile was weary. "Like it or not, you *are* the Council now, Sara Wilde. Welcome to the show."

CHAPTER SEVEN

Over Dr. Sells's strident objections, I checked myself out of the clinic a few hours later after looking in on Nikki. She was still asleep, but it was a natural sleep, Sells assured me, not one that was medically induced. Progress.

Once outside, my first thought was to return to the festival, but that felt foolish at best. If anyone recognized me…

Then again, screw that. If anyone recognized me, they'd know their little attempt to shut me down had failed. That seemed far more important than managing my own safety.

"You could also disguise yourself, Miss Wilde."

Also a good point. Carefully restoring my mental shields to allow for communication but not random thought rifflage, I focused on the general direction of the Magician, but spoke aloud. "So, I'm good to travel? The goop is out of me?"

His response was not as quick as I would have liked, but it was still a response. *"You are good to travel. The poison that struck your system was made with a combination of technoceuticals and microorganisms — a combination Dr.*

Sells is now researching as quickly as possible. We anticipate data soon."

"Microorganisms." I made a face to the sky. "You mean bugs."

"Superbugs," Armaeus said. *"If my hypothesis is correct, and there is a 99.875% likelihood that it is, you were poisoned with a substance that is, in fact, in developing usage among the spectral opposition warriors to counteract the effects of magic. But they clearly are not the only ones experimenting with the formulation."*

"Well, that's encouraging. Is Sariah okay?"

Another pause, this one more annoying. "What?" I demanded.

"You forget, Miss Wilde, that your sister, for lack of a less disturbing word, was formed of the same stuff and stubbornness that you were. This means that she has many of your same strengths, though in far more rudimentary, truncated forms."

"She can also pickpocket other Connecteds' abilities. How come I was never able to do that?"

Armaeus's return thoughts were wry. *"Another aspect to your sister's personality is her willingness to eagerly take that which isn't hers. While you have a hard time taking even that which is thrust upon you."*

"Could you not judge me for just ten seconds here?" I retorted, but my lips twitched at the familiar gibe. It suddenly occurred to me that nobody on this earth knew me as well as Armaeus did. Even people I'd worked with longer knew parts of me, but only Armaeus had the unique perspective of having crawled around inside my neural circuitry and lived to tell the tale. Of course, that level of insight was not without its liabilities. "So what you're saying is that Sariah is blocking you. You can't track her because she's putting up the same kind of mental barriers I am, only she's better at it."

"Not better," Armaeus corrected immediately. *"More stubborn, perhaps. More desperate. Sariah has spent a very long time avoiding beings who sought to control or dominate her. The idea of allowing anyone, even a benevolent searcher, to find her is likely anathema to her."*

"So I'll have to do it the old-fashioned way."

"It would be wise. What would also be wise is what you will find in your pocket."

I frowned but put my hand into my jacket pocket, drawing out a small metallic device. I rolled it around in my fingers. "This is a tracking device."

"The council is also not without its resources," Armaeus said. *"The subject of Sariah has been vexing me, but the most likely manner of tracking her is one recommended by the Fool, of all people."*

I grinned. The Fool of the Arcana Council had many skills, but one of the most important was his ability with technology. Simon had gotten me out of difficult scrapes on more than a few occasions, so often I could almost forgive him the occasions where he'd gotten me into even worse scrapes.

I squinted at the small device. "He thinks that Sariah won't notice this?"

"He believes, based on limited experience that he has with your sister, that she won't even think to look. Another thing the two of you share is a sense of personal recklessness, particularly when it comes to anything regarding your own safety. While it is not one of your most charming attributes, it is one that we can put to good use in this case."

"Hey," I protested. "I'm standing right here."

"Which is another point of curiosity," the Magician observed. *"I would have thought you already well on your way back to the festival."*

I gritted my teeth. "You know it's not as easy for me as it is for you. I got this whole firebomb thing I've got to go through first. Maybe you and Simon should put your heads together and come up with a solution for *that*."

The Magician, however, was already gone. Rolling my eyes, I destabilized, the familiar burn almost welcome as it confirmed my powers hadn't been irreparably damaged by the poison someone had so rudely insinuated into my person. I reappeared at the festival at the same place where Nikki and I had first claimed our beers a few hours earlier. If anything, the place had gotten more crowded. From the looks of it in that quadrant of the festival grounds, the spectral opposition warrior group was putting on some kind of demonstration involving glittering lights. I turned myself in the other direction without hesitation. I'd had enough of them for one day. I was all for people protecting themselves against the Connected, but I preferred to believe that most Connected weren't out to hurt each other. Dare to dream.

I found Sariah's tent without too much difficulty. It was lit from within, casting a cheerful glow out into the walkway. There was no one waiting at the door, so I ducked my head inside — only to find no one there. I moved to the back of the tent and noticed that a seam had been sliced into the fabric. Sliced by Sariah or by somebody else?

Given that there was no signs of struggle, my money was on Sariah.

Which meant she'd known I was coming.

I scanned the space, flicking open my third eye, and rocked back slightly on my heels. The Connected energy here was...an absolute mess. I could almost see — I thought I could see — Sariah beneath all of it. But whatever was Sariah was completely buried beneath a mass of conflicting circuits, some barely glowing, some flaring with angry sparks, glittering even as they faded with her departure. In any event, Sariah hadn't left long ago. If I ducked through this same slit in the tent...

"Mistress Malificorem?"

Shifting my gaze back to normal sight, I turned at the hesitant voice, not at all expecting the young woman it belonged to. She was a tall, slender black woman with tight, curly hair cropped close to her scalp, her fine brows arched, her striking face devoid of makeup from the tips of her long lashes to the fullness of her lips. She stood at the front of my tent looking straight at me, but she couldn't see me. Her eyes were clouded over, hazy, and she clutched the harness lead of a muscular, white-muzzled German shepherd.

"Um, well—"

"Oh, good," she said, her shoulders dropping into a near boneless slump. My third eye flipped open without prompting, and I watched her energy jump again, more powerful by far than it should be. "The little boy said you would be in and out, and I've already stopped by a few times. I was here just a minute ago and I thought you were here, but you didn't say anything, and—"

She waved a hand in front of her face, and my heart clenched. *Dammit, Sariah.* My guts twisting, I stepped around Sariah's small table and crossed the short distance.

"How can I help you?" I asked.

She smiled nervously, the faintest blush darkening her cheeks. "Thank you. My name is Lainie Grant, and the boy—I mean, he was just a boy, so it's possible he really had no idea... Now I feel a little silly."

I reached for her hand, helping her toward the seat. "He, ah, didn't give you any cards, did he?"

"What? Oh no." She shook her head. "He just talked to me. I think he liked my dog."

"I can understand why." I smiled, trying to swallow my apprehension. I could sense the problem with her eyes—she wasn't born with the affliction, and I was pretty sure it'd been caused recently. The fact that she was still clutching the harness of her dog meant she hadn't had him for a long time, and she didn't have the ease of movement of a long-term blind person. I tugged on her hand, and she came forward, her face moving up and to the wrong direction until I guided her to the folding chair. Then I scooted around to the other side and sat, drawing in a deep breath.

Sariah, of course, had left no cards behind, but I wasn't without my resources. I pulled my own tattered deck out of my hoodie pocket and set them on the table, squaring the edges. I glanced over to the dog, who was watching me with his soulful doggy eyes.

I'll do the best I can, buddy.

He bobbed his head up and down, and I gave him a grim smile. Did dogs do that, like, randomly? Or had I seriously just talked to a dog?

The young woman had begun visibly trembling, and I loudly shuffled the cards on the table.

"So, Lainie, would you like a reading?" I began gently. "Or how can I help you today?"

"I—I think I would like a reading," she said softly. "I mainly want to know how...like, how I can fix what happened to me. Or if I even should."

Oh, honey. I lifted my hand and simultaneously opened my third eye again. There was a veil over Lainie's eyes, but the eyeballs themselves were also damaged, severely damaged. Beyond those destroyed eyes, however, that deep well of psychic ability loomed.

"Can you tell me how it happened? I can read the cards without that information, but it helps to have as much context as possible."

This sounded like a cheat, and probably was a cheat for some of the people who'd set up shop at this festival. But the truth was, it was easier for me to direct a reading if I knew specifically what the querent wanted to know. The cards were equal opportunity servers—I could pull the exact same reading for a love question as I could for a reading about a job search or whether or not someone would find their lost wedding ring. But knowing what particular circumstances were driving the reading always helped.

"Sure. I…so, I work, well I *worked* at the Mt. Potosi Observatory. Do you know it? It's not far from the city."

"I've heard of it, yes." I hadn't, but the answer seemed to please her.

"It's really great. One of the best observatories out there, and such good people. Anyway, I was doing some research for a college paper several weeks ago, and—well, there was the strangest constellation pattern in the sky. It didn't make sense. So I…" She hesitated as she colored, but my stomach was already sinking. I knew where this was going.

"I b-broke the rules of the observatory and recalibrated the scope to see more clearly. I've done that before, and it's never been a problem. But this time when I looked, there was a sudden bright surge, and—" Lainie looked away, a tear snaking down her cheek.

"And you were blinded," I said, as gently as I could.

She nodded quickly. "At first, I didn't realize it. I fell back and hit my head. I passed out, apparently, and someone heard the commotion and sent for an ambulance. But when I came to, they told me the news. I was blind."

I winced, and the need to reach out across the table, to heal this woman, suddenly overwhelmed me.

"Miss Wilde." The Magician's voice sounded in my mind instantaneously, his tone careful and soothing, but firm.

I know, I know. Armaeus and I had discussed this many times—that I couldn't go around healing people indiscriminately. I'd done it before, though, and it hadn't come back to bite me...well, not really. Most of the people I'd helped were in dire circumstances, not literally walk-ons off the street. *But you know what she was looking at.*

"Yes. She was looking at you, or what you created. But this may well be the path she came into this world to follow. Who are you to decide to alter that path?"

I'm the woman who altered it the first time by blasting her retinas into the back of her head? I could anticipate his quelling response, so I turned down the volume on Armaeus Radio and refocused on the young woman. "What happened after that?"

"See, that's the strange part. My parents, God love them both, had enough money to get me immediately into treatment, and then I was paired with Night here." She reached out, and the dog obligingly ducked his head under her palm, allowing her to pat him. "But ever since the accident, the strangest things have been happening. I've been, ah, seeing things. Like, not with my eyes."

I straightened, once again noting the flare of Connected energy rioting through the young woman. "You mean like a psychic?"

"Well, that sounds ridiculous—no offense intended—but yeah. The first thing was a series of numbers, so of course I joked to my mom that they were for the state lottery, and she went right out and got a ticket."

I winced. "And you won."

"It was three million dollars," she whispered. "More than enough to take care of me, my mom kept saying. She didn't want to tell my dad that she'd even played the lottery, but she went and got the money anyway, and after she deposited it, she caved. We had a meeting that night, and my dad told me not to tell anyone. They've been super scared ever since. I hate that."

"Of course," I said, keeping my words low and easy. I looked at her dog again, and he stared back at me with earnest sincerity. "What else did you see?"

"I saw more numbers, but I refused to play after that first time, refused even to tell my Mom about it so she wouldn't check. But it wasn't only numbers. It was people and situations too. And some of what I saw was terrible. My grandmother fell in one of my visions, and my Mom was so freaked out she made my aunt go spend the night with her. Grandma didn't fall that night, of course. Which kind of made it worse."

"Free will," I murmured, and I realized I'd picked up the cards and was shuffling them. "You can very often affect the outcome of an event simply by changing one element leading up to that event. Your aunt being with your grandma was not an expected action, and it forestalled an accident."

"But the problem is, what happens if I see something and don't do anything about it? I've tried that too." Her words broke on a sob. "There was an accident."

"Oh, honey." This time, I did say the words aloud.

"So my question is…is it wrong for me to want to go back to the way I was? To not have this burden on my shoulders anymore? Is that wrong? Or should I, like, embrace it." She gestured awkwardly around the small tent that she couldn't see. A tear slipped from Lainie's eye and flowed down her face, but she kept going. "Honor the ability I have, try to do some good with it?"

I placed the cards in front of her and folded her hands over them. "Go ahead and shuffle. When you're ready, cut the cards. I'll just do a three-card spread to see what message the universe has for you."

And the universe had better not dick me either.

Whether Armaeus heard that or not, he didn't respond.

"Okay," Lainie said, her voice soft and scared. She shuffled and cut the deck, then sat back. I chose the second pile and put it on top of the first, then quickly drew three cards, laying them out.

Her brows leapt as she stared down at the table. Then she reached for the cards.

"Oh my God," she whispered.

I swallowed, my mouth suddenly dry. "You can see them?"

"I can." Her hand started to tremble. "That's a picture of a tower, like, with fire," she said, correctly identifying the Tower card while neatly avoiding any mention of the people who were falling out of said tower. "And that's a lady in a chair. Actually, both of these are ladies in chairs." She gently touched her fingers to the other two cards. "One with like those weighing scales things, and one with like a little moon above her head."

"The Tower, Justice, and the High Priestess," I said, pressing my hands over hers. She was the only one trembling, but it was a near thing. Because Lainie Grant was sighted, even though she could not see, and the cards could not have been clearer about where she needed to go, or who could help her. "You were right to come here today, and your path was right to lead to me. But I'm not the one who can help you, ultimately."

She looked up hopefully. "Someone can?"

"Oh yeah," I said, grimacing. "She's known as the High Priestess, and she knows her stuff. But brace yourself. She's kind of a drama queen."

"I'm okay with that." Lainie nodded. "Really. I just want—I just want to understand."

I lifted my hand, eyeing the young woman's dog, who also seemed to be regarding me with a placid "don't do it" expression on his face. And in truth, it really wasn't my place to heal this woman. She hadn't asked for it. She'd only asked for understanding. Eshe, the High Priestess of the Arcana Council, could give her that. Or she could give her a headache and a deep desire to smack something. It was kind of a toss-up.

But the pressure inside me to help grew too strong, and I broke beneath it. I drew in a deep breath, my fingers starting to tingle despite the dog's low, cautionary whine. "So, um, in addition to understanding, is there anything I can do for you?"

"This card." Lainie reached out and pulled another card from the deck, handing it to me. "You can pay attention to this card."

"I—ah, what?" I took the card from her, glancing at it before setting it faceup on the table. "That's Temperance. That—that doesn't make sense with your situation." Temperance was all about finding harmony, blending disparate forces, and making primal magic, but it didn't feel at all right for the blind seer in front of me. It also was a card I'd never been a fan of. No one would accuse me of going out of my way to find harmony in life.

"It's not for me." She shook her head, confirming my suspicions. "It's for you."

I made a face Lainie couldn't see. "Well, thanks. I'll add it to my next meditation cycle."

The flap of the tent fluttered again, and all three of us jumped at the noise, two of us craning our necks to see.

"Ah, Mistress Malificorem?" Brody asked, shooting a startled glance at the woman in the querent's chair. "Sorry to interrupt. But we've got a bit of a problem."

CHAPTER EIGHT

B rody and I stalked across the festival grounds, which once again looked entirely too normal for everything that had gone on today. Celtic music played cheerfully over in Celtlandia, while some strange tribal chants were happening in spectral warrior-ville. But neither group so much as looked at each other, so it appeared that, for the moment, the Hatfields and McCoys had signed a truce.

Which was weird.

"Is this about the boy handing out the postcards?" I asked, unable to contain myself any longer.

Brody shook his head. "No, we never found the boy. But there's been no reports of anyone matching his description reporting any distress or going missing, nothing like that. So that's a bit of a dead end, I'm afraid."

"Of course it is." Feeling uneasy about the fate of the towheaded child, I jerked my thumb back to the tent. "Did you see the girl getting a reading in there?"

"I heard you saying something about the high priestess. And I saw she was blind. You recruiting for a new Oracle?"

I stumbled a little, and Brody's hand instantly went out to steady me. "What's wrong?"

"What's wrong is...what you just said. Everything about it."

"You mean—"

"Don't say it again! Once was enough." I held my hands to my temples, willing the sudden pounding of my brain to subside. I couldn't, *wouldn't* believe that the sweet Lainie Grant from the observatory was being led to the High Priestess of the Arcana Council as an acolyte, but perhaps more importantly, I didn't know why the possibility of her doing that was upsetting me so much. Eshe wasn't necessarily my favorite Council crony, but she had helped me in the past, and she more or less had my back. She was haughty, condescending, and cruel when she wanted to be—living over two thousand years would do that to a person—but she wasn't a villain by any means. So what was I so worried about?

I pushed the idea away, tabling it until I had time to focus. "Okay, so Sariah, then. You found Sariah."

"No, but I haven't been looking for her. Sariah's never lost by mistake." There was a curious flatness to his tone, the universal pitch that exes who were left behind employed when speaking about the ones who got away. Brody seemed not at all in the mood to talk about his troubles with Sariah, but nevertheless, I persisted.

"What happened with you two, anyway? I thought you were chummy."

"We're plenty chummy. We'll continue to be chummy."

Okay, so maybe this wasn't a good idea after all. The idea of Brody and Sariah together was charming in the abstract—at the time of Sariah's creation more than ten years ago, my seventeen-year-old self had been hopelessly in love with Brody Rooks. So while I'd gone on to forge a distinctly Brodyless life by choice, Sariah had been holed up in Hell with nothing but her daydreams to keep her company. Brody was her first true love and — I'd thought — still her true love. But I preferred thinking of their romance against a background of Disney princesses and chirping birds, not Fifty Shades of Ew.

Brody, however, kept going. "But Sariah is kind of like an addict, and I know that type way too well."

I frowned. "An addict of what?"

"That's the problem. Everything. She's constantly in search of the next high, only in her case, it's not limited to drugs or booze. It's experiences. It's abilities. It's feeling. She doesn't know who or what she is and she's more than ready to find out, but that problem is only made worse by her little kleptomania problem. She literally doesn't know who she is, and when she finds something she likes, she knows she can't keep it."

"Yet apparently, she's not the problem right now. She's not where you're taking me." I didn't know how to feel about Sariah, but I did want her to be safe. After all she'd endured, I worried more about her than I did myself, which, arguably, wasn't saying much. But still.

He scowled. "No." Then he clammed up and kept walking, leaving me to take in the rest of the festival. There remained only this last evening of it and tomorrow morning, then it'd be done again for another year, but for a moment, I wondered what it would be like if it *wasn't* done. What if this *was* the future of the world, little enclaves of specially skilled Connecteds living in the open, offering magical experiences to non-Connecteds in a more visible way? Would they be accepted? Or would the almost pathological fear against the other eventually knock them back and keep them down?

Being left alone with these thoughts was less than awesome, but it wasn't until Brody got me into his car—the beat-up brown sedan, unfortunately, not a sleek Town Car from the Justice Hall parking lot that had been allocated for my use—that Brody even looked at me. I could tell he was working up to a doozy of an announcement, but I didn't know which way it would break. He wouldn't have held out on me this long about Nikki, because then he'd be dead. Which left me with a whole lot of no ideas.

With a grim curse, he started the sedan and pulled it out into traffic, taking us roughly back toward the Strip. "Spill it, Brody," I finally said, not bothering to hide my irritation. "It can't be that bad."

He drew in a deep breath, then released it. "Dixie called me. We're heading to the Chapel of Everlasting Love in the Stars. There's been a death."

"Okay, fine. It can be that bad."

I deliberately avoided glancing his way. Dixie Quinn was one of the most well-known Connecteds in Las Vegas, and up until a relatively short while ago, she'd been dating one Brody Rooks. Why couldn't all his exes live in Texas?

Still, this didn't make sense. "I didn't realize she was up and running again. Heck, I can't believe she survived detox after the hit of technoceuticals she'd taken. How is she back to marrying off showgirls and sugar daddies?"

Dixie had gotten caught up in a low-level drug-running operation of high-level technoceuticals, drugs spiked with arcane or magical properties. Though not directly as a result of her transgressions, some people

84

had died, and some — including her — had nearly died. She wasn't my favorite person right now.

"She's on probation," Brody said. "That doesn't restrict her ability to run her chapel. Which she's been doing, quietly and successfully. Until tonight."

"Who died?"

His jaw worked, and the way his hands were clamped on the wheel, I was pretty sure he was going to pop a knuckle. "A young woman by the name of Alison Kay. She came to the chapel with another woman, Lenora Drake, earlier this evening, wanting to get married. Dixie, being Dixie, had no problem with that. Only, they didn't want to get married to each other. They wanted to marry an absent party."

My brows went up. "How absent?"

"Absent as in he was Skyping from Ireland."

My stomach twisted on itself and doubled back, a Möbius strip of queasy. "Ireland."

"You can see why I thought you'd be interested."

"But how is that even legal? Isn't there, like, marriage license paperwork that has to happen?"

"According to Dixie, the women appeared to have all their documents in order — separately — to marry the same man under two different aliases. But to be clear, she doesn't make it a policy to refuse anyone a ceremony. A wedding at the Chapel of Everlasting Love in the Stars doesn't legitimize an illegal act, and she states that right up front. That said, if a man comes in and wants to marry his poodle, she makes it happen. That's just who she is."

"It certainly is."

Dixie may have a unique capacity to jump on my last nerve, but the petite, vivacious blonde, known for her killer curves and pink cowboy boots, hadn't officially done anything illegal…directly. She was a Connected of moderate ability who wanted to have far more of that ability than she did, and she was willing to do about anything to make that happen—including putting unsuspecting people at risk as she stitched together her get-Connected-quick schemes. She hadn't been convicted of intentionally harming anyone, and she'd denied leading that technoceutical drug ring with every bubbling bounce of her being.

The real kicker was this: since the technoceuticals she trafficked weren't controlled substances, her lawyers had argued that it would be the equivalent of her getting the book thrown at her for selling Love-Me-Not pills to lonely hearts with a daisy allergy. The judge had bought it, or the lawyer had bought him, if I was feeling uncharitable about it. Either way, Dixie was back in her chapel.

With a dead girl on her hands.

"How'd it go down?" I asked. "And why were you able to leave the scene to come get me?"

"Two women showed up, one knifed the other. We have the attacker in custody. And I could leave the scene because I didn't catch the case. Despite the location, there's been no whiff of a Connected connection. I wasn't even tapped to ride shotgun. They've given that role to a rookie."

I eyed him. "And that chafes your chaps?"

"Nah, she's a good kid. She does seem to have a particular knack for working homicides, though, which is the second reason I wanted you along." He shot me a weary grin. "Not that I have a problem with her being Connected, if she is, I just want to know what I'm dealing with."

"Fair enough. And the first reason?"

"The guy the women were all hyped up to marry? He went by two names, both of which start with a G and a K. George Kerry and Geoffrey Kent."

"And that's important why—" And then I got it, of course, as I imagined the names in my mind's eye. GK also stood for Green Knight. "Seamus McCarthy's kid, Conal?" I asked. I'd sent the McCarthy family tree over to Brody earlier. Apparently the detective had been busy.

"We're tracking down anything we can on the guy. Given that he's operating across international boundaries, we've also pulled in Interpol."

I grimaced. "Of course you have." I'd had more than my share of run-ins with Interpol, and most of them weren't pleasant. It was not that I didn't understand their interest in me. Interpol had a particular interest in crimes that crossed international borders, and the Connected drug trade did that on an almost daily basis. I was the most connected Connected they'd ever spoken to, and they knew I was an important link. They just also weren't entirely sure I wasn't a criminal. It made for tense fireside chats.

"But you're not involved in this case," Brody countered. "I'm not involved in this case. And as of this moment, Interpol isn't involved in this case. Which means you can come in, talk to Dixie, meet this rookie detective, and see what you see about the scene. I've already been to it, and something about it strikes me as hinky, but I can't quite place what."

"What does the rookie detective say?"

"Unknown. She's working with her partner, and he and I aren't mutual fans. So she's playing it smart and keeping her eyes on the dead body right now."

"Noted." We swung into the parking lot of the Chapel of Everlasting Love in the Stars, a lot it shared with several other businesses, none of which were doing a brisk business given all the police tape cordoning off the area around the chapel. Just another day in Vegas.

We exited the car as two CSI techs left the building, nodding at Brody with their grim, no-nonsense gazes. They paid no attention to me, but I was working on being unnoticed. This was a slightly different skill from being disguised, but I seemed to be developing the hang of it.

"Why, Detective Brody, as I live and breathe. You came back."

Dixie Quinn was dressed in her usual attire of white minidress and pink cowboy hat and boots, only a bit incongruous given that a murder had just taken place at her chapel. Her gaze swung to me and widened. "And Sara! It's been too long. How's Nikki doing? We sent over a brigade of well-wishers as soon as we heard she'd fallen ill. That Dr. Sells is ever so prickly, isn't she? But we convinced her that the best cure for Nikki was the love of those who loved her."

Despite myself, I smiled. Love her or hate her, Dixie did have her moments. "I think that'll definitely help."

"Let me bring you right in," she said. "I'm not technically allowed on-site, but Detective McGeery is being particularly charmin' about all that. And I *do* appreciate it so."

She prattled on as Brody and I exchanged a look. Even as rookies, homicide detectives were rarely charming.

When we got to the chapel, however, we had another surprise waiting for us.

Homicide detectives were rarely staked to the floor either.

CHAPTER NINE

"What the *fuck*!"

Brody bolted forward, yelling for the other cops, who were in the secondary chapel where apparently witness interviews were still ongoing. I was right behind him, my third eye flickering open—

I reared back, sending another of the cops into the wall.

"Sorry." I stepped to the side and steadied myself against the plaster as the men and women in uniform thundered by me. It took only a few seconds for them to descend on the rookie. She was out cold but alive, weak heart rate, bleeding heavily from a shoulder wound. I stood off to the side, forcing myself to swallow my bile, and refocused on the room.

The electrical currents in the place weren't simply erratic, they were off the charts. Spinning and whirling and flying wild, like a class of third graders set loose with a thousand cans of silly string. These currents vibrated differently than they should, not merely humming along like good little circuits usually did, or hissing angrily like frayed circuits tended to do. But crashing, wailing, moaning, crying, as if all the sins of the world had come home to roost…

"Dixie," I murmured to the woman cowering beside me. "What *exactly* is going on?"

She stiffened, reluctantly pulling herself off the wall. "Well, as you can imagine, I'd like to know that myself. I don't even know where the first knife came from, let alone this one. I can assure you, neither of those women brought any such thing with them. Not that we checked for weapons, of course, but something like that, I would've noticed."

"I'd like to think so."

The knife that stuck out of the detective's shoulder was easily a foot long, the blade wide and not particularly sharp looking below the ornamental hilt. Nevertheless, anything pointed could be a weapon in the right hands. The hilt wasn't jeweled or made of precious metal from what I could tell, but the leather wrapped around its base was intricately worked, a riot of dyed green-and-brown designs. It didn't look like a traditional witch's athame, and while it may not have been razor-sharp, it had more than done the job on the rookie. "Were the women Irish? And where's the living one, anyway?"

That seemed to be the question of the hour. A fresh uproar in the interview room revealed that the homicide suspect, one Lenora Drake, was now mysteriously missing, while of course the homicide victim Alison Kay, had already been whisked off to the coroner's office for further examination.

"She was sitting there all huddled over, not saying a word, practically rocking in place," spluttered a beat cop who'd clearly been assigned to watch her. "Then I heard Detective Brody shout, and I looked over. When I looked back, just that quick, she was gone."

"Bullshit," an older detective growled, and I realized this must be the man Brody didn't like, though I had a hard time blaming the guy for his frustration. It wasn't normal for women to just disappear on you like that, unless you were Connected. "You left your post."

"My eyes did, absolutely," the man protested. "My feet were right here. And she would have had to go past me to get outside. I mean, her *clothes* are still there."

That made me stiffen, immediately recalling me to the banshee I'd encountered at the festival. What were these women, merely illusions? Wraiths?

No. Illusions didn't die. Nor could they stake living people to the ground.

Right?

"How'd the bride die exactly?" I asked Dixie abruptly. She didn't hesitate.

"Same type blade as that sweet Detective McGeery took, same thrust. I heard a knock on the door, I turned, and one woman, Alison Kay, was on the ground just like that, knife in the heart, while the other one had fainted clean away. I screamed for someone to call the cops, and they came. I got the unharmed woman, Lenora Drake, to come to, and…" She glanced at me. "And I wish I'd had Nikki with me, I'll tell you that."

I felt the slightest twinge of guilt. Before I'd come along, Nikki had been Dixie's right-hand woman. The two hadn't been the best of friends the way Nikki and I had become, but they'd been close, and Dixie had relied on Nikki's unique skills probably more than she'd realized until the day she looked up and Nikki was no longer there. Dixie blamed me for breaking up the band, but she and Nikki weren't enemies by any stretch. Still, I could understand her missing Nikki. I'd been without the woman for a matter of hours, and I already felt like my arm'd been cut off.

"You're no slouch yourself, Dixie," I said, as graciously as I could manage. "I suspect you held your own."

"Well, I can tell you this. Lenora Drake was out of her mind, babbling, frightened. She'd seen something more than her friend getting knifed, like a ghost, a demon…something. By the time the cops got here, she was barely coherent. And smaller too, it almost seemed. Withered."

I frowned. "Like she was fading?"

"Exactly like that." Dixie nodded. "Only, that doesn't really make sense, right? Ordinary Connecteds can't do that."

I sharpened my eyes on her. "She was Connected?"

"More so than her friend, yes. But after Alison got stuck—"

"By Lenora," I put in.

"Well…" Dixie bit her lip.

"You were right there," I said severely. "How did you not see what happened?"

"Because nothing *did* happen," she insisted, her eyes rounding. "I heard the knock, I looked back, and the women were on the ground. One right in front of me, the other several steps away. There was no one here, Sara, I swear it. And they didn't have knives!"

"Who was in the room with McGeery?" Brody barked, drawing my attention.

"No one," another of the beat cops said, the one we'd shouldered by at the door. "I know that doesn't make sense, but no one passed us until you did, coming in or coming out. McGeery said she wanted to look at the scene with the room empty, and Detective Robbins was interviewing the witnesses."

Brody narrowed his eyes at Robbins. "You were talking to the bride who's now escaped?"

"No, I wasn't," huffed Robbins. "I was handling other interviews. Not that this is your case."

Brody pointed at the strange athame sticking out of McGeery's shoulder. "That thing makes it my case. Who did talk to her?"

"Well, McGeery did. She's a chick, the vic was a chick."

I winced at the blatant sexism, but no one in the room seemed to take notice.

"So you didn't talk to the bride—what's her name again?" Brody raked his hand through his hair.

"Lenora," Dixie said in her sweet drawl. "Lenora Drake."

"You didn't talk to Miss Drake at all, Robbins?"

"I hadn't yet, no. Woman was gibbering like a freak of nature. I couldn't make any sense of it." The surly detective closed his notebook and stuffed it in his jacket's inner pocket.

"But Detective McGeery could."

"I have no idea," Robbins said gruffly. "But she was talking to her. Then, all I know is McGeery stood up, patted the woman on the shoulder, announced she wanted to check out something else at the scene, and took off. I wasn't too worried because we had Las Vegas's finest watching every doorway and window. Little did I realize—"

"We got that part," Brody interjected wearily. "Who else did you interview?"

"There was another couple waiting to get married. They left to, I assume, go get drunk." Robbins rocked back on his heels. "They saw nothing out of the ordinary, nothing coming in or going out. Same story with the receptionist and wedding planner, both of whom are in the lobby. It was fucking Schrödinger's brides in here."

"What about the groom? The guy from Ireland?" As Brody asked the question, his eyes were on Dixie, not the detective. She frowned back.

"Why?" she answered defensively. "I don't understand. He wasn't even here. It's not like he could have sent a knife through a Skype call."

The EMTs chose that minute to arrive, and as they hustled forward, I braved another third-eye peek toward the center of the room. Once again it was a mass of electrical static, but this time, there was a distinct difference. I had a clear shot of Detective McGeery, and I could tell at a glance the damage that had been done to her. I could also tell that she had Connected abilities that were off the charts. And that she was dying. There was no reason for it because the wound from the athame hadn't hit anything critical, but darkness flowed out from that blade like an insidious wave, darkness that had been continuing to flow out while I'd been chatting with Dixie. Outrage shot through me, and I surged forward even as Dixie squeaked in alarm. Without giving it much thought, I robed myself in the appearance of an EMT, even as the real EMTs were running down the aisle of the chapel. All that mattered was that I reached McGeery first.

"Miss Wilde."

Stuff it.

I had no interest in playing by the Council's rules on this one.

I dropped to my knees by Detective McGeery, taking in her blonde hair and Nordic features. From her name, I'd assumed she was Irish, but this woman looked far more like a Viking than a Celt. She was also taller than I first expected, though lying flat out on the ground with a knife stuck in your shoulder would make anyone look a little puny. Still there was no doubt she was

Connected, which wasn't a bad thing to be for a detective.

Someone huffed behind me. "Who the hell are—"

I pressed my hand down on the detective's sternum and yanked the blade free.

The psychic flow that followed rocked everyone behind me off their feet, Connected and non-Connected alike. The power held within the crude-looking athame was ancient, far more ancient than the blade itself. I tossed it into the hands of Detective Robbins, who was out cold on the floor next to McGeery. When he came to in a second, though, he'd want to have the blade handy. Cops tended to be big fans of chain of evidence, and I wasn't about to get Brody into any more trouble from my antics.

Then I got down to work.

Unlike when I had attempted to heal Nikki, I wasn't operating in some sort of magic sinkhole, nor was I injured any longer. So my abilities to reach deep into Detective McGeery's life essence weren't hindered in any way. And, truth be told, I was more than a little pissed. There was too much going on that I didn't understand, and I was tired of being fed the information in dribs and drabs. I jolted McGeery with enough power to raise an elephant from its sickbed, and her eyes flashed open as she drew in a startled, agonized breath. Like Dixie, I missed Nikki in that moment, because knowing what was going through the woman's mind would have been nice. It would also have to wait.

"Don't let them sedate you until you talk to Brody," I murmured, and her eyes flared even wider at the implied threat, but there was nothing I could do about that. I released my hold on time and let one of the other EMTs push me aside, then moved among the crowd, switching outfits with each step. First EMT, then cop, then detective, then EMT again, then finally, Sara Wilde.

"We are going to have a nice long chat about scene protocol one day very soon," Brody muttered under his breath, keeping in lockstep beside me through every change.

"She was going down faster than anybody realized," I mumbled back. "I had to do something."

"Understood. And in this case, it's not a problem."

"Brody?" Dixie's voice reached us from the top of the room, distracting us from the buzz of EMTs around McGeery. Her cell phone was in her hand, and she looked fiercely at us as she stepped back into the hallway.

Without hesitating, Brody and I headed up the aisle of the chapel and followed Dixie down the hallway to her office. Leaving the door open, we stepped inside after her, with Brody in position at the doorway. "What is it?" he demanded tersely.

"After the drugs were found in my office—drugs I did not put there," Dixie said, eyeing me in particular, "I worked with Simon to create a better surveillance system for the chapel."

The Fool of the Arcana Council helping Dixie? That surprised me. She wasn't exactly running in the right circles to wrangle a favor from any Council member. So why were they so eager to assist?

If I seemed a little distrustful of the Council, well...it's only because I was.

"I already showed the primary surveillance footage to the police, of course. There's nothing on it, not even a twitch until a bright light flashes and I start screaming. Nobody could explain where the bright light came from, or the knife—knives—but that's beside the point now. I just got the feed from the system that Simon set up streamed to my cell phone. I didn't want it on any hardwired equipment here in case the police confiscated it." There was such an uncharacteristic flatness to her tone that, for the first time, a chill skated down my spine.

"You think they won't confiscate your phone?" Brody asked dryly.

"Why, of course. Which is why this is a burner," she retorted. She flipped it around and handed it to Brody. "Look at it. Both of you."

We did. The scene was in the chapel, with Dixie standing off to the side as the two women adjusted their tiaras. They were wearing actual wedding gowns and emerald-green velvet cloaks overtop, despite the fact that it'd been a warm day in Las Vegas. Either of them could've been hiding the knife in the folds of their skirts, so that explained that.

I realized with a start that I recognized them. They were the same two women I'd seen at the psychic fair, tiaras and all.

Then Dixie pushed a high-tech stand into position between them, where she had placed a tablet on a small tripod. She'd just hit Play and turned to the women, all smiles, when a bluff, attractive face appeared on the screen.

I leaned forward. "This is the Green Knight? Conal McCarthy?"

"Well, they didn't call him either of those things. They both had different names for him...Kerry and Kent, I think." Dixie said. "Here we're splicing back out to a wide angle of the room."

The view changed as the man on the iPad began to speak. I didn't know the language exactly, but I could understand it just the same. More than that, it was a language I'd already heard once today.

"Welcome, masters of the deep, the dark, and the unknown," the Green Knight intoned. "Your brides await you. A gift to bring life to your souls."

I blinked as the faintest outline of a rectangle flared to life at the far end of the room. "What the heck is—"

"Shh," Brody growled. Suddenly, the rectangle flash of light disappeared, and the room was filled with huge, dark figures, long-limbed giants with ruined faces.

"What the hell is this?" Brody muttered.

"According to Simon's analysis, they're something called the Fomorians, the mythological enemies of the ancient Irish," Dixie supplied, her voice barely a whisper. "But watch what happens next."

CHAPTER TEN

What happened next made no sense at all. There was a loud sound in the front of the room. Dixie looked up. The woman on the right, Lenora Drake, turned to the woman on the left, Alison Kay, then lifted her hand and knifed the poor girl in the chest. She hadn't even pulled an athame out of her gown—it'd simply appeared in her hand.

The creatures around them erupted in movement, rushing for both women. Their combined force pushed Drake away from her victim, where she immediately collapsed, mouth stretching wide. In the blink of an eye, all the creatures turned to mist and plunged down her throat.

"Jesus," Brody muttered.

"Yeah," I agreed, staring in horror. These were the creatures that a much younger Seamus had unwittingly called out of the ether, when he'd gone dialing for the Tuatha dé Danann? Talk about a wrong number.

And now Conal was stirring them up, hoping to wake the Tuatha dé Danann from their long slumber? This case just kept getting better and better.

The moment passed, and the on-screen Dixie shook herself hard, looking in confusion at the woman on the floor and then swinging her head wildly to locate Lenora. But that wasn't the end of it. After her meal of a roomful of Fomorians, Lenora shuddered and split into two. Then one of her turned and ran up the aisle as Dixie opened her mouth to scream. The sound had barely emerged from Dixie's throat before the woman was gone.

"I never saw that—her leaving," Dixie said. "I never saw two of her until just now."

"Son of a bitch," growled Brody again, his eyes pinned to the screen. "She was never here in the first place. No wonder that cop lost her. That wasn't actually a person. Which means she was what?"

Fairy, my mind whispered, before I could stop it.

Brody demanded this last while looking at me, but I had nothing. Well, that wasn't true. I had a disappearing banshee, I had ancient Irish demons who might be on the warpath for a self-exiled druid, I had dead people and almost-dead people, and maybe a possessed soon-to-be dead person. I also had a nearly dead Connected detective. All that put me in mind of a whole lot of Death.

"No clue, but I've got an idea of who does," I said grimly. "You guys stay here and do *not* show that to anyone. I need to take a walk."

"Don't take too long," Brody sighed. "We're going to…" He shook his head. "No. We can't show this feed to anyone. This is the LVMPD, not *CSI: Paranormal Investigations*. We cop to this and everyone's going to lose their shit, which will totally derail the investigation."

"I do believe you're right," Dixie said. Her voice was thin and wavery, and she looked like she was on the verge of tears. I managed to escape before any waterworks broke free, but the odds weren't looking good for Brody to avoid it, especially if he still harbored any feelings for Dixie—which, judging from the quick glance he shot her, was likely. I wanted no part of that, and I took off.

It took me only a few minutes to work my way past the cops and out into the cool evening air. I quickly moved across the parking lot to enter the fluorescent confines of DarkWorks Ink, the merry little bells jingling incongruously as I stepped inside the tattoo parlor. There was nobody in the front of the shop, which was not too surprising given the number of police cars in the parking lot, I supposed. Cops would tend to turn off a fair number of prospective customers.

I took a moment to glance around. I hadn't been back to Death's official place of business in a while, but it looked the same as it always did. The walls were covered with pictures of happy customers with their newly inked arms, coronas of angry red skin glowing in mute protest around brightly colored masterworks. In books lining the walls as well as countless pictures pinned up to the drywall, there were all manner of flash designs posted. Butterflies, fairies, dragons, flames, skulls of every description, Hello Kitty in ever more unlikely poses. If it was something that some misguided college kid on spring break might consider cool to put on her ankle, it was here.

While I was admiring a particularly involved tattoo of a serpent coiling around a carved staff, a door opened and shut deep in the back of the shop. I looked up to see the small, pinch-faced figure of Jimmy Shadow slouch into view.

"She's not here," he said by way of introduction. He nodded at my elbow. "You need a touch-up?"

"I do *not* need a touch-up," I said, flinching reflexively. I'd received several tattoos in this shop, as well as a newer image from Death at a tattoo convention in LA that'd felt like my skin had been lit on fire. Since engulfing myself in flames was becoming a regular pastime, you'd think this last one wouldn't have bothered me so much. You would be wrong. "Is she in town?"

"She is, but she got summoned by the man in the High Castle. I'm thinking either you got the same summons, or you're about to, or you're ignoring him."

I scowled but let my barriers slip slightly, staggering back at the strength of the Magician's voice pounding against my mind. Yes, I'd been issued an invitation. I clamped my barriers tight again and scowled at Jimmy. "What's it about, do you know?"

"It's a meeting, which is enough. She hates them, and the Magician knows that, so for him to be summoning the crowd means there's something big going on. Probably the same thing that just ripped a bunch of slimy Fomorians out of the primordial ooze." He grinned with yellowed teeth. "That wasn't pretty either."

"Death knew that was happening? She didn't stop it?"

"She wasn't on-site, no. She came screaming in like the Fourth Horseman she is about an hour ago, more pissed than I've ever seen her. But she no sooner came than she stopped cold. They were there, then not again, is what she said, a door opening and shutting, quick as a wink."

The important part of that statement should've been the bit about the door, but it wasn't. Instead, I stared at Jimmy. "She said quick as a wink?"

He grinned with dark glee. "Well, she didn't put it quite that way, no. Her language was more to the point. But then she ran out of here like her hair was on fire. By the time she came back in, she was drenched in sweat, looking haggard. And this is *Blue*. She don't look haggard. That's not her deal. But she said she was too late."

Blue was Death's most recent appellation, for those mortals who got a little hinky calling her Death, and served as her calling card for both her tattoo clientele and vehicle owners looking for high-end airbrushing of their muscle cars. Basically, if it involved guns of ink, Blue was the one you wanted.

"Which means those Fomorian things were real. And — she hates them why?"

Jimmy looked at me oddly. "Ahhh...how much d'you know about how Death came to be Death?"

I grimaced. "Not a heck of a lot, honestly. She's one of the oldest members of the Arcana Council — the oldest, before Michael showed up anyway. But as to how she got that way..."

Jimmy rocked back on his heels, eyeing me speculatively as he went through a laundry list of rationalizations, all of which I appreciated. I was a rationalization kind of girl. "She's never told me not to tell you. I always got the impression that you knew. She's inked you with some of her best stuff. She doesn't have friends, she doesn't have hangs, but she seems to like you. She's let me add to her own designs without frying them right off your skin when she's had the chance — "

I blinked at him. "Wait, what? She can do that?"

"*And* we've got a new little hordelet of Fomorians running around, which pretty much are her Ebola. So that's a good reason too. You could help her. Not that she would ever admit to needing help, but still."

"And that's enough reason for me to do it right there," I said, the soul of loyalty and logic. "So, spill it, Jimmy. If Death is at all linked to whatever's going down with the Neo-Celts, this murder, the whatever-they-were that just showed up and infested a bride-to-be next door, or this asshat in Ireland, then I need to know, like, right now."

This wasn't how I'd expected this conversation to go, frankly. I hadn't expected to find Jimmy alone, and I certainly hadn't expected him to be in such a talkative mood. Jimmy Shadow was a chain-smoking, hard-drinking tattoo artist who was more than Death's right-hand man, he was very possibly her reformed-demon familiar. I'd never quite figured that out for sure, and I'd never wanted to investigate too closely. We all have our secrets. Jimmy was entitled to his.

That said, I was up to my eyeballs in questions right now, and it was past time that I started collecting answers. For Armaeus to be as concerned as he seemed to be about this Green Knight character, something was going on here that I was clearly missing.

Sometimes being the last kid to the party was less than awesome.

Jimmy seemed to agree. "They say a picture's worth a thousand words, so I'd show you if I could, but Death has done her level best to remove any and all inscriptions, images, historical accounts, songs, or artwork about those dark times. She only tells me the story when she's wasted, but she's told it often enough that I can remember it line by line. You repeat any of this to her, though, and my next tattoo will be delivered to me by her foot on my ass. I don't want that."

"Understood. If I can avoid telling her, I absolutely will. And if I need her to know what I know in order to help her, which would be a bad day all around if that's necessary, then I'll bring you ice for your ass. That's the best I can do."

"Fair enough." He shifted uneasily. "Come on back, then." He switched the OPEN sign of the tattoo parlor to CLOSED and slouched past me again, heading to the rear of the shop. Passing by the inking rooms, Jimmy didn't pause until he pushed the heavy door at the end of the hallway, leading us into the wide garage space where Blue kept evidence of her other pastime — vehicle airbrushing. Three motorcycles and a gleaming muscle car sat at odd angles in the wide space, all in various states of augmentation. The detail of her work was breathtaking, earning her a cultlike status in all the circles where she wasn't already a rock god for her tattooing abilities.

The reason for our transplant to the back of shop quickly became obvious as Jimmy picked up a battered pack of cigarettes and slipped one out.

"Is that a good idea with all the paint fumes back here?" I asked, eyeing him as he lit up the cigarette.

"If I was going to blow up, I would've done it a long time ago," he said casually. I frowned, not quite following that logic, but Jimmy kept going. "So Death was kind of a unique son of a bitch from the very beginning. She lived around 3000 BC, in a village near the west coast of Ireland. She was a druid priestess and sacrificed just about everything to the cause — family, husband, children."

I blinked, taken aback by the barrage of information, but his last words caught me in particular. "You mean she gave them up? Or she, um, *sacrifice* sacrificed them."

He grinned at me, smoke streaming through his weathered teeth. "Exactly the same question I asked at this point in the story, so don't feel bad. She's a tough nut. But no, she didn't kill anyone. But she gave up her position in the tribe, which apparently was quite a big deal, since she was the daughter of the chieftain and her mother, supposedly, was one of the fae."

I lifted my brows. Given my own questionable parentage, I had no room to judge. "The Tuatha dé Danann? Really?"

"Really. But giving up her position meant she could never marry—or have children. And that was a big disappointment to her tribe. She's never admitted as much to me, but apparently, when she was young, tales sprang up around her like daisies in springtime. She had an unusual affinity with everything bright and beautiful. Flowers burst into bloom around her, the chatter of children would follow her wherever she went, like that."

"This is Death we're talking about here."

He shrugged. "Well, she wasn't known as Death then."

"Fair enough. But seriously, the chatter of children? And if you tell me there were little people dancing around her, I may have to kill you. Consider yourself warned."

Another long drag on his cigarette. He was almost down to the filter already. Were cigarettes really that short-lived? Or was Jimmy an expert inhaler? "You believe in gods, right? Since you've been up to your ass in them?"

"Of course."

"The fae were gods. Nothing more, nothing less. Gods. You can wrap your head around that?"

"Of course," I said. "But—"

106

"No buts. I'm not here to argue sprites and brownies or fairies whispering limericks in the shadows. They're just the foot soldiers. What you need to focus on is the original fae, the reason behind all those stories. The Tuatha dé Danann, or the Tuath Dé. They weren't the first gods of the Irish, those were the Fomorians, but the Tuatha dé Danann get all the press. They conquered the Fomorians, who are generally portrayed as the dark and ugly stepcousins of the swamp monster, while the Tuath Dé were not only supernatural, they were supernaturally beautiful. Not too surprisingly, they're the ones who went on to capture thousands of years of Irish literature and the world's imagination.

"Well, I happened to get a good look at the Fomorians, if those were the creatures who hopped a ride inside Lenora Drake. They were looking pretty spry for a conquered race."

Jimmy made a face. "Why do you think Death was so pissed? And before you tell me, she already knows about the Irish guy at the festival. Seamus McCarthy. Apparently, she gave him some pointers when he messed with the Fomorians the last time. She knows he didn't pull this."

"She'll keep him safe?"

He snorted. "She'll make sure he doesn't die by the Fomorians' hand. Beyond that, no promises."

I considered that, then shut it up in its own blinged-up box of crazy for the moment. "Okay, so keep going. Death was a druid priestess."

"One of the best."

"According to her own story." I grinned, defanging my words. Jimmy grinned too.

"Yeah, which pretty much means that she wasn't one of the best, she was *the* best. By a long shot. Without her coming right out and saying it, she had the entire fucking western half of Ireland by the short hairs, and she had more woo than she knew what to do with at her fingertips. But it wasn't enough."

"Why's that?" I asked as he shook another cigarette out of the pack. "What was going on in 3000 BC that was that big a problem? Besides basic survival, anyway."

"Like I said, the Tuatha dé Danann defeated the Fomorians, but quite a while later, the Tuath Dé had their own battle to fight with the mortals themselves. The humans defeated the Tuath Dé, but they didn't defeat them entirely. They more sort of came to a truce, where the humans agreed to live in the upper world, and the Tuath Dé disappeared into the mists, never to be seen again."

"Seems like the humans got the better end of that deal."

"You'd think so, but there was always something slippery about the Tuath Dé. They never made a deal where they didn't have the upper hand. It was kind of a thing with them."

"Yeah, I read Shakespeare too."

"Exactly," Jimmy said, though he didn't really seem the type to go in for The Bard. "And that was what was vexing Blue so much. Her name wasn't Blue back then, but even with as lit as she's gotten, she's never told me what her original human name was. I get the feeling it was a name of great and terrible power, and probably something quite beautiful. Names mattered back then in a way they simply don't now, but that's all I've been able to get out of her about it. That and that she decided to ascend to the Council only after she helped dispatch the Tuath Dé once and for all. From what I could tell, that was a bitch of an experience in more ways than one."

I rubbed my jaw. "Was she hurt?" The only person older than Death on the Council was none other than Michael the Archangel. But he wasn't the type to sit around the campfire and tell stories about the way things used to be.

"She never said, but something hinky definitely went down. And when the Council came knocking on her door, she took the offer they made. The same offer they gave you, in a manner of speaking. Ascend to the Council, and you'll have more power than ever to keep the gods at bay, particularly the gods that pissed you off the most. She bit."

"But why, after all she'd done—after knocking the Tuath Dé out for good—did she choose to ascend as Death, if bunnies and rainbows scampered around her wherever she went? Was that the only position that was open on the Council at the time?"

"Nah…" Jimmy broke off then, and turned to look at the wall for a long moment. When he started speaking again, he still wouldn't look at me. "Blue wasn't an idiot. She knew what she was giving up and the toll it would take on her family, her tribe. She'd already sacrificed so much to keep them safe, and she couldn't bear to leave them. So she took the one role where she'd be guaranteed to see them again, each according to his time."

I stared at Jimmy in horror. "Because they were *dying*?"

He nodded. "She inked each of them with her inscription so that at the moment of their death, no matter where she was, she would be able to find them, to hold them, and to help them over to the other side. Death can shepherd any soul, but she doesn't have to shepherd all of them. Those she chooses to aid make the passage filled with joy. To be marked by Death in that way is sort of a gift and a curse all wrapped up in one."

I frowned. "Curse how?"

"The gift is that she will be there when you pass. The curse is that she knows you'll pass before her." He stubbed out his cigarette in a tray filled with about five hundred others and pointed at my arm. "You look close sometime, you'll see you've been given that tattoo too, deep in the mix of all the others."

I frowned, looking down at my arm, willing myself to see through my sleeve. "Well, when I met her, I was mortal. She wasn't. Of course, she thought she was going to live longer than I will."

"You keep telling yourself that." He lifted his own hand, and a tiny blue tracing flared to life amid my ink. "It's a gift. And a curse."

Chapter Eleven

I barely made it out of DarkWorks when my barriers finally gave way to Armaeus's demand — with unfortunate timing. A knot of LVMPD's finest was standing and arguing about something, the missing Lenora Drake most likely, but my exit from the closed tattoo parlor did not go unnoticed. I suspected that neither did my super-smooth self-immolation move, or its attendant yelp of pain.

I stepped back into real time at the base of the Luxor casino, the corporeal starting point for the Magician's fortress, Prime Luxe, which soared above the Luxor with spectral magnificence. Many of the Arcana lived along the Strip in lofty residences that only the most powerful of Connecteds could see, but the entrances to these shadow casinos were almost always embedded within the lobbies of the casinos they surmounted. In other words, in order to access the spectral wonderland of the Arcana Council above, all you needed to do was enter the kitschy, flashy lobbies of casinos like the Luxor, Flamingo, and Excalibur — and know where to look.

Here at the Luxor, I could easily spot the onyx-and-silver elevator doors for Prime Luxe, wedged between the golden glam of the kitschy casino's primary bank of elevators, but I didn't approach it right away. For one thing, I was still a little singed. For another, I felt ill-equipped to face the full brunt of the Council quite yet. It was my first official meeting since becoming a full member, and I hadn't even brought cookies.

I pulled my Tarot deck out of my hoodie and, with the ease of long practice, shuffled the deck as I walked, thinking back to the young woman in Sariah's tent. Lainie Grant had far more reason than I did to be afraid of what her future held. She was beset with psychic visions for the first time in her twenty-odd years, whereas I'd built up to this point gradually, even if I hadn't fully realized it at the time. Granted, I wasn't used to the Magician going max corporate on us all and demanding a staff meeting, but I shouldn't be feeling quite so uneasy about Armaeus's summons. What was going on here? What was I missing?

I drifted to an unoccupied blackjack table and sat down, grateful that even at this late hour, the casino wasn't stuffed to the gills. Shuffling my well-worn deck a few more times, I quickly drew three cards, laying them facedown in front of me. I had a strong urge to do a traditional reading too, which struck me as odd. I hadn't pulled a full Celtic cross in longer than I could remember. Then again, I was dealing with a problem that centered in Ireland, so maybe I had shamrocks on the brain.

Either way, it was too late now. The cards had been dropped.

Quickly, before I could draw too much attention, I flipped the three cards upright. And rolled my eyes. The Magician, The Devil, Death. Well, that was super helpful. I suspected if I kept going along this route, I'd probably draw the entire seated Council and that would prove nothing at all.

Sighing, I gathered up the cards, then shuffled them a second time. As I did so, a slender woman with golden-blonde hair in a pit dealer's uniform stepped into the dealer's position at the blackjack table.

"We tend to frown on gamblers bringing their own cards," she said with an easy smile.

"Totally understandable." I nodded. "But would you mind if I take up this table for another thirty seconds or so? I promise you I won't be long."

"Those are Tarot cards, aren't they?" she asked, leaning over as I continued shuffling the cards. "You're a reader?"

I leveled a glance at her and could tell without even activating my third eye that she had no Connected ability.

"I'll be quiet, I promise," she whispered, and I proceeded to drop the cards.

There are ten cards in a Celtic Cross reading, but how you lay them out is a matter of personal preference. As usual, I ignored the Significator card entirely and dove straight into the reading itself. I laid two cards out—one upright and one crossing. These formed the first impression of the reading as a whole, and in my case, they were doozies. The Magician crossed by Temperance.

The fact that I'd drawn the Magician for the second time in a row was not lost on me, there was something here I should be paying attention to. But Temperance as a crossing card was also interesting, because we did not currently have a Temperance on the Council. In fact, I'd never even heard of a Temperance Council member.

And yet Lainie had pulled the same card, so clearly something was going on.

Taking Temperance purely at its more esoteric meaning, this was a card of taking a pause, finding harmony as I pursued a middle path, blending disparate forces, and mixing primal magic. Since this reading was technically about what I was about to walk into, pulling two Major Arcana cards right out of the gate meant today's meeting was not going to be the typical Monday morning overview. Fair enough.

A shiver played along my arms as I dropped the next round of cards in quick succession, forming a clockwise circle around the first two: What lies beneath me, what lies behind, what crowns me, and what lies before me. These cards made a little more sense. What lay beneath me was the Six of Cups, or an issue with deep roots in the past, or it could simply have represented all the kiddos at the psychic fair. What lay behind me was the Five of Wands, the garden-variety fight card that'd also already played out earlier today. What lay above me, or crowned me, was the Seven of Swords.

I wasn't a fan of the Seven of Swords. This was the card of diplomacy and guile and being strategic, all things I was never very good at, so having the Seven in the crowning position meant I wouldn't be playing to my strengths.

Then there was what lay before me, the Six of Swords. Another interesting card, it meant travel over water, or the idea that there were smoother waters ahead. It could also portend a journey toward a great psychic deepening. I was already pretty deep into my psychic best, so I wasn't sure if this was a good thing or a bad thing, but either way, I felt quite sure I'd be packing my bags, and soon.

Next came the staff of cards that lay alongside the Celtic Cross, four cards that helped to define and flesh out the reading. Once again, I dropped these quickly, all in a vertical line. The first card made me smirk because it was Justice. I always enjoyed it when the cards were literal. The second card, which traditionally represents the environment or what other people are thinking was…the Moon.

I studied the card, frowning slightly. The Moon is a fascinating card in the Tarot deck, because it was one of the ones that was dependent upon the reader as much as the answers being sought. It could alternately mean deception, trickery, and deceit—or the deliberate confusion of the matter—or it could mean the embracing of psychic ability, the magic of the world around us, and the acceptance of the unknown.

In other words, super useful. Moving on.

The ninth position card was what's commonly known as the Hopes and Fears card, or the Manifestation card, and generally signified the attitude of the person asking the question. I was not at all happy with that card either, as it was the Nine of Swords, traditionally called the nightmare card. Neat. Clearly, I needed to cowgirl up and stop making such a big deal out of whatever was about to befall me.

Or, that would ordinarily be my take on the reading, if it wasn't for the last card I laid out. Death. Also a card I've been seeing way to much of today.

Taken in general terms, the Death card was pretty straightforward, no matter where it fell in the reading. It meant transformational change, just like death can evoke in any person's life. But given that I was about to go into a meeting with someone who'd taken on the mantle of Death, and she was significantly involved in the deep history of my newest case, I wasn't entirely sure where all this was leading me. I spread the remaining cards in a quick fan and drew three more cards. Then, looking up at the dealer, who was still watching with wide-eyed fascination, I asked her to draw a card as well and hold it. She did, and I dropped my three cards faceup, both of us leaning forward.

The cards I'd drawn made me feel better, I had to admit. The first was the Ace of Pentacles, demonstrating a healthy new beginning, the second was the Two of Cups, signifying unity, and the third was the Devil. While in a lot of cases the Devil was a card that could incite fear and panic, I happened to have an in with the guy. Chances were good that the Devil held a key to all this, and unlike many of the members of the Arcana Council, he was a big fan of sharing the truth, no matter what. Granted, his truths generally ended up being more than you wanted to know, but I'd still take it.

The dealer practically bounced on her toes opposite me. "I don't know what all that means, but it looks pretty awesome. Are you ready for the card I drew?"

"Sure," I said, gathering up the rest of the deck as she slapped her own card down. Then she watched me with patently worried eyes.

"This doesn't look so great. Are you going to be okay?"

I smiled slightly, squaring the card on the baize table surface as I took in its dire imagery.

"Oh, it's okay," I murmured. "That's the Ten of Swords. Like most of the cards in the deck, it can mean a lot of different things. It could mean the end of the line, that something's going to end whether you like it or not. Or, it could mean a realization that's been a long time in coming—a truth you knew but didn't want to face. It could also mean something like back surgery, depending on who's asking the question."

"Back surgery!" she said. "You don't mean me, do you? I can't afford that."

"I'm sure it's not you." I glanced up at her, quickly surveying her circuits with my third eye. Still not Connected, and not in line for back surgery. "Though you might want to get out into the sunshine a little more. Your energy's low."

As her eyes bugged out, I glanced back to the card. "But no matter what it means or what ending is presaged, it also speaks of the shattering of an illusion that needed to be shattered, the turning of the corner, and the bringing of the new dawn."

"Dawn," she echoed, pointing at the card. "Like what's behind the dead guy."

I nodded, my eyes still fixed on said dead guy. "That's right. The only problem is, before the sun rises, like it or not, you've got to get through the darkness. That's what this card is all about."

A couple showed up, another man right behind them. "Are you open?" they asked the dealer eagerly.

By the time she looked back to me, I was gone, with barely a glowing ember to mark my passage. I was feeling pretty good about that.

Right up until I poofed into the middle of chaos.

CHAPTER TWELVE

The Council of the Major Arcana was in nearly full force. Up until a short while ago, it'd been positively sparse, with only a few core members holding it together. Then Armaeus had taken it upon himself to recall the sitting members who had drifted away, and added a few new members as the opportunity presented itself. Most of those members were now there, with a few notable absences—Gamon, whose role was Judgment, and Willem of Galt, whose role was the Hermit. Both of them were inveterate recluses who didn't play well with others, but witnessing the group before me now, they'd clearly chosen the better course.

Half the room was screaming.

It appeared the altercation was divided more or less along party lines. The traditionalists of the Council, those who favored strength over subtlety, were lined up on one side of the long conference room table: the Emperor, the High Priestess, the Hanged Man, and the ever-bickering duo of Lovers. On the other side, stoically allowing all the shouting to continue while restricting themselves to a few shots across the bow, were the Fool, the Magician, and the Devil. Standing off to the side, looking like they wanted to be anywhere but here, were the Hierophant...and Death.

At issue seemed to be a name I'd already heard once today, and one too many times at that: Temperance. I jerked to attention, trying to follow the thread of the argument.

"There is no way you can install Conal McCarthy into the role of Temperance just because he's a troublemaker," the Emperor ground out, his haughty voice matched perfectly to his elegant Aryan features and fastidiously styled blond hair. He wore a vaguely military-cut suit, adding to his air of Emperor Asshattedness. "It's unthinkable."

"You do know that's how you secured your spot," Kreios observed blithely.

"That is not at all the point." Eshe, the High Priestess, snapped. I focused on her, wanting more than anything to warn her about the young woman about to seek her out, but now was not the time. Especially when she was in full dither. Granted, even in full dither, Eshe was a stunning woman, her rich Greek features, long dark braid, and flashing eyes the perfect complement to her usual toga, this one fashioned in a deep, gold-trimmed midnight blue. She tightened her glossy lips into a stern rebuke.

"We have grown too quickly. Look at these two, they can barely stop fighting with each other long enough to make any sort of valid contribution to the whole." Eshe's far-flung gesture swept toward the Lovers, another duo dressed in traditional Greek garb, but her criticism was not unwarranted. After they'd been trapped on this side of the veil after last winter's Showdown of the Gods™, Hera and Zeus had been accepted into the Council in large part to keep them from making any more trouble than they already had. The Emperor, Viktor Dal, had been installed for the same reason. To say that the Arcana Council was a collection of misfits and menaces was perhaps an overstatement, but nevertheless had some merit.

"Oh?" Hera turned and addressed the High Priestess. Surprising, since the goddess rarely took her eyes or her attention off her husband. "You are one to talk. You're simply jealous of me as you have always been jealous of me, High Priestess Eshe."

"Oh, for the love..." Eshe muttered, rolling her eyes.

"If Conal McCarthy is as strong as early indications say that he is," the Magician said in his most reasonable tone, his voice containing the weariness of a man who has repeated himself too many times, "then we owe it to ourselves to bring him to the Council. Not only for the world's safety, but to control and target his abilities more effectively."

"For your benefit, perhaps," the Hanged Man sneered. With his ascetic, sharply cut attire, sleek black hair fastidiously combed back from his face, narrow features, and excessive early twentieth century civility, nobody could sneer like Nikola Tesla.

A new voice sounded beside me. "Do you know what's going on?"

Startled by the sudden presence, I turned to see Gamon eyeing the chaos with the same level of bemusement I had. So that meant only one person wasn't present and accounted for: the Hermit. Given his role of holding together the veil between the worlds, I remained perfectly okay with him skipping out on this little meeting.

Gamon, Judgment of the Arcana Council, stared around the room, her wonder at the arguing Council members obvious in her hard, dark eyes. In all her mortal years, which were particularly long-lived in her case, she'd made it a policy not to negotiate with anyone. If they'd been in her way, she'd simply rolled over them.

"The short of it?" I asked. "There's a guy in Ireland making a lot of noise, and he's apparently determined to raise the ancient dead gods and hand Earth over to them. Along with stopping that little plan of action, the Magician wants to maybe possibly elevate the guy to the Council as Temperance."

"Temperance? Seems reasonable enough," Gamon mused, eyeing the escalating anger in the room. She was another of the Council members who'd gained her seat in part to muzzle her abilities. Still, she shot me a look. "I thought you'd stopped the gods from coming through. Beyond Hera and Zeus, obviously."

"So did I. It looks like there were a few back doors I wasn't aware of. And this guy seems to have a fistful of keys to them."

As I said the words, I shot a look at the Magician. How much did he really know about Conal McCarthy? If the pattern of the past held, far more than anyone else in the room — but if so, why hadn't Armaeus warned me about Seamus's son? For once, there wasn't anger driving this question...merely curiosity. But it was curiosity I needed to have resolved.

"Then we should probably bring him on board," Gamon said. "So what's the problem?"

Eshe turned on her, her robes flying, though Gamon's question had been muttered only to me. "The problem, *Judgment*, is that this idiot human has done nothing more than stake his claim in Connected dirt with his band of followers. I hardly think that's enough cause to raise him to the Council. Even you caused more trouble than that."

"Nothing more?" This time it was Death's voice that sounded over the room, and her dire, resonant voice immediately silenced everyone. It seemed to swell out from her, icing my very bones. She didn't move from her slouch against the wall as she continued. "We have just fought a galactic war to keep the gods on their side of the veil. And not only did this Conal McCarthy manage to set loose an entirely new set of gods to attack two mortals in barely the blink of an eye, he did so without us even noticing. That's not Connected-level skill, it's Council-level skill. And yet there was only one position on the Council who could conduct such magic so stealthily, utilizing the In Between, and it's not the Magician."

My brows shot up. The In Be-what?

Death's gaze shifted to Armaeus, but to my surprise, he only nodded. "Temperance," he murmured, sounding more intrigued than dismayed. That was okay, though, I had enough dismay for both of us.

"You think a *past* Temperance has returned?" I dared to venture as my mind tried to wrap my head around that idea. So was Conal McCarthy acting as himself, or was he a past Temperance reborn…and if so, how was that even possible? When it came to Council-level woo, any level of weird was possible, but still. Explanations. I needed them.

"If the ancient tomb passages connecting our world to the far side of the veil are opening, we have to consider it," Death said. "We have lost too many of our own to those mists and shadows. More pressingly, the first wave of gods has slipped through the old passages, breaking the hallowed seals. They won't be the only ones to do so."

I pursed my lips. The Fomorian lizard people had appeared to walk through a sort of door to enter Dixie's chapel, so had that door opened from this In Between place? The term sounded vaguely familiar, but only in a pop culture kind of way.

"I saw Simon's video too," Eshe countered, recalling my focus. "If those were the ancient gods you so fear, I'm not impressed."

"Dude, I'm telling you. They were totally Sleestaks," Simon countered. He was now practically bouncing, his young face bright and inquisitive beneath his mop of dark hair barely constrained by his skullcap. He wore a short-sleeved T-shirt over a long-sleeved T-shirt and faded jeans above his Chucks, and he looked around as if expecting a bigger reaction. "You don't mess with Sleestaks."

"You dismiss the Fomorians at your peril," Death continued mildly, ignoring Simon, which was probably for the best. In her voice, the word Fomorians took on an odd, arcane sound, menacing and foul. "As Seamus McCarthy did once before—and yes, Sara." She nodded to me. "He will be protected. If he's smart, he's already in the wind."

"Thank you." Seamus had enough problems without being hunted down by lizard people. And I still needed him to keep a leash on the spectral opposition warriors.

Death turned her attention back to Armaeus. "But again, the rogue Fomorians are not our only problem now, and neither is the idea of a past Council member returned. Whether he is Temperance reborn or not, if you think for one moment this self-appointed messiah is going to be content with the adulation of his little sect of followers after having stirred such an ancient power, you are deeply and profoundly mistaken. Because regardless of what *he* wants, those he has awoken want far, far more. He has rekindled in them a desire for nothing less than to rule Earth as theirs. They've done it before, and they always promised they would do it again."

"Fairies," the Emperor sneered, sounding so much like me only a day ago, my stomach turned. "You're talking about fairies."

Death's gaze on him was withering. "I'm talking about the Tuatha dé Danann. They have been silenced for many an age, waiting and wanting and dreaming," she said. "For all your strength and fury, Emperor Dal, you are no match for them. In their haunting, harrowing songs, they will gather the souls of the unwary and stitch them together into cloaks of fire. In their fiery need for power, they will not, cannot stop. Should they set their eyes upon you, they will draw the very blood from your veins and turn your bones to water, all to paint their magic upon this world they loved so long ago—and lost."

There was absolute silence for a long, harrowing moment.

Then the shouting started up again.

CHAPTER THIRTEEN

I t took another twenty minutes before all the arguing settled down, and then mainly because the Council members all seemed to lose steam at once. I surveyed the group suspiciously as my right hand started to tingle, the Nul Magis detecting the slightest flare of unexpected magic. Unexpected magic was only to be expected with this group, of course, but it still put me on edge.

"It seems we've reached some agreement, no matter how discordant," Armaeus said. "We need to determine if this new player, Conal McCarthy, is an incarnation of Temperance and handle him accordingly. If he is, we should consider recalling him to the Council."

"Depending on which incarnation he is." the High Priestess said. "If he's the one from the 1500s, you can keep him. All that idiot wanted to do was try to figure out how to turn lead into gold. Which made him a hit with all the ingrates of society, but relatively useless in terms of Council business, as you no doubt recall. The one we pried away from Queen Victoria wasn't much use either."

I perked up at this. The Justice immediately previous to me had served around that time period, and I remained desperate to learn every detail I could about Justice Abigail Strand. Talking to one of her contemporaries would make tracking down this rogue Temperance worth it all on its own. "When was the last incarnation of Temperance on the Council?" I asked.

"Nineteen eighteen." It was Death who spoke, but her face was drawn. "He didn't survive the transition, though."

"That wasn't our fault," Eshe snapped, her tone defensive. "He was already sick."

Beside me, Gamon stiffened ever so slightly. She and I were the newest Arcana Council members, and while Armaeus had mentioned that our transition wasn't an assured thing, that we might have more trouble ascending than we expected, neither of us had. I'd assumed his concerns had been merely a hand-waved, obligatory warning.

"It was our fault insofar as we did not properly understand the nature of his illness," the Magician said, not meeting my eyes. "I can heal what I understand. What I don't understand, I must study. That study doesn't take very long, but it does take time. Time that Temperance Danny Wilson did not have. He came to us too late in the cycle. His extraordinary psychic abilities shielded us from learning about the attack on his body until well after the disease had taken root. At that point, given the unique nature of anyone suited to the role of Temperance, he had already transitioned to the other side."

"Ahh…unique nature?" I asked. Sometimes sitting on the Council was like discovering a game in your grandmother's basement. You sort of intuitively knew how to play, but you still were missing most of the rules.

"Different positions require different sacrifices. Temperance is the alchemist. Constantly in motion, constantly blending, constantly changing. He was already in the wind before his body knew there was a breeze blowing." Eshe glanced to Armaeus. "Do you think he has reincarnated? Truly?"

"It's possible," Armaeus said.

"Wait—how?" I frowned. "I didn't think you people could regenerate."

The Magician shook his head. "In this case, regeneration isn't necessary. Consider it more that the young man stepped across the veil where it was thinnest, into a space between worlds, where doors may open and close without warning, joining the living and the dead. The In Between. You've traveled it yourself, after a fashion."

"I've crossed the veil," I countered. "But not in Ireland. I'm getting the idea that it's a bigger deal there."

Armaeus quirked a smile. "It would seem you're correct. Before he was lost to us forever, Temperance Wilson was last seen in Dublin. He was Irish, poor, and working class, but his family was spread out across the countryside. Ireland in the 1900s was not an easy place to be. He had a hardscrabble life. If he transitioned into the space between and did not truly die…"

"He died," Death interjected starkly. "His soul was shown the way. What he chose to do with that information was up to him, I suppose. If he chose a different path…it's possible he could still return. I was there for his passage, but he was so young, his light still so bright."

Had Death personally escorted him? After chatting with Jimmy, I had to wonder who would make the trek with any Council member, just to be sure they went where they were supposed to go.

"No." Death tightened her jaw, rejecting her own words. "No. I don't believe that young man has returned as this zealot. Danny Wilson had no love for the old wives' tales of his family. He wanted to move his country forward, not backward. He doesn't feel at all right for the Green Knight."

"I'm inclined to agree with you, but we need to make certain," Armaeus said.

The other members of the Council remained silent. Even those who'd been alive in the early 1900s — everyone except the Fool, Gamon, and myself, actually — weren't offering more commentary on this topic. It was clear that the passing of this young Temperance Wilson had affected them on a deeper level than usual, maybe because he'd died in transition. Nothing like a little unexpected death to dampen your bid on immortality.

"And, ah — the other guy you mentioned?" I put in, trying not to sound too hopeful. "The one from the Victorian era? Could it be him?" I wasn't at all sure how I felt about elevating a man to the Council who had quite possibly put Nikki into a coma. But I was more than happy to be the one who got to him first. What happened after that…was impossible to predict.

"Temperance Bartholomew Simms," Armaeus said. He glanced at Death, but she only shrugged.

"I wasn't nearby when he passed. I don't know."

She appeared unwilling to say anything more, which seemed odd, but Armaeus continued. "And if this Conal McCarthy is not Temperance of a previous incarnation, we need to consider making him part of the Council on his own merits. To contain him, yes, but also to use him."

"Oh, like you've done a splendid job using the rest of us to our fullest potential," Viktor sneered.

The Magician flicked him the briefest glance, but I caught the amusement in his eyes. "Your role within the Council is very much appreciated. Please always know that," Armaeus said blandly. Viktor scowled at the Magician with a hint of mistrust, which made me unaccountably happy.

"So what's the plan?" Simon piped up from the far corner of the table, where he'd taken a seat. He slouched and swiveled his chair back and forth. "I gotta lot of surveillance in play right now, and I should probably get back to it."

My brows went up. What was the surveillance he was working on?

Apparently, it wasn't high on the Magician's priority list—or at least not as high as the current crisis. "Actually, I need you to go with Miss Wilde," Armaeus said, his voice completely neutral even as his gaze finally met mine. "If Temperance is reincarnated, there are precious few members of the Council he will not recognize. Namely, Viktor, Gamon, Miss Wilde, and you, Simon. I think you can understand why we might not want his reintroduction to the Council to be handled by Judgment or the Emperor.

Gamon smirked. "I guarantee he'd come back if you sent me for him."

Armaeus slanted her a look. "Unfortunately, his mind may already be in a fragile place."

Her smile deepened. "Then I'm probably not your best choice, no."

Simon, however, was leaning forward. "Really? You want me to go to Ireland?" He broke off abruptly, realizing how eager he sounded. "Well, ah, sure. I guess. But I've got some things to get cleaned up in a hurry, then."

"You have until ten a.m., tomorrow," the Magician said. He gestured lazily with one hand, and a door appeared in the far wall of the conference room. Without asking anything further, Simon spun off his chair and strode away, his entire manner galvanized into action.

When the door closed behind him, dissolving back into a wall, Armaeus fixed his gaze on the rest of the Council. "You know the danger here," he said. "We must be careful."

"You will *not* sacrifice Simon to your need for power," Death said, her voice stony.

I blinked. Wait, *what?*

"I have no intention of sacrificing him," Armaeus countered. "He has Miss Wilde to ensure that."

The Emperor huffed. "Who doesn't even know what she's—"

If it had been anyone else in the room, I would have accepted the slam about to come out of Viktor Dal's mouth with equanimity. I knew very well that I had much to learn as Justice, and even more to learn about the unique nature of my abilities.

Still, the Emperor and I weren't friends on the best of days, and this had decidedly not been a great twenty-four hours. I lifted a hand, magic erupting in licks of fire around my fingers, and the Emperor froze.

Like, actually froze in place. Didn't know I could do that to a Council member. Or anyone.

Didn't so much mind being surprised, this time.

"Miss Wilde."

"What is it you need me to do, specifically? And why is Simon at risk?" I asked, ignoring Armaeus's silent reprimand as the other Council members straightened carefully in their seats. An act of aggression against one of our own was probably not a typical agenda item for Council staff meetings, but I didn't have it in me to care about that. I could hear Gamon chuckling beneath her breath, while I kept my focus on Armaeus. "Now that I can hear you clearly."

His lips didn't so much as twitch. "The space between worlds is unmapped territory, blocked to most members of the Council by powers set in place in ancient times, by means and agency we don't understand. I have searched endlessly for information on the restrictions to the In Between, to no avail. We know only for sure that Justice, Temperance, the Fool, and Death may walk its byways."

"You're not getting me in there again," Death said flatly. "Full stop."

Armaeus nodded. "Agreed."

"Um — why not?" I asked, swinging my gaze between them both. "What's in there that you're afraid of?"

"It's not fear that stays Death's hand," Armaeus said, while Death remained silent. "It's restraint. She could do great damage to the remaining passages, and not all who tread them deserve such treatment."

"They shouldn't be open to mortals at all," Death huffed. "Stupid druids."

I blinked, knowing what I now did about Death's past, but Armaeus continued. "However, we aren't completely without understanding of the byways of the In Between. One entrance to the space between worlds is contained in the Trinity College library, and information on how to travel therein is inscribed in a book that has been largely overlooked in favor of its more famous brother, the Book of Kells. Both volumes, however, are important to your search."

"What sort of information are we talking about here?" I pressed. "Like a map?"

The Magician's lips tightened. "Regrettably, I don't know. The chamber where it is housed is also forbidden to me, and has been since the founding of Trinity College in the late 1500s. I know only that you'll understand the message you are supposed to receive when you see it. The information it presents will not be easy to decipher, but that's where Simon's presence will be beneficial as well."

I nodded. Simon had a gift for interpreting maps and for making his way through games. Beyond Temperance not being familiar with him, I suspected the Magician had multiple reasons for including the Fool in this journey. Multiple reasons, and one big warning sign.

"Why is Simon at risk, though?"

"Because he's the Fool," Death snapped. "As always, that's reason enough."

Armaeus sighed. "Temperance isn't the only Council member who entered the spaces between the worlds and didn't come back. For whatever reason, the In Between proves to be an insatiable lure to certain personalities."

"Fools rush in." To my surprise, it was Gamon who murmured the line from the Pope poem, but I was already moving on.

"Who else is going with, then?" I asked. "I want Nikki with me."

Armaeus's gaze met mine. "She's not ready yet."

"Then make her ready."

He shook his head. "It's not quite that simple, Miss Wilde. You had multiple layers of magic to protect you against the spell that was cast at you both. She did not. We don't have the complete—"

"What?" I cut him off, stiffening in surprise. "You *still* don't know what's wrong with her? That makes it like this Temperance Danny Wilson guy all over again. She's been hit with something you haven't seen before, and you can't cure her outright." Even saying it made my heart hammer, my lungs constrict. "How is that possible? How can you not cure her outright? Why can't I go back in and try?"

"*No.*" This time, Armaeus's urgency was echoed by Death, Kreios, and even Eshe.

I looked slowly around the room. "What's going on that I'm missing? Because I'm clearly missing something."

"Only this," Armaeus said, lifting a hand. "We don't know what is afflicting Nikki, only that she's afflicted — but she is stable. Meanwhile, we cannot risk you getting further damaged. We have a threat that you are uniquely qualified to address that is urgent. After his successful attempt with the Fomorians, all indications are that Conal McCarthy will summon the Tuatha dé Danann on Beltane. That's now only forty-eight hours away. We must be in place to combat him by then."

"Or we could blow him out of existence right now," Gamon said, saving me the trouble.

To my surprise, it was Death who replied. "Sadly, no, we can't. Conal — whether he's Temperance reborn or simply an opportunistic Connected — is only a key that unlocked a door. The door remains, and more keys will be fashioned now that the ancient gods know that a pathway exists through the In Between. Killing him would serve no purpose if we don't close off those passageways for good."

"Fine. I'll do — whatever it is you think I'm supposed to do. But *you* had better take care of Nikki," I said, pointing at the Magician. "I mean it."

Armaeus grimaced. "I assure you, she's our highest priority."

"She'd better be," I breathed, and a wave of energy skittered through the room, a mix of panic and unfixed anger. I barely whispered my next word. "Please."

The Magician met my gaze. "She will be made whole, Miss Wilde. I swear it."

I drew in a shaky breath and nodded, and the room seemed to release a collective breath.

"Though I won't go with you into the mists, I'll be in Ireland too," Death said before Armaeus could speak again. She looked at me. "I pray you won't need me, but I'll be there if you do."

I expected Armaeus to object, but instead, he merely looked at Death with concern. "That isn't necessary."

"Temperance Wilson won't object to me being there, if it's truly him calling the ancients to life — which, again, I don't think it is. Still, I was the last grace in his life, and he recognized that. More to the point, I need to see this Green Knight. If he's truly planning to summon the Tuath Dé, it is my place to stand with Justice and oppose them. And if he's not — if this is all a pretty fairy tale to impress his followers — it is my place to stand with Justice and beat the crap out of him."

After Nikki, Death was seriously my favorite person ever.

CHAPTER FOURTEEN

Death left the Council meeting then, and the others followed swiftly behind. Within ten minutes, everyone was gone except for the Magician, the Devil, and me. We stood staring at each other from opposite ends of the table, the tension in Armaeus's lofty conference room thick enough to cut.

"Come *on*, you guys," I protested, fire trickling once more around my fingers. "Something is *still* going on here that I don't understand. What aren't you telling me?"

Armaeus blew out a long sigh. "You're correct, but it is…a delicate matter. Death has been a member of the Council since before the time of Christ. Only the Archangel has been here longer. Which means only the Archangel can truly understand what she experienced in the time leading up to her ascension to the Council."

I looked around, but there was a decided lack of Casper the not so friendly Archangel going on. "Then why isn't he here?"

The energy in the room snapped again, and a new voice sounded.

"Because Death is also not an idiot," Michael said, slowly fading into view. "If she knew I was hanging around for a sidebar after the meeting, she would never have left. And she has much to prepare herself for."

"Fair enough." I narrowed my eyes on Michael. While I'd actually gotten a kick out of the Archangel when he'd first rejoined the Council after an extensive sojourn in Hell, he'd definitely worn my patience thin since then. For the record, his return hadn't aged well on him either. Gone was the almost boyish joy he'd first expressed upon stepping foot back among the children of God, as he called them. Now his hands were full with a demon infestation that had occurred during the last attempt by the gods to return to Earth. I didn't approve of everything Michael was doing to handle that attack of the horde, but I had no say in how he managed his affairs.

If he was going to put his nose into *my* affairs, however, that was another thing entirely.

He continued before I could prod him. "When Death ascended to the Council, she was also on the verge of death after a long and arduous battle."

"With these same gods," I hazarded a guess. It was the only thing that made sense. "The Tuath Dé. They defeated the Fomorians, then she helped defeat them."

He nodded. "While she was successful in turning them back, she was very damaged by the experience, and the conflict had rendered her into a near god to those who harbored her injured body. She was forced to rely completely on the humans who gathered around her, who nursed her back to health despite their fear of her. She survived in large part because of those mortals, and that's part of the reason why her compassion for the human race runs so deep. She does not ascribe to the beliefs of the Father or to any modern faith, but she has a deep and abiding respect for human grace. So her anger here is twofold. She absolutely refuses to see a recursion of the gods against whom she personally sacrificed so much to keep out of the world. Beyond that, she has limited patience for any individual who would lead others astray by convincing them he's a god on this earth. To her, the man who styles himself as the Green Knight is doing just that. He's leading mortals and their inestimable ability to trust that which they don't understand, down a path of danger and deception, and she cannot abide that."

"Understood." I swung my gaze to Armaeus. "But why were you so worried about her returning to Ireland, not just this In Between place? Surely she's been back before now."

The Magician grimaced, but it was Michael who spoke. "She hasn't. I was not idle in all my years away from the Council. I watched, I saw. Death has never once set foot upon the Emerald Isle, not since she last walked its rich soil three thousand years ago. For her to return is more meaningful than any of us can imagine. Meaningful, and dangerous."

I shivered, the ink that Death had inscribed down my arm tingling forcefully. "Will they know she's there?"

"The Tuath Dé? Oh yes. But they're not the only concern. Death was a druid priestess. That is an ancient and twisting pagan faith that has diminished but never quite died, tucked into the forest primeval of the human soul. When she returns to Ireland, she will not be left to her own devices. Her acolytes will be drawn to her, whether she likes it or not."

"Haven't they been drawn to her all this time?"

"Of course, to some degree. But there is something about the rolling hills of Ireland that works a change on the spirit. You've been there before?"

"Well, yeah." I shrugged. "But I don't remember it all that much. There was a whole lot of Guinness happening on that particular job."

Michael managed to effect rolling his eyes while still staring straight at me. "If it was some time ago, you can be excused from feeling its effects. But rest assured, Justice Wilde, you'll feel it this time. Magic found its home millennia ago on the shores of the Emerald Isle. It will respond to you in ways you cannot imagine."

"Kind of strange words coming from an angel of God."

"Not at all," Michael said with a twist to his lips. "When the Lord created the world in the image of all that was good and true, there are those who believe he fashioned Ireland first. Who are we to gainsay them?"

My phone rang in my pocket, the sound jarring all of us. I pulled it out. "It's Brody," I said to no one in particular. "He's got news on the attack in the chapel, though heaven only knows what the LVMPD is making of all this."

I glanced up to Michael, but he was already looking more transparent. "Okay, give me the rest of it. These Fomorian creatures are responsible for the death of one woman and the kidnapping and probabl death of a second. And that's a very real, very human problem we're going to have to deal with. Anything else I need to know about them?"

"Only that they know they're bait," he said. "And they're not happy about it." Then he faded from sight altogether.

"I'll return to the side of Miss Dawes," Kreios said, nodding as I shot him a startled glance. "She remains in a coma, but she seems to be closer to the surface when I'm present. I prefer to think of that as a good thing."

There was nothing in Kreios's tone to indicate that he was at all concerned, yet he wouldn't look at me directly. Instead, he turned to the Magician to give him a short nod. A moment later, he also was gone.

Leaving Armaeus and me alone.

I studied the Magician for a long minute, struck anew by how little I still knew about him. He was the Great and Powerful Oz of the Arcana Council, but the curtain he most defiantly refused to pull back was the one shrouding himself. At the same time, he'd opened up his mind and his magic to me like the ultimate playground, encouraging me — often dragging me kicking and screaming — to reach out, discover, explore. He knew so much more about me than I felt I could ever know about him, but he wasn't holding out on me, exactly. He wanted me to know. He just didn't want to make it too easy.

Or perhaps couldn't. The thought whispered through my mind. The Magician had lived a long and twisting life — who knew what deals he'd been forced to strike along the way to reach his current pinnacle of power? Who knew what trials he might yet face to continue surging higher?

Because as all-encompassing as his abilities were, I'd already been faced with an unexpected weakness of his. One that struck all the way to the bone.

He couldn't heal Nikki.

"Sooo…" I began almost cautiously, shifting my gaze away. "Tell it to me straight. How much do I truly need to worry?"

It seemed impossible to wrap my head around the idea that she was actually sick. Nikki had been an unstoppable force in my life since I'd met her on my first job in Vegas. Back then, she'd been moonlighting as the Council's chauffeur, ready to drive me anywhere I wanted to go. The idea that I'd not been able to heal her struck a pang of insecurity deep within me.

"Not too much, Miss Wilde," Armaeus said. There was something odd in his voice however, and I glanced sharply to him. His eyes were not resting on me, but were fixed on some far-off point, as if he were working through a hundred thousand different scenarios with a twitch of his pupil. Maybe he was. "Miss Dawes has a great deal to live for, and far more strength than she has yet revealed. I could give you the probabilities of her recovery versus her decline if you would like, but the odds are overwhelmingly in her favor. Particularly if you leave for Ireland before the festival of Beltane begins."

"I can leave right now."

"No, you can't." Armaeus shook himself back to the present moment. "Simon must prepare, Death as well, each in their own way. Further, there is more we need to determine about the breach that allowed the Fomorians to gain such a deadly foothold in a mortal. Once that woman dies—which she likely has already, if the ancients haven't left her—they will be free to roam again. Even if Seamus McCarthy has managed to hide himself, others will be at risk. This is but one incursion of these creatures. There will be others."

"And then there's the Tuatha dé Danann."

He nodded. "According to Irish legend, the Fomorians ruled the island before the insurgent Tuath Dé arrived, and their battle for control over the exalted isle was long and harsh. But in the end, the Tuath Dé overthrew the Fomorians and, little by little, edged them from this world entirely."

"And then Death helped knock the Tuath Dé off the planet in turn. Did she ever come up against the Fomorians?"

"She did not, not directly. By my calculations, however, she will engage them this time. That could prove a deadly choice for her."

I narrowed my eyes at the pun, trying to decide if it was intentional, then pushed on. "Keep going. What's going on in this In Between place that's so horrible, especially to Simon? Why are the Fomorians roaming through there like kids in a fun house if they were so soundly routed all those millennia ago? And, finally, why would Death taking on the lizard guys be so bad?"

"I'll start with the In Between, because I have so little to say about it." Armaeus turned to face the window, his jaw working with irritation. "The truth is, I have *no* knowledge of the Irish passages of the In Between— none. And yet, I have the impression of having *had* knowledge."

I blinked. "Um, once more for the cheap seats?"

"Simply this. I know nothing of the In Between, but I should." He glanced at me, and there was no discounting the frustration in his dark and simmering gaze. "I *should*. I was born during the dark ages. I excelled in all forms of the mystical arts. Part of my training—a considerable part—included studies of druidic magic. I have a deep and unassailable knowledge of that magic, as well as scores of books, manuscripts, and memories attached to it. But I have not one *shred* of information in written or memorized form about the In Between. Not where it stretches across the Emerald Isle."

"But it does exist."

"It most definitely exists. The lore that I can access— scarcely more arcane than Wikipedia, you should

141

know — suggests it is a quantum physics anomaly, a bending of time and space that allows for instant access between two discrete points. Doorways and passages, opening and closing. The descriptions get more detailed from there, of course, up to and including passageways stretching throughout the world. Those passages are no more better mapped than in Ireland, if you believe the hype. Which I am forced to do, without an alternative source of information."

"So you're sending Simon to map it on your behalf."

"I'm sending Simon to provide me data," he agreed. "Data I should already have access to. There's no reason for me not to have it."

"Makes sense." I'd known Armaeus long enough to understand that information was his catnip. Being barred from it all these centuries would have been a violation. "So why didn't you send him in earlier?"

"Because..." The Magician tightened his lips, once again glancing away. "The previous Fools have been too weak of mind or spirit, for all their myriad gifts. I have seen many outcomes, many twists and turns of fate regarding our present, mercurial Fool. In 67.13% of them, Simon dies in a place where I cannot get to him in time. There is currently only one place on this earth that fits that description."

I'd gone completely still. "Please tell me you're joking."

"I am not. When I discussed it with Death, suffice to say, she's aware of the probabilities as well. Remember, there are only a few members of the Council who can walk the In Between. How do you think we came by that information?"

"Jeez," I muttered.

"As to your next question regarding the Fomorians, they can travel through the In Between once again because they have been invited—there's no other possibility than that. Which means that whether he is Temperance or not, Conal McCarthy is very powerful indeed. And finally, regarding Death confronting the Fomorians...you must understand. She was the vanquisher of those who vanquished them, ages upon ages ago. It's uncertain how the Fomorians will react to her."

I lifted my brows. "As in, the enemy of my enemy is my friend?"

He shrugged. "Perhaps. Or perhaps they believe she is merely the first barrier they must break down on their road to redemption. First Death, then the Tuath Dé."

"And she knows that." I thought of what Jimmy said about Death, racing after the Fomorians and not finding them in Dixie's chapel.

"What Death knows of the Fomorians, I cannot say, but I have predicted that outcome as well. The probabilities are—"

"Stop," I ordered, lifting my hand. "I think it's safe to say that's not a percentage I want to know. But she *can* survive it?"

He hesitated, then nodded. "It would be best if you were there with her. As it would be best if you remain with Simon at all times in the In Between."

I scowled at him. "You had to throw that last part in there? You couldn't have simply said yes?"

The Magician bowed slightly. "I prefer being as accurate as possible."

"Of course you do." I blew out a long breath. "So, where does that leave us? What else do I need to know?"

Armaeus's expression grew a touch wearier, and his gaze seemed almost gentle. These were the moments that scared me most about Armaeus. That he knew so much and could only tell me the barest fraction, because the truth might break me.

"At this point, there is nothing I can tell you that will help. You must go to Trinity College tomorrow, and see what you will see. But first, you are needed with the detective." His eyes got that faraway look again. "There is so much more for us to learn."

I searched his face — was the bronzed skin paler now than I remembered it? Were the dark eyes more deeply sunk? Any weakness at all in Armaeus was unnerving, and I struggled to fight back a flare of panic.

"Can you come with me?" I asked quietly.

He blinked back to the present moment, and the smile he gave me was soft, almost apologetic. "I cannot. I have much research still to do if we are to find a solution for Nikki. Modern medicine has done many things, but perhaps nothing so valuable as create an expectation of life in the minds of those who believe in its powers. Nikki is graced with a very strong belief. In herself, in you, in me, and in Dr. Sells. She's in perhaps the best, most supported situation possible, but that doesn't release me from my obligation to find a cure that will return her to complete health as quickly as possible. Time waits for no man, as they say."

Another jet of unwarranted panic spurted through me — and not for Nikki this time. For him. For us.

"But you're not a man," I reminded the Magician. "And neither am I."

I lifted my hand as Armaeus's elegantly arched brows shot up. I stiffened in my resolve to carve this moment, this breath out for the both of us. For someone who commanded extraordinary power in so many ways, the Magician was curiously loath to do anything to disrupt the temporal progression of time. He, more than most, understood the ephemeral nature of our life span upon this planet. Even those who were immortal were not deathless, and our work for the Council was becoming ever more dangerous. Despite that, slowing and even stopping time must take some sort of toll on him for Armaeus not to employ it more. A small part of my mind begged for me to have a care with that toll, but I willed myself to ignore that clamor for a moment.

I needed so little—so very little from the Magician. But I did need this.

"Miss Wilde," he exhaled softly, lifting his hand to match mine, his eyes suddenly lit with a deep, infernal fire.

And time…simply stopped.

It was as if the heavens themselves were caught in the midst of exhaling, and a curious pressure lifted from me even as the world went silent. I didn't hesitate. I rushed forward, and Armaeus's arms opened wide, grabbing me and holding me close as he turned to carry the weight of my body against him. I tilted my head up and his lips came down on mine, and in that kiss, I found absolution, promise, hope, and forever. All the answers to all the questions I never realized I'd been asking. It was like this every time I kissed the Magician, a completeness so immense it made everything else seem impossibly meaningless. I pulled back, hauling in a deep breath, then sagged against him as his hold only tightened, his hot mouth and questing lips roaming up my cheeks, my brow, branding my skin with a trail of scorching kisses, his own need seemingly as great as mine.

"Miss Wilde," he moaned again.

His breathy sigh set every circuit in my body alight, heat exploding through me with an undeniable, carnal need. I needed him on me, in me, through me, in a way that defied both reason and sensibility. "You draw your power from sex," I countered. "What sort of lover would I be if I didn't help you refill your well?"

I didn't give him a chance to respond, instead pulling his clothes away from his body, ripping his shirt free of his pants as buttons flew. Without lifting a hand, Armaeus stripped my own clothes away, incinerating them in a fiery poof. Within moments, we were both tangled on the floor, naked and driving, skin against skin, heartbeat against heart, magic against magic. As always, the Magician was more than a match for my passion, but I sensed in him a level of urgency I had not sensed before. In this moment, he was more than willing to take from me than ever before, more than willing to siphon the power off that I so desperately wanted to give him.

"*Sara,*" he whispered, and his use of my given name only heightened the panic building within me. I didn't know what Armaeus needed, what he wanted, I only knew that I was an open, throbbing current of power, desperate for him to be strong, to be sure—

To be safe.

Another flare of panic shot through me, a stab of ice and fire.

"Armaeus," I breathed, the word sounding wrenched from my very toes. "Take it. All of it. I'll give you anything you need, you *have* to know that."

"You don't know what you're saying." His words were little more than a moan, but his hands only tightened on me.

I flailed for him as well, blue fire sparking from my fingers. "I don't need to know. All I need to know is that you love me. That's it. That's always been it. Just that you love me."

He rolled me to my back and levered his body over mine, and I arched beneath him, willing him to seat himself deep within me. Still, he hesitated, and I reached up and grasped his hips, pulling him down, until finally his shaft sank deep, plunging hard, filling me as I nearly exploded from the surge of electrical power that flowed out from Armaeus, blanketing the world.

"More than magic itself, my beautiful Sara," he murmured against my hair. "More than magic itself."

CHAPTER FIFTEEN

M y eyes snapped open, and I was alone.

Reeling against the conference room table, I gaped at the world around me. The bright sun shining vigorously over the Vegas Strip was proof enough that time had started again while I'd slept bonelessly on the floor of Armaeus's conference room. I knew it'd started again, but my mind, my body, even my soul seemed to cry out at the shock and wrongness of it all.

Was this why the Magician resisted the urge to stop time so forcefully? Because the human psyche couldn't process such a violation without wanting to shut down completely?

Either way, I was here, my clothes were here—and Armaeus, of course, was gone. Making him one of the few men alive who would never have to endure the walk of shame.

Sucking in a deep, shuddering breath, I swung my gaze around, trying to get my bearings. I couldn't afford the time to process what'd just been shared between Armaeus and me, and if I was honest…I didn't want to process it. I wanted it to stay fixed in place, as pure and inviolate as the stars in a far-off galaxy, a perfect, frozen kaleidoscope.

I didn't know what the future held with Armaeus— but we'd had that moment, at least, that breath of time out of time. And we would always have that moment.

My phone was on the conference table, and I stumbled over to it as it angrily buzzed. Brody again. His text made me chuckle as the world once more righted on its axis.

Where are u? Get to D's. Now.

I crackled out of the conference room and back into the space outside Dixie's chapel in a blink. This time, the expected skiff of heat and pain was almost welcome, grounding me further in the here and now. Around me, the place was almost deserted. It was midmorning, according to my phone, and police tape still encircled the chapel, rendering it officially closed for business. None of the businesses around it appeared open, and only one vehicle was in the parking lot. Brody's beat-up unmarked sedan.

He pushed himself off his vehicle as I brushed embers from my shoulders. "Are you seriously telling me that's the most efficient way you have of getting around now?"

"I was completely on the other side of the Strip ten seconds ago," I protested. "And I didn't have to embarrass myself in your car. You tell me."

"Well, prepare to be embarrassed now. We've got a dead body, and you're not going to like where she ended up."

I thought about the worst possible scenario. "The psychic fair? So why didn't you ask me to meet you there?"

"Because I need you to *pretend* to be a little normal for the sake of our collaborating partnership, without drawing too many questions from my peers. Arriving in a car is normal. Arriving in a ball of flames is not."

I smirked. "You're such a baby."

Brody grunted something, but waited until we both got into the car and he'd fired up the beast, pulling out of the chapel's parking lot before continuing. "Lenora Drake has been discovered on the grounds of the psychic festival, behind one of the tents in the spectral opposition warriors' camp. Only, she was already dead when they found her—and the CSI guys are backing that fact up, pending a full report from the coroner. She's been dead awhile, it seems. Like, as far as they're concerned, she died right around the time she got married."

"She wouldn't be the first. But how is that—oh." I shuddered. "Decomp."

"Decomp," he agreed. "I get where they're coming from. I've seen the body, and it's already in an advanced state of decay. Whatever those things were that leeched inside her, they did a number on her."

"And her body was dumped at the festival?" I winced, imagining the panic at such a horrific sight. "Has it gone viral yet?"

"That would be negative, which in and of itself is pretty much a supernatural event. Her body was tucked out of sight, thank God, and all the tourists were encouraged to leave early without raising any alarms. Nobody's left on the premises but the vendors, and most of them have already departed, especially the ones who weren't local." He waved off my relieved sigh. "There are two notable exceptions to that rule, of course. Our spectral opposition warrior friends, and the Neo-Celts."

"Oh, jeez."

"Pretty much. The warriors are remarkably chill about the whole thing, while the tree huggers are losing their minds—but they're not posting what they're finding online that we can tell. We're sure they're sending it somewhere, but not out for the general public to consume. Which is interesting in and of itself."

"You want me to get Simon on it?" I asked, pulling out my phone.

Brody made a face. "Well, that'd be easier than me explaining to my people what the arcane web is, yeah."

I typed the quick request to Simon, and he responded immediately. Simon had never met a tech challenge he didn't like. He also let me know he was ready, willing, and able to head to Ireland, and I gave him a time to meet me at Justice Hall.

"He'll text us both back when he picks up the data trail. What about the Fomorians that were in Lenora? Where'd they go?" I asked, drumming my fingers on my knees. "Everyone's saying they're bait, but bait doesn't usually eat people."

"Well, it does if it's pissed off bait," Brody answered reasonably enough. "We have had no further word on the Fomorians' next victim, but we got the intel on Lenora. She's a Neo-Celt all right, one of the tribe that met here at the festival. So was Alison Kay. The Neo-Celts are all in various states of shock, but one thing that's consistent—they both signed up for this. They were also going for the role of god consort, not trying to marry Conal McCarthy."

"So they were signing up as human sacrifices, you mean." I looked at him in horror. "That makes McCarthy a murderer twice over."

"Technically, it makes him an accessory to murder at best, and even that is sketchy. In an apparently lucid and fully aware state, Lenora Drake and Alison Kay agreed to take part in what the others described as a fun, harmonious marriage ritual to make them the brides of the gods. By the time they showed up at Dixie's, both of them were high as a kite, on a mixture of stuff so effed up, the coroner's office will have to centrifuge their blood six times over to figure it out."

"Premarital counseling might have been a better bet," I said, my heart twisting. This was exactly the reason why Death was so upset. Humans were far too easily led.

"Yeah, well. As far as the forensic evidence is concerned, midway through the marriage ceremony, Lenora turns on Alison and knifes her, Alison collapses, Lenora leaves the crime scene and is found dead several hours later of an overdose that induced advanced and accelerated necrosis. So the Fomorians didn't kill her, and neither did Conal McCarthy. In the eyes of the law, it was a murder-suicide."

"And how do you explain the rookie detective getting a knife to the shoulder?"

"I don't. The going theory is that there may have been a third, hidden accomplice who got the jump on her and fled. All Dixie's cameras were turned off at the time, apparently."

"Even Simon's extra special cameras? I can shoot him another text."

"I assumed so, but maybe not. Excellent idea. Not admissible as evidence, but...I'll take what I can get." He drummed the steering wheel as he drove, while I typed out the second request. "I saw Death too," he said, casual as all hell.

I stiffened without quite knowing why. "You did?"

"Yeah." Brody shivered. "She showed up outside the tattoo parlor when the scene was still a mess. I've never seen her so pissed. It was a pretty scary look."

"I can only imagine. What'd she say?"

"She told me that once I found Lenora Drake, not to touch her skin without gloves, and not to let her breathe on me. She also wanted to let you know that the Archangel Michael doesn't know as much as he thinks he does, and not to jump to any conclusions until the two of you chat. What was that about?"

"That was about me navigating a hostile workforce of ten-year-olds." I sighed. "She say anything else?"

"Yeah. She said if we found Lenora dead, that we should know the woman had felt no pain once the Fomorians took over her body. That she'd felt nothing at all, in fact. Death seemed unreasonably broken up about that, though." He scratched his chin offhandedly as he drove. "I'd think in her line of work, you would get used to people getting capped after a while."

"I'd think in her line of work, it's probably best that you never get used to it."

He considered that, nodded. "Fair enough."

We reached the festival grounds less than ten minutes later, and as promised, there was a decidedly smaller group of people there, all of them circulating amid law-enforcement personnel. The Neo-Celts and the spectral opposition warriors were segregated to either side of the clearing where the body had been found, while an older couple huddled together as they were being interviewed.

"Those are the festival directors, the Carltons," Brody said. "But they're pretty useless. Lenora Drake wasn't there—and then she was, smack in the middle of the walkway, dead as a rock, no outward sign of distress or trauma. Initial hypothesis is that she had a heart attack, but then she started leaking and—"

"Got it." I grimaced.

"Also, she smells funny."

"Well, leaking bodily fluids will do that to a person."

"Not like that." He shook his head. "She smells like Nikki did, and you too, though much less so, when I saw you both at Dr. Sells. I thought if maybe you could identify what was on her, or, like, look at her and determine what she was poisoned with somehow, it could help Nikki. I'm not supposed to let anyone get close to the body, and of course nobody knows about the connection between Lenora Drake and Nikki, but..."

Brody had barely parked the car when I bolted out of the vehicle.

"You're brilliant," I shouted, not waiting for him to catch up. As I ran, I shifted through several disguises that I drew from the people I passed, ending up with the most likely one: a low-level CSI tech scurrying up to the body to collect some last-minute required evidence. Nobody looked twice at me as I knelt down by the woman and flipped open my third eye.

I flinched immediately. Lenora Drake was burnt from the inside out, every last one of her circuits dead, not even a glow to indicate the life that had gleamed so brightly here just a short time before. The exuberance of a woman who thought she was going to get married to the gods, even if she was getting married over Skype. She'd had a future ahead of her, a future in which she might have realized the error of her ways, but now that choice, that realization had been forcefully taken away.

How close had Nikki and I come to this exact same fate? A renewed jolt of anger knifed through me, sharpening my senses. I raced through what was left of the husk of Lenora Drake, bitter tears cresting my own lids as I searched for a hint of what had harmed her. This woman had been Connected, though only slightly; this woman deserved justice. She would get it too. But first she had to help me.

One of my tears fell on her lifeless body—and then I saw it. As my tear slid down her cheek, I saw the other stains of Lenora's own tears, tracking down her temples. Precious fluid still remained caught in her lashes. I reached out blindly, and Brody was there with a small evidence vial he'd procured from God knows where. I held it up against the woman's lashes and delicately teased the fluid in. I handed off the vial to Brody, who stoppered it, but I couldn't...couldn't quite resist the pull of those tears. I turned back to Lenora Drake's still form, and touched the fringe of her lashes.

Instantly, my body jerked back, an all-too-familiar queasiness sweeping through me. But this time, the suppression of my abilities wasn't the only reaction. I spun to the side, my gaze drawn inexorably to one of the few remaining tents standing open...

There, in its shadows, stood the Fomorians.

The creatures from the darkness beneath the world. Tall, lean, their skin oily and dank, their faces long, their eyes hollow. Some had claws for hands and feet, some were almost human in appearance, but all of them were hunched, waiting. Waiting, wanting, and hungering. How many thousands upon thousands of years had they been lingering at the edge of the world, desperate for the chance to return?

When we'd banished the gods back beyond the veil, we'd only been looking up. I'd never thought about the possibility that we should be looking down as well.

Down and across, in the unknown passages of the In Between.

I staggered to my feet, heading toward the Fomorians who waited for me, drawing me closer with their hunger, their pain. If I could just speak to them, somehow understand—

"Sara—Sara!"

155

The pain across my face was so abrupt, so unexpected, that my hands immediately broke apart in abrupt defense, though no fire spurted forth at first. Brody wheeled away, smart enough to get out of range, and I sank back to the ground.

He dropped beside me. "What is wrong with you?" he asked, helping me back to my feet. "You looked like a goddamned zombie, and I need you to focus. What do you want me to tell Sells when I hand her that vial?"

I shook my head, trying to re-center. "Tell her the compound that afflicted Nikki and me is definitely in the mix of whatever Lenora Drake ingested and in her tears, I don't know in what concentration, though. Still, it has to help."

"It will help. And it will help even more if you pull yourself together. Go sit in my car until I can get us out of here."

"I'm fine—"

"You're green," he cut me off. "Trust me, green is not your color. Go. And don't set anything on fire while you're at it."

"No promises," I muttered.

Chapter Sixteen

Though I much preferred simply fireballing it back to home base, I waited like the good little collaborating partner I was. I used the downtime in Brody's beat-up sedan to use Brody's phone for research...and catch my second wind. The pull of the Fomorians on me had been unnerving, to say the least, and unnerving wasn't good if I was supposed to help Death stare these creatures down.

When Brody finally showed up to escort me back to the Palazzo Hotel, Mrs. French was waiting for us, wringing her hands nervously as she eyed a contraption that looked exactly like the Skype kiosk Dixie had used to pipe in Conal McCarthy for his very own red wedding.

"What's that?" I asked, striding toward the contraption as Brody shut the door behind us.

"Mrs. French." He nodded.

"Oh! Oh, good. Detective Brody, I'm so glad you're here as well." She drew herself up in her proper Victorian-era business gown, all starched lace at the collar and wrists and thick buttons down the front, and focused on me. "This, ah, machine is Nikki."

"What?" I skidded to a halt, immediately imagining the worst. "What are you talking about? She's locked in a computer now?"

"No, no," Mrs. French said as she wheeled the machine around to face me. On it, I saw Nikki sitting up in her hospital bed, grinning wearily. She looked a little wan, but the pink sheets definitely helped put some reflective color back into her cheeks.

I squinted, looking more closely. Those were pink *satin* sheets. "Where are you?"

"Still at Dr. Sells's." Nikki's voice was barely more than a rasp, and I stiffened, trying to wipe the concern off my face. As usual, I didn't do a great job of it.

"It's okay, dollface." Nikki smiled. "Apparently, I should have been dead several times over with as much juice as I got hit with. But the fact that there's no *way* I could have been so afflicted by just touching a damp postcard is freaking everyone out, especially Armaeus. He's been at my side almost constantly, I gotta tell you, even when I suspect he's other places too."

"It doesn't make sense, I agree." I fought to keep my voice steady. "Has he found anything out?"

"That would be negative. He feels like he's missing something obvious, some nugget of information that he should know but doesn't. But I'm sure he'll track it down, and I look forward to spending the rest of my life yelling at him for not doing his job in a timely manner."

Her gaze shifted to Brody. "Detective Delish! How goes it?"

"Good…" he allowed, glancing at me. "Why aren't you asleep or something? Why are you wearing yourself out talking to us?"

"Because I had an idea about how I could help, even in quarantine, and this is the only way they'd let me do it," Nikki said. "I've had a lot of time to think since I've been forced to do nothing but lie around and contemplate my manicure. And it occurred to me, I touched Seamus's wrist, right? Enough to know that he legit believed the line of bullshit we thought he was giving us."

"Right." I nodded. "But all that's been verified now. His son is really a problem."

"I know, I know," she said. "But what if there's something I know about him that I didn't realize? Something that imprinted on my mind but didn't seem important? I can't stop thinking about it. That maybe I know something but just can't quite reach it. Like it's right there, but I need to reach for it to bring it into focus."

I blinked. It wasn't an unreasonable thought, but I didn't see how it could help us, and I told her as much.

"I thought the *same thing*," she practically crowed. "And I was complaining about it to the Devil as one does. Let me tell you, the Devil is not a dumb spirit, I don't care what anyone says."

I could hear Kreios snort in the background, and my heart gave a tight little shimmy. I was glad he was with Nikki, keeping her company in her sterile hospital room. Some people could handle the isolation of a quiet room with no distractions, but Nikki was not one of them.

Now she was looking off-screen. "You want to tell them?" she asked, but Kreios's noncommittal answer was clear enough.

She refocused on her camera. "Kreios said I would reveal my most important truth if he demanded it of me, but Dr. Sells started screaming bloody murder, that I was too weak, not right in the head, an idiot, and a few other choice descriptors I'll leave to your imagination.

She refused to sign off on it without approval from my medical power of attorney."

I made a face. *I* was Nikki's medical power of attorney. "Nikki…"

"I'm telling you, I think I know something," she insisted. "I can't see Seamus in person, even if I wanted to, not right now. My immune system is too compromised. But I don't need to see him again. I already have any information he could provide inside me. I just need to bring it out. How dangerous could it be for me to simply talk?"

She appeared to be asking this question off-screen, and the camera spun to Dr. Sells's unforgiving face. "The Magician has calculated the odds of this procedure contributing to Nikki's recovery versus impeding her progress," she informed me icily. "Do you want to know his calculations?"

I winced. I didn't want to know. But I did need to understand everything that Nikki did about Seamus.

Mrs. French piped up beside me. "I've not been sitting on my hands either, Justice Wilde. But I don't have anything current. There've been no calls to Justice from the druids since the late 1800s. So I can't help you with the present troubles, I'm afraid."

"It's okay," I told her. I'd been afraid of exactly this problem. There was just too much we didn't know, and to Armaeus's point, too much we should know, needed to know.

I refocused on the screen. "Kreios? Let's do it."

As Nikki flashed me the thumbs-up, the Devil moved into position beside her. His expression was unnaturally intense, his normally soft, mobile lips now pressed into a hard line. I didn't understand the exact nature of his relationship with Nikki, but there was no one I trusted more to love her and keep her safe.

"Go," I said.

Kreios reached out his long fingers and gently brushed Nikki's cheek. With a soft smile, she looked up at him — and jerked back.

While I couldn't see what she saw, there was no mistaking the physical reaction that followed. Nikki's body convulsed, her eyes widened, and the monitors all around her started emitting chittering screams. She stared up at Kreios, her eyes imploring, her mouth falling open. For one long moment, no sound came out. And then when it did, it was in such a tangled rush of mixed languages, it was my turn to jerk back.

Nikki wasn't only sharing Seamus's truth. She was sharing the truth of all he represented.

A truth that rooted me in fear to the floor.

As quickly as it started, Nikki's oral dissertation ended and she slumped back, the monitors still gyrating wildly. Kreios moved his hand to her forehead, and I could see his lips move, though I couldn't hear what he said. The effect, however, was immediate and deeply gratifying. Nikki slumped into a boneless sleep and the monitors blinked out — then came online again, once more showing perfectly placid readouts.

"She should rest now," Kreios murmured, though he didn't take his gaze from Nikki's face.

The screen went dead.

"What was *that*?" Brody demanded, turning on me. "What did she say?"

"She said — Seamus said — that the coming of the Green Knight presages the end of the world," I reported, my words dull. "It's a title that's been known among the druids for thousands of years and rarely adopted because of its fell warnings. But the real concern here isn't that Conal is the Green Knight, but that he's the Hallowed Knight."

Brody rolled his eyes. "And what's *that*?" he asked, exasperated.

"A druid blessed by the ancient gods, sent here to do their bidding. If that's who Conal is, then even if we defeat him, we're too late. The damage has been done, the seed has been planted, the candle lit. Nothing will ever be the same."

"Oh. Is that all." Brody scowled at the empty screen. "Which leaves us where?"

"It leaves us with a problem." I passed a weary hand over my brow. "There's more, too. The spectral opposition warriors have started their own movement in earnest, opposing the Neo-Celts in my name. Seamus is their underground leader, though no one knows that, not even most of the warrior sects. He's not simply allied against his son, he's afraid of him, particularly if Conal's this Hallowed Knight. He's using some of his druidic woo to manage the spectral opposition warriors, and…and he thinks I'm pretty much the Easter bunny. A god-human synthesis, at one with earth and sky."

Brody rocked back on his heels. "Well, that could be handy."

I grimaced. "I sincerely hope not."

"Given all that, what I've found makes more sense," Mrs. French said. She offered me a thick file. "History of druid complaints up until the late 1800s, both by and against them. Something for you to be reading when you get to Ireland. "

"Ireland?" Brody demanded. "When are you going there?"

There was a knock on the door, and I glanced at the clock on the wall. Ten a.m. sharp—which would make it 6 p.m. in Ireland. Perfect timing. I took the file from Mrs. French and gave Brody a weary smile.

"Now," I said. "Keep the home fires burning for me."

CHAPTER SEVENTEEN

"Are you seriously kidding me with that pack?" I demanded fifteen minutes later, staring at Simon with genuine dismay as he stood in the middle of the lobby of Justice Hall next to a backpack almost as tall as he was, its contents spread out on the floor. "I didn't expect you to pack for a European tour."

"What?" Simon protested. Behind him, Brody sat on the couch, enjoying the show with a cup of Mrs. French's tea. "We need this stuff. I've got collection tubes and a digitizing scanner and two separate laptops in case one gets deep-sixed, one of which has access to the Arcana Council's network no matter where we go."

My mind, of course, went immediately to the In Between. I didn't think we'd have much in the way of hot spots there. "No matter where?"

"That's what I'm going to test out." Simon nodded enthusiastically, already refilling his pack. I handed him Mrs. French's folder for good measure. "If we can get computer access In Between, we can begin to understand what it really is. What its chemical composition is, whether or not people can survive— even people we thought were dead—and whether or not this is simply a new and improved way to breach the veil. It's important stuff. Your dad dropped off the mother of all maps on me, and I haven't had time to digitize that bastard, so that's in here too."

I narrowed my eyes. Willem of Galt, or the Hermit, hadn't made an appearance at Armaeus's Council meeting, but that was to be expected. His job was to protect the veil between Earth and the outside plane where the gods still roamed.

"You actually saw him? How's he doing?" And more to the point, how long was my own father going to continue to ignore me?

"He didn't drop it, drop it. Like, not in person. It was just waiting for me when I got back home from the Council meeting. Sitting right there in the lobby of the Bellagio, addressed to me. Once I opened it up, I was seriously jacked."

I frowned, and Brody and I exchanged a look. Even Mrs. French sniffed with concern.

"You're sure it's from the Hermit? It couldn't have been someone else trying to mislead you?" I pressed.

"Totally not that," Simon said, his words absolute. "I may look young, but I'm not an idiot, you guys. This map is the real deal."

"Okay, well, good." I sighed. "Next question: How well do you know Trinity College?"

"Are you kidding? I love that place. I was there just last summer to do some research for Armaeus, and it's incredible. I can't believe you've never been there."

"I've been there, it's just been a while." I'd logged some major Google Earth time in Brody's car to jog my memory, but this particular trip was definitely going to test the boundaries of my need to know where it was I was going. "You're going to have to have a real specific picture in your head for this to work. You good with that?"

"Of course," Simon said, reshouldering his pack. "I'm picturing it right now, clear as day."

"Excellent. And that pack is flame retardant?"

He frowned with surprise as both Mrs. French and Brody backed up several steps. "What do you—hey!"

I collared Simon and burst us both into the requisite flame. Truth be told, Simon did have the ability to transport himself incorporeally as well. But while my travel requirements involved me catching on fire, his involved leaving all his clothes behind. And in his case, his clothes didn't regenerate when he did. Whoever was handing out powers in the basement of the Arcana Council, they had a sense of humor.

Nevertheless, reaching the library in the heart of Trinity College proved easier than expected. We stumbled onto a sidewalk and caught ourselves before sprawling into the mud, which was more difficult than you might expect given Simon's enormous pack. Once we patted our clothes free of sparks, though, the trek to the Trinity College library took us less than five minutes. I swept the outside of the building with a quick, cursory glance, and, well, it looked like just about every other European library I'd ever seen: an old weathered stone facade, three and a half floors, arched roof. Despite the cool springtime temperatures and the late hour, the area around the library was packed with tourists too. I couldn't imagine how crowded it would be in the summer.

"Are we supposed to meet anyone here?" I asked. "Or are we on our own?"

"According to Armaeus, one of the library caretakers will usher us through to the reading room, but he didn't give me any indication who that would be. He just said we'd be recognized."

"Well, it can't be because we're American. Half the people here look American."

"Yeah, well. Can you blame them?"

I snorted a soft laugh, surveying the area. From their broad, flat accents to their bright smiles and terrible sweaters, college-age American students choked the green in front of the Trinity College library, almost too many to be believed. Then again, I had to imagine that Ireland was one of the coveted "gets" in a study-abroad program. Just enough of a foreign experience to say you'd been to Europe, a thick enough brogue that even English was difficult to discern, and all the Guinness you could drink. A student could do far worse.

We elbowed our way into the library, which involved some slight sleight of hand on my part, given Simon's pack, but nobody paid us any mind. Despite the signs announcing that no oversized packs were allowed in the hall, we weren't the only rule breakers. It was surprisingly loud too, the sound surely an affront to the miles of books that were stacked floor to ceiling. I stared around the room, trying to get a sense of the age of the place, the history, but I found it strangely lacking. It was as if I was staring at the veneers on an old, revered Renaissance masterpiece. I was more interested in what lay beneath, but I couldn't quite get to it.

"I feel like we're still on the tourist track," Simon muttered, echoing my thoughts. The library was absolutely beautiful, but it felt...oddly incomplete.

"Justice Wilde." The quiet, polite male voice startled me with its thick Irish accent, like a cork bobbing along in an American sea. I turned and saw a slender man who appeared only slightly older than Simon, if Simon hadn't actually been born in the 1960s. As it was, the

Fool grinned at this clear sign that our fortunes had improved.

"You're our guide?"

"I'm William Gray, yes." The man blushed as he nodded to Simon with awkward deference. "It doesn't feel right calling you Fool Simon, I must admit."

"Just Simon is good. The Fool stuff usually takes care of itself." Simon hefted his enormous backpack up on his shoulders. "We good?"

"I'm surprised they didn't make you check that at the front door," William said, eyeing the pack with patent amazement.

"I—" Simon frowned, looking over his shoulder, but I nodded William on.

"You're taking us to the Long Room, I assume?" I asked as he led us toward a well-worn staircase. "Armaeus said we needed something from the Book of Kells."

"Oh, I've already got that," Simon interjected. At my startled look, he grinned. "Dude. The Internet. Armaeus wanted me to catalogue the animals and various animallike whozits the ancient scribes used in their illustrations. I didn't need to be here for that. It's all catalogued on my laptop."

"We'll be going to the Long Room anyway," William said, agreeably enough. "The library, you see, for all its nooks and hidey-holes, was built on a very simple plan. To get anywhere, you need first to go to the Long Room. As you'll see, in reality, there's quite a bit more to it than it seems."

We entered the main room and, as the floors below had been, found it chock-full of people. At the front of the room was a beautiful Celtic harp that caught my attention, but I didn't know why. When I flicked my third eye open, it glowed with a unique energy, but not a strong one.

"That's not Ireland's most impressive harp, but you're on the right track," William said beside me. I glanced at him, startled that he'd caught me looking, and he nodded to the harp. "That one is what we call Brian Boru's harp, and it's pretty enough, to be sure. An early wire-strung cláirseach dated to the fourteenth or fifteenth century, and, as they say, one of the three oldest surviving Gaelic harps. But it's not the oldest, not by a longshot. That'd be Scáil An Bháis."

"Scowl unwashed?" Simon repeated the word phonetically, frowning at him.

"Shadow of Death," I translated. I felt a chill slide up my spine when I said the harp's title, and I didn't miss the operative word. Death had been a druid priestess, and druidic harps were well documented in ancient literature. I'd never known Death to play any instrument, but… "Um, how old is the harp you're talking about?"

"Nobody knows for sure, and that's the truth. They said it was the harp of a woman, and it could be true. It's not a massive instrument, but it'd still take some strength to wield it."

"You make it sound like it's a weapon," Simon said, eyeing Brian Boru's harp.

"In the right hands, isn't everything? And the legends about Scáil An Bháis are long and twisted indeed. According to our most ancient stories, whoever plays it stirs the soul of the world itself, a soul that, should it heed the call of the harp, could be made flesh, to wreak terrible vengeance or glorious reward, but no one knows which. We only know that to play the harp too long is to break the world in two."

"Oh," I said, my voice sounding very small. "And, um, where is this super special harp, again?"

William smiled. "Lost in the In Between, it's said. But come, we've got much to see." William moved us along the passageway, past the busts of philosophers and men of note who'd been affiliated with Trinity College over the years. All the faces blended together after a while, serene expressions masking once-active minds, minds lost now to all eternity.

Or were they? I thought about the In Between and how little we knew about it. While in Brody's beater sedan waiting for my head to stop spinning, I'd spent some quality time roaming the Wikis and Reddits of the world, but everything I found seemed to double back on itself, seeming almost deliberately confusing. Was that by chance? Or were the druids and other agencies trying to cover their own shadowy tracks? I'd stowed Mrs. French's druid file in Simon's pack when he wasn't looking, but it would make for interesting reading.

"So, William," I began. "What do you know about—"

"Gabh mo leithscéal—Pardon, Justice Wilde. In a moment, you'll see all you need." William had reached the end of the Long Room where a spiral staircase stretched up to the second tier. He glanced back over his shoulder. "Up you go."

Simon immediately started up the stairs, but I didn't miss the jump of electrical currents that swirled along the iron railings as he did so. "What's up there?" I asked.

"A doorway. But there are those who would see what they shouldn't if they looked at the wrong time, so if you would, we need to be quick about it."

Without further hesitation, I clattered up the metal staircase, oddly reassured to hear William coming up behind me. I wasn't certain I believed him about his concerns of us being watched, but he seemed credibly worried. When we all reached the second level, though, William didn't head down the narrow passage. He turned to the blank wall.

"There's a good lad," he murmured as he pressed a panel that appeared exactly like the other panels in the wall — only this one shifted. A thin passage opened, so narrow that Simon had to shoulder off his pack to sidle inside, and I followed quickly after him. William came last, and just that quickly, the panel slid sharply back into place.

I blinked, looking around the dim space as William hit another switch. Illumination sprang to life in electric sconces lining the room, which contained a table, benches, and two short stacks of books. Bookshelves lined the room except for right beside the door, where there was a small stone shelf set into the wall, used at one point for holy water, I assumed, though now it was dry as dust. That didn't stop William from miming a blessing with it as he entered, before he turned to the stacks upon the table.

"They came," William said, his voice once more reverent.

"Who came?" I was immediately put in mind of my own Mrs. French, all the way back in Las Vegas. It surprised me how much I missed her in this cold, archaic library where everything was so stark and still, halfway around the world. "What are these books?"

"Well now, these are the books you came all this way to see. The Book of Kells is perhaps the most famous of our tomes, but it's not the most precious, I should say. Not when you start to speak about what truly lies in the mists of Ireland, hidden away from all to see."

I eyed him. "You're talking about the In Between. You believe it exists as well."

"Believe! Well, of course I do. I've been in it—though not traveling far, to be sure. The ways are treacherous for the unwary, and I'm new to the study." He glanced at Simon. "I was told you might be a serviceable guide, for all you've not been there yourself."

"Well, maybe not so much a guide," Simon demurred. "That's usually Sara—Justice Wilde's thing. But I plan to map everything I see, and if that survives…"

"Ohhh." William nodded, excitement lighting his eyes. "That would be something."

"But you've been in it," I said again. William was definitely Connected, but I didn't consider him supremely so. "How many others have? Do you know?"

He cut his glance to me. "You have to understand, Ireland isn't a large isle, for all that it looms large in the minds and hearts of her people. If you were to compare it to an American state, it's no bigger than your Indiana."

I frowned. "I've never been to Indiana."

"And I would venture to say many people from Indiana haven't had the chance to visit Ireland either." William chuckled. "But we're about three hundred miles long and one hundred and eighty miles wide. It's not a lot of space for such a proud people. We've long been keen to stretch our boundaries without leaving our place, you could say."

"You make it sound like this is common knowledge to the average Irish person, and I know that isn't true."

He spread his hands. "Well, perhaps not the average Irish person you'd meet in the city, but there's much about our isle that's been lost to those who live only in the cities. You'll need to learn the byways as well if you're going to stay here any amount of time."

I glanced around the small, cozy room, already itching to be gone. It was remarkably plain for a room that was supposed to start enchanting me. "Yeah, I don't plan on that."

William gave another soft laugh. "This island has a way of seducing even the hardest of hearts, Justice Wilde. Don't say I didn't warn you when the time comes and you're sad to let us go."

Having leaned his pack against the table, Simon was busily opening the books that'd been laid out for us.

"This is *amazing*," he murmured as he fished in his pack for a long leather tube that he shook out over the table. A slender coil of parchment slipped and immediately spread open, its edges weighting themselves to the surface of the table without assistance. "And look how it matches up."

William and I stepped closer. The map Simon had laid out next to the book was an ancient chart of the world segmented only by significant landmasses, not by individual countries. Still it was easy to find Ireland, the distinctive island perched in a cluster with Great Britain. Overlaying the different sections of the world was a tracery of fine lines, some thickly woven, some barely etched. Over Ireland, there was only the barest hint of lines, as if there'd been a layer once, but it had long since been erased.

"So there's no veil over *all* of Ireland?" I asked, scowling at the map. "That seems…kind of dumb."

"There is, but watch this."

Simon reached out, grabbed one end of the map, and turned it a quarter turn to the right. Now Ireland had as much coverage as anywhere else in the world, with no unbroken lines.

173

"It's an illusion. I noticed the discrepancy once I unrolled the map a few times. It starts out with these gaping holes, not just over Ireland, but over about a third of the planet in various places. Then you turned it, and you were okay. That's what I wanted to look at in these books."

"And the Hermit didn't give you any ideas as to why the map changed?"

"All he said is there were veils, and then there were spaces, and the two weren't alike, but they both protected the world as needs demand. I hadn't even thought of the idea of the In Between serving as a form of protection until the Council meeting, but—look here."

The map he pointed to next was in a large two-foot-square book, bound in musty leather. He had it open flat, and the island stretched out before us, its edges elaborately illustrated with crashing waves and dragons, while the land itself was colored a rich emerald hue, peppered with inscriptions for ancient towns and churches, all with distinctively Celtic symbols ringing certain locations throughout both northern and southern Ireland.

"This is Dublin," he said, indicating the large cluster of symbols along the east coast of the country. "This symbol is repeated here, here, and all the way up here." He tapped a section of the country far to the north. "There's healing powers going on in these areas, as well as entries into the In Between. I still don't know what any of this means, and definitely not how to navigate, but I'm hoping once we get inside, we'll understand more."

"Your Magician said you were looking to bring Temperance back to the fold of the Arcana Council, if he's roaming the shadowed passages," William said, and I looked up at him with surprise.

"He told you that?"

"He did. He wanted me to understand what I was sending you into and what you hoped to bring back. But I think he is mistaken. Danny Wilson's soul isn't what you'll find between the worlds. He was blessed, he truly was, for all that his body was wasting away with influenza. He knew what awaited him on the far coast, and he yearned for it."

"Oh." I rocked back on my heels. "So you're saying we're wasting our time here."

"Not at all," he said. "Danny Wilson, well and good, *he's* not hovering between the worlds, waiting for a peek back in. But the Temperance before him, Bartholomew Simms, well, that's another story altogether. He's the type what would've held on to this plane with everything he had. He was in love with another Council member after all."

I stared at him. "You don't mean...."

"Aye, Justice, I do." He smiled at my surprise. "Justice Abigail Strand, the very same."

CHAPTER EIGHTEEN

How do you know this?" I demanded. Simon glanced up, so engrossed in his book of architecture on the old library that he was only paying us the barest attention.

William smiled. "Well, at Trinity College, we have access to a lot of books we should have and a few we shouldn't. And some of those books may once have been in Justice Hall. When Danny was ascending, he gained access to your library, and he right pilfered what he could without being noticed."

"Really," I said drily. "Two problems with that. One, there was no Justice at the time, so there was no one there to let him in, and two, he was a Council member. Council members are strictly verboten in the library of Justice Hall."

"Not the Irish ones," William said. "You see, Abigail Strand was in love with Bartholomew Simms too. When she established her protections for her library, she didn't want them to extend to her lover. Simms, being a proper Irishman in his own right, saw perhaps a bit farther down the path than his true love did. He knew some things she didn't."

I narrowed my eyes. "How long had he been Temperance when Abigail ascended?"

"Going on five hundred years, I should say. There'd been Justices off and on all through that time, an' he knew the trouble it'd caused him when there weren't Justices favorable to him in session."

"So he preyed on Abigail."

"Oh, it's not like that. He just wanted to be sure future Temperances, his kinsmen, after all, wouldn't have to rely on the good graces of Justice to get the information they needed to do their job."

My head was starting to hurt. "How do you know all this? And why didn't Armaeus tell me?"

"Because this library has its wards too," William said smugly, gesturing around the small room. "And you can guess who's been kept out."

I stared at him. "Temperance had the ability to keep Armaeus out of Trinity College?"

"Not Armaeus specifically, but the Magician in whatever incarnation he finds himself, yes."

"I'm going to need a cheat sheet," I muttered.

"It's a simple enough construct. The Magician bends the elements to his will. It's what he does. But Temperance works a different sort of magic. He—or she—*blends* the elements to his will. The sum is never different from its parts. They remain real, constant, whole. The Magician can create an entirely different construct and leave the past behind. Not Temperance. He takes a more organic approach."

"I've found it," Simon announced, leaning over yet another book. "There's an entire wall behind this wall, only there can't be. We're flush against the outside wall of the library."

I frowned at him, then gestured to the wall. "And that schematic is of this building? Not something that got torn down a long time ago?"

"It's this building," Simon said. "But what it's showing is a structure that extends down into the basement—far down. Like past the edge of the foundation." He looked at William. "Are there catacombs beneath the library?"

"Well, there are catacombs beneath every sacred building in Ireland, it could be said, especially those in Dublin. The city grew so fast, but the dead always keep pace in the end."

"So I'll take that as a yes." Simon looked at me. "I can't say for sure this is In Between space, but there's a very real *something* space that goes behind this wall and straight down. That's where we need to go. Armaeus was adamant that the trail to find Temperance started here."

"Well, it makes sense he would think that since he searched everywhere else, and this was the one place on Earth he couldn't get to." I glanced at William. "This *is* the only place from which the Magician is blocked, right? That you know of?"

"That I know of." William nodded. "But I will say, I've only set foot inside the In Between at Newgrange. I don't know anything about a passage to the catacombs here. I've been the caretaker of this room for years, and there's been plenty of odd doings—spectral visions, mists out of nowhere, rushes of cold, and books appearing when you least expect it. All of those would be consistent with a passage to the In Between. But we've searched many times for one, as you can well imagine. We've even done infrared testing to see through the stone itself, let alone the books. There's nothing here. It's all blocks of granite."

"And there's nothing in the books that say how to...I don't know, open the wall?" I asked Simon.

"Nope." He closed the last one with a thump. "Which makes a certain sort of sense. You wouldn't want it to be too easy."

"Of course not," I groused. Fortunately, I had other options. I fished in my hoodie pocket for my deck, pulling the first cards that came to hand. I flipped them over on the stone table, and we all stared at them. There was Temperance, the Star, and the Tower.

"Hey, all Major Arcana," Simon observed. "That's significant."

"It is," I allowed. "Temperance is almost a gimme, but the Star is more interesting, I think. She's kneeling and pouring water into the pool. Temperance also has a thing with water, you see?" I tapped the card showing the white-garbed angelic figure pouring water from cup to cup. "That's significant too."

Simon pointed to the third card. "Probably less significant, however, than these people falling out of that tower. That seems like it would be more significant by a longshot, especially if those people are us."

"Those people probably are us," I agreed. I could already see how this was going to go, but I needed the catalyst...

I regarded the far wall. As William said, there was nothing particularly special about it. No hooks for artwork or built-in shelves, no ledges or spurs of any kind. The stone floor extended the length of the room and was partially covered by a thick rug. "The rest of this floor of the library is wood, isn't it? The walkway and alcoves of books?"

"It is," he agreed. "Only the outer rooms have stone floors."

"Alchemy is the blend of two disparate elements to create a third. Lead and the philosopher's stone makes gold," I mumbled. I once more took in the basin built into the near wall and moved over to it, running my hands over the shallow, scalloped lip of the basin. "How long has it been since this was filled?"

"Probably the eighteen hundreds, I tell you plain. Water and books don't mix, just as fire and books don't. The moment we got electricity in to light these rooms, we embraced it. Before then, besides their blessing to those who worked here, those basins were used to douse any flames that couldn't be safely extinguished otherwise."

"Simon?"

"On it." He rummaged again in his pack until he came up with a metal water bottle. "But this isn't blessed, if that's what you're going for."

"It doesn't need to be. The stone is." I poured the contents of the water bottle into the basin, my jaw tightening.

Nothing happened.

"I'm telling you, there's no way that holy water in that basin was the trigger for anything," William said. "Otherwise, it would have been documented a long time ago. You're not the first people to think there may be a passage down to the catacombs from here—it only makes sense. It... What are you doing?"

I cast my hand over the still water, feeling the energy crackling off it, the strength buried deep in the stone transferring to the liquid. I refilled the water bottle to about halfway, then stepped away from the basin. "William, there's no need for you to come with us."

"Are you daft? There's every need in the world," he countered. "I've been working here for ten years, and I've *never* found a passage. I'm not leaving you now, and that's for certain." As if to emphasize his words, he sidled up alongside me. Simon crowded in on the other side, his pack in hand.

"Are you seriously going to take that thing everywhere we go?" I asked the Fool.

"Well, I can't exactly leave it here."

He did have a point. Without arguing further, I stepped forward to where the floor extended out from the stone wall and chased under the thick rug. There didn't seem to be anything to indicate where a good point would be to pour the water. Further, now that I was right up against the wall, there was also no indication this wasn't simply a very dumb idea. Then again, if it didn't work, I wasn't out anything except for a little pride.

I poured the water out onto the floor.

The water sat on top of the stone for a long moment, apparently spiteful at the audacity I had to dump it out so unceremoniously. But as we watched, it didn't so much settle into the stone as…get sucked into it.

And then, so did we.

All things being equal, it probably wasn't our best move to scream at the top of our lungs as the floor fell away beneath us in one smooth, sickening drop. There was no crumbling, no stairway that formed, no rings suddenly appearing hammered into the wall. It was simply that, one moment, there was a thick granite floor, and the next, a black hole opened wide and swallowed us whole.

We dropped down a deep chute of smooth stone, banging against either side of the narrow shaft. For whatever reason, Simon seemed to hit the ground first, his body sprawling as his pack bounced and crashed beside him. I dropped heavily next, missing Simon by inches as I thudded onto his pack, and then spinning around just in time to catch William as he tumbled into the black pit.

A resounding crack seemed to rock the very foundations of the building, and far, far above us, the thin rectangle of light winked out.

"That's it?" spluttered William, staring high above him. "That's all it took? All these years, all these theories, and blessed water from the basin is all that was required? I can't believe it!"

"Simon?"

Simon had reached his pack and pulled out a computer, which he set up on his pack after drawing it deeper into the room.

"No signal," he groaned, shaking his head. "There should be a signal. There's no way there's not, frankly. Maybe…lemme try another device. Some of these should be gathering data even if we're off the grid…"

"What's this stone made of, anyway?" William asked, frowning at the wall as Simon's voice devolved into muttering. "I can't quite—ouch." He flinched back from the stone, rubbing his nose. "Smacked right into it."

"No, you didn't." I flicked my third eye open, surveying the surface. The wall was there, all right—only there was more of it now. More where there shouldn't be more. "The wall smacked into you."

"Well, that serves me right, I suppose—"

"No, I don't think you understand. Simon, do you have anything else handy to lead you to Temperance if he's stuck in here, anything at all? Enchanted compass, pixie dust, Magic Eight Ball?"

"What?" The Fool stood, reshouldering his pack and waving a shiny glittering screen at me. "No. Not without a functional laptop. This thing's working, but it's not getting connection either. I mean, I'm recording,

I'm pretty sure, but as far as nav goes, you probably have a better chance at reading your cards than I can offer—and again, that shouldn't be the case. The connection should have been strong enough."

"Right," I said, taking a careful step away from the wall as I watched it closely. It seemed to shift with me, tracking my movement, tracking William's too. The strands of its energy reached out for him hungrily, like the twining serpents of a Celtic illuminated page. This was not benevolent magic here. This was a trap.

Why had my cards led me into a trap?

"Guys," I said quietly, glancing around quickly to where the energy patterns split, the first rustle of quiet laughter reaching my ears. "There's a path out of this room over there. Do you see the door?"

Simon pivoted with his typical good cheer, swinging his pack around. The wall stretched toward him another crucial inch. "I sure do. But what's wrong with your voice, Sara? Why are you sounding so strangled?"

"Do. You. See. The door."

"Yes, *yes*—I see the door," Simon said, as more giggling slipped around us, this time to my left. "Geez. You'd make a shitty dungeon master."

"Start edging toward it. Edging, not running. Not even walking. Edging. Like you're an amoeba. You know what an amoeba is, William?"

"Yes," he whispered, his glassy eyes on the wall. He flinched at the next roll of laughter. He'd gotten an inkling of the truth, I thought, even if he couldn't understand it. "Why are we being an amoeba, though? That seems bad."

"It's a little bad," I agreed. "Amoeba, Simon."

"But there's something close to the wall like this," Simon said, looking down at his handheld and ignoring me. "I think I might be able to get a signal here. And there's another blip right through the door. Yesss..." Oblivious, he fist-pumped, turned, and held up the device, not seeing what I was seeing, which was the eager movement of the wall toward him, forming a land bridge that stretched out like an accusing finger toward the Fool. Simon either couldn't see it or didn't care, but beside me, William started muttering the Lord's Prayer in Irish.

"You guys, seriously, you've got to look at this," Simon said. "This is amazing what I'm picking up!"

Apparently tired of waiting for us, Simon turned and dashed through the door.

Behind us, the wall hissed with excitement and bulged forward, a burst of laughter rising up with it, this time with discernible words. *Hallowed*, the very rocks breathed. *Hallowed, hallowed, hallowed!*

"Run!" I squeaked. Dammit! I was supposed to be *protecting* the Fool down here—not letting him dash off like Alice through the looking glass. "Simon, stay with us!"

I shoved William ahead of me, then took off after them both, pausing only once I was through the doorway to cast twin balls of flame back into the walls— which was a mistake. First off, my fingers barely emitted a thin crackle of energy. Secondly, the stone surfaces seemed to move even faster after that, a wave of thick rock bursting forward, filling the tiny carved doorway and spilling out into the corridor. Assaulted with yet more mocking laughter, I took off pell-mell down the passageway after William and Simon, who was racing ahead, his laughter a mix of pure joy and excitement that didn't stop even when he shouted about a cavern of bones.

It was difficult to hear him above the roar of the rock cavalcade behind me.

We ran and ran, and at one point, I turned back to try my magic again to no avail, only to find the passages had shifted when I turned back forward again, while Simon and William were nowhere to be seen. With the rock closing in around me, I had no choice but to choose one of the remaining options and take off.

But though William and Simon weren't with me, that didn't mean I was alone. Chittering, rumbling, and yet more giggles accompanied me on my mad dash, along with something new: rustling and racing feet. I got the impression of bodies — short, squat, monkey-like bodies — which didn't make me feel any better. I didn't know if I was hearing things or if there really were other creatures in this infernal place, but I couldn't slow down to check. I finally spilled into a wider space — I don't even know how long after — but of course, neither William nor Simon were here either. I heard laughter far off, but it was too low, too dark to be either the Fool or the Irishman.

I stood, swaying on my feet, my lungs heaving as I tried to get my bearings. I prayed that the two of them had taken a different turn than I had, but there was no way of knowing. Simon could have fed an army of twelve guys for a month given the size of his pack, but knowing Simon, he'd filled it full of video games, not rations. And of course, *I* was supposed to have protected *him*. Wasn't that what Armaeus had asked me to do? Yes. Yes it was.

Instead, Simon and William were lost — and so was I.

Aces.

I sighed, inching forward through the darkness, trying manfully not to employ magic of any sort, the shard of Nul Magis aching in my palm. It was the second time in only a few days that my abilities hadn't been as useful as they should be, and for the record, I wasn't a fan.

I rummaged in my pockets, pulling out my cards, then tensed, waiting to hear the telltale sound of *Hallowed* in the whispering rock. But there was nothing. I pulled a card out, squinting to see it—then almost cried out in pain as a shaft of bright light suddenly burst into existence in front of me, practically searing my retinas.

I flinched away before getting a glimpse at the card, then rolled my eyes at what it portrayed. The Hermit, depicting a cloaked and hooded man holding up a lantern, a beacon in the darkness.

While in front of me stood a cloaked and hooded man holding up a lantern, a beacon in the darkness. Gotta love how literal the cards were in Ireland, I'd give 'em that.

"Welcome, Justice Wilde," the man in front of me intoned. "We've been waiting for you."

CHAPTER NINETEEN

I didn't move. Despite the lantern and threadbare robes, the man in front of me was not the actual Hermit of the Arcana Council, though I sure could use some illumination right about now. Or even a fatherly hug. But I didn't know if this figure was friend or foe, or even alive. Was this some phantom of the In Between?

"I'm not alone," I warned. "Or I wasn't. There were two men in these tunnels with me."

The hooded man in front of me said nothing, and my temper spiked.

"So, word to the wise, I'm a little stressed out here," I continued. "You either stop me with magic or get out of my way, but there are two men in this tunnel that I need to take care of, and if I don't get really clear on where they are *right* now, it's not going to be pretty. I'm not sure what the end result will be of me going Hulk smash when my abilities aren't tracking the right way, but I know for a fact you're not going to like it."

The man remained unperturbed. "Your companions are safe, but they've sustained injuries. I will take you to them that you may heal them in divine order."

That didn't sound too promising. I flicked my third eye open, and this man definitely had the goods. Magic didn't merely swirl around him, it rolled off him in waves. And he wasn't alone. With the aid of my third eye's second sight, I was finally able to see that the energy spike extended beyond this man and into the next several rooms, where, eventually, there were four more little glow balls waiting for me. Why hadn't I been able to see this before? "You guys having a party down here I should know about?"

"You of all people can appreciate the value of keeping to the shadows, Justice Wilde. You simply have once more stepped closer into the light. The walls will no longer follow you now. You're safe. Seamus told us to expect you and to prepare. We hope we have done both."

"Right. So you're, uh, human."

"Very much so." I could hear the smile in his voice as he answered.

"And you're currently alive, not some phantom of the In Between."

"I remain a humble servant of earth and sky, wind, and rain," he agreed. I couldn't get a fix on the man's age from his voice, but he talked with a certain gravity that gave him a sense of having logged far more years on the planet than I had, though I didn't get the feeling that any of his psychic abilities were currently bent toward extending that age. If anything, the man had a sense of being almost obscenely pure in his magic — if there was such a thing as a vegan Connected, this guy would be it.

"And you've got Simon and William? They weren't eaten by the monkey trolls?" I asked the question defensively, going for humor, but the man stopped, turning to me sharply.

188

"The guardians of the In Between," he murmured. "So the stories are true."

"Ahh…stories?"

"You're very lucky, Justice Wilde. Lucky, or stronger than you realize. The creatures that roam the In Between are many, but none are so voracious as the stone imps you encountered. For them to be on the move…there is fell magic indeed coursing through the In Between. Did they say anything?"

"Well, something did. Hallowed."

"Oh. We should be going then." Without saying anything further, he led me into another very small, nondescript chamber that was empty, significant only because of the door at its far side. That door gleamed with carvings inlaid with silver, a tree with branches that extended skyward and roots that stretched down deep. As soon as I saw it, a chill ran through me, and a few pieces of the puzzle dropped in place. So did the memory of the rectangular door that'd appeared right before the Fomorians had poured through to enter Dixie's chapel. The magic here was deep—and old. Very old.

The druid moved toward the door, but I held out a hand to stop him. I'd heard Seamus's side of the story of his rogue druid son, but I wanted more context.

"While I've got you all to myself, bring me up to speed. What's your take on the Neo-Celts?"

"Is that what they're calling themselves now?" the druid asked, again with a cadence to his words that made him seem as old as time. "It's never enough for the old ways to make a resurgence. They always must be remade, refashioned, reborn. It's as if those in the newest generation are always too embarrassed to embrace a belief that's existed for centuries untold before them. Instead, they must reform it to make it their own. It's the way of the untutored and the neophyte. But there are times that the teacher must be taught, and it is the student who can show the way."

"That's beautiful," I deadpanned, then repeated, "So what's your take on the Neo-Celts?"

"I think they are a threat, if that's the answer you're seeking. I think they are stronger than even they realize, and certainly stronger than anyone around them realizes. Once that realization is made, however, by the greater world around them, it will go…poorly for them, I think."

I nodded. I suspected he was right. "And Conal McCarthy?"

"One of our greatest successes, and most abject failures," the druid said, his matter-of-fact tone oddly incongruent with the heaviness of his words. "Conal swore he would usher in a rebirth of our order, and we wanted to believe him. We did believe him, for far too long. When he fell away from the order and defied Seamus, he drew some of our youngest, strongest druids with him. Unfortunately, his path is not one of rebirth, but of chaos. He seeks to incite untrained Connecteds to public acts that will result in their persecution, not their celebration. And he's grown far too strong, too quickly, for us to handle him as we would prefer, quietly and secretly."

"Uh-huh. So is Conal the Hallowed Knight?"

Long pause. "We sincerely hope not."

I looked around the darkened room, hung with gloom except for the gleaming door. This was an order that had existed in the shadows for millennia. Had it not been for the surge of magic during the battle of the gods, they might have been able to police Conal, but the Connecteds as a whole? No. Seamus was right to have summoned me. Me, and the Council at large.

So I'd best be getting on with things. I gestured to the wooden panel before us. "Where does this go, exactly? And why is it so sparkly?"

"This is one of the most popular entrances into the In Between, and as it happens, it's also your fastest way out," the druid said, his voice warming with enthusiasm as if he was giving me the location of a famous Dublin pub. "It thrives from the energy of all those who pass beneath its blessed arch."

That maybe sort of made sense. "Exactly how many of you travel these passages on a regular basis? And is it only druids? Or are there other groups that use these byways too?" Like super-scaly lizard groups?

"Well, you clearly can use them, Justice, though they're not well known among your Council. Except to Death, of course."

"Yeah, except her," I said. "Though from what I understand, she doesn't usually make it back for the St. Patrick's Day party."

"That she does not. I sense the other questions within you, but they are not mine to answer. We don't know how many Fomorians are walking the passages of the In Between. We do know they are very dangerous, and that the deaths in Las Vegas are only the beginning."

"They'll kill more?"

"It's inevitable. We also know very little of Death in the present age, other than that she refuses to return to the land of her people for reasons unknown. Whether it's a grudge or a pledge or a personal vendetta—we have no idea. She's given us no hint whatsoever as to her true thoughts."

"That pretty much sounds like the Death I know."

"Then perhaps it's time we renewed our acquaintance with her. It has been far too long."

I wasn't liking his odds for a cheerful family reunion. Part of my mission here was to protect Death, but I didn't think these guys were going to be a problem for her. "If she shows up, be careful. She's carrying a several-thousand-year-old chip on her shoulder, and you don't want to be the one to knock it off."

"In that, I would agree with you, Justice Wilde."

The druid placed his hand upon the panel and murmured something beneath his breath that I couldn't quite catch. Though I could decipher any language I heard, there remained the small problem of needing to hear it. The panel, however, seemed to hear it just fine. The silver inlay glowed brightly for a moment, then the door swung open into the room beyond. A room that was far more distinct in its shape and form than the one we'd just left, for the record. We stepped in. The illumination was brighter here. My eyes were drawn immediately to the two men lying on the stone floor, surrounded by a bunch of guys in bathrobes.

Simon and William, out cold. *Dammit.*

"What happened to them?" I asked, forcing myself not to set everyone on fire.

"Nothing, so far as we can see," my guide said, unperturbed. "They appeared to both be struck down by some force we cannot identify, but it's a force that's left no visible signs of injury. They're unconscious but asleep, and they appear to be more or less unharmed. We didn't want to move them when we realized you were following, for obvious reasons."

My third eye was still in full operation, and as I moved forward, I immediately knew that the druid was correct. William and Simon were out cold, but that was all. There was no magic suppressing their activities or their movements, and there was only the faintest beginnings of bruises at their temples.

"This wasn't done by some random, nebulous force," I mused. "This looks more like they were clubbed. Who else is roaming through these passages besides the Fomorians?"

I'd asked this question once already, but yet again, I didn't get the answer I wanted, mainly because I didn't get any answer at all. The group was completely silent, and I looked up in irritation.

"Look, you can tell me now or you can tell me later, but either way, I'm going to find out. There's no use having a secret from me, because it's not going to last." I stopped short of saying, "we have ways of making you talk," for which I believed I deserved a medal.

"There have been rumors," my druid guide said at length, "of others taking the byways before the recent arrival of the Fomorians. Some of the demon horde, for example, and even darker creatures, lurking in the gloom. It takes someone with the ancient knowledge to open the passages and close them again without any of us catching on. But every now and again, you'll find a door to one of the tomb passages left ajar, followed by the story of a spelunker gone missing and reemerging hundreds of miles away. It happens so infrequently that we can always shrug them off, and of course there's long been the popular bias toward suppressing stories of this nature to aid us in that effort. Though that too is changing, as so much is in the world."

I settled back on my heels, looking up from Simon and William. "What do you mean?"

"We live in a world of transparency, of winnowing everything down to its core. It's not the kind of world that does well with magic, for all that the New Agers profess to want to embrace it. Everything needs an explanation now, everything must have a purpose and a place. Everything must be recorded to be believed."

"Do you yell at kids for playing on your lawn as well?"

"It's easy to be smug, but you're running up against it as well, Justice Wilde. Far more so. The rule of Justice is not merely to protect the Connected from themselves, it's to protect the Connected from themselves."

"You do realize you just repeated yourself."

"Not at all. You've seen it yourself in a small way. In the altercations you've experienced this very week in your own city."

"The Neo-Celts squaring off against these spectral opposition warriors or whatever they're calling themselves? That sort of thing is bound to happen."

"Beyond that," he said, shaking his head. "You watched users of magic unafraid to use their abilities in public where anyone could see, in a world where everything is captured on cell phones and transmitted all over the world. There are no secrets in a world such as this, not that can last very long. You don't think the fight at the festival grounds wasn't noticed?"

I narrowed my eyes. Though the psychic festival fight had been hella concerning, it also hadn't technically happened. Armaeus had rolled back time specifically to keep it from happening. "How do you know about that?"

"Time passes differently in the In Between. And there are many doors that need not be opened fully to serve their purpose."

"Needlessly vague, but okay." I shrugged. "But there has always been magic to be had for those who were willing to look. The black market of the Connected community has thrived as long as the Connected community has existed. The knowledge isn't new."

"Granted, but now there is magic being shown to those who had no intention of looking, who don't even know how to fully process what they've seen. In the span of a few short months, you've experienced significant weather disturbances in your efforts to keep the gods from piercing the veil, an influx of demons that, like it or not, is bubbling up into the mainstream of society, and now you have wielders of illusion and fire who are bold enough to use their abilities in public without concern for collateral damage. Even in a country as lax as the United States is when it comes to gun laws, everyone will rally around the idea of not being attacked by a magic ball of fire."

"That's probably true," I allowed. I thought of the spectral opposition warriors. I really needed to do something about them before they got out of hand.

"It is also the real reason why we wanted to meet with you today, why we entered the shadows of the In Between to pull you gently toward us. Though we didn't know you'd face such trials."

I tried to not think about the monkey trolls. "What, you guys don't hang out down here on the regular?"

"No." Though my question was flippant, his answer wasn't. "The In Between is meant as a passage, not a dwelling place. You stay within its confines too long at your own peril."

I blew out a long breath, hoping he was right about Conal not being a past Temperance. It sounded like anyone staycationing in the In Between wouldn't end up in great shape.

The druid's gentle voice continued. "You must understand the importance of this altercation you're about to have with Conal McCarthy, Justice Wilde. The Neo-Celts and their leader believe they are pure of heart. They have the fire of zealotry to guide them and real magic to prove that what they believe is the truth. They will not back down simply because you tell them to. Civility has fallen away in every corner of our world, and the idea of following the guidance of others simply because it is for the good of the whole no longer holds sway among these people. They will act because they can act, and perhaps in part because they've never had the strength to act before."

"More like Conal and his followers feel entitled," I scoffed.

"Call it entitlement, call it what you will, but the reality of magic falling into the hands of a populace who has grown up in such relative luxury among the developed world is not an ideal situation."

"Not all places on Earth are developed. Half the world doesn't have clean water, yet the entire world was affected by the last surge of the gods. It isn't only rich white people who got a power boost," I challenged.

"Justice Wilde, most of the Neo-Celts haven't suffered great deprivation," he harrumphed. "Magicians and sorcerers who have suffered greatly in their lives, assuming they have not been wholly broken like Judgment was, can often handle the advancement of their abilities with far greater discernment. But for those among us who have never suffered and who now have powers at their disposal heretofore unexperienced, powers that are going completely unchallenged... It creates a dangerous environment. The forces of the non-Connecteds will rally against all of us."

"You mean like SANCTUS," I said, referring to the quasi-religious, quasi-governmental hatchet men loosely tied to the Vatican. In my efforts to protect Connecteds from the asshats of the world, I'd nearly been killed by that group several times over, but they hadn't caused me much trouble of late. "They're pretty much scattered to the wind."

"Organizations like SANCTUS always scatter to the wind, the easier for them to fly back together as one," the druid observed blandly. "But no. I'm talking about the governments of all major nations. I'm talking about the UN, Interpol. I'm talking about police forces at the federal, state, and city level in your own United States. I am talking about witch hunts, and I'm talking about mass hysteria. It will come. I suspect your Magician has foreseen it. I suspect that's why he is so eager to bring Temperance back to the Arcana Council, now more than ever."

I narrowed my eyes. "That's an awful lot of information you've gathered for a group of guys who hang out in dark closets. Was there a bulletin or something that went out without me realizing it?"

He didn't answer, not that I expected him to. I pushed on. "So, since we're on the subject of Temperance, is the Green Knight a past Temperance reincarnated, or is he his own special snowflake?"

"An excellent question, and one that any member of your Council who'd been alive when Temperance Wilson was seated, albeit for a brief time, would know. Yet I see not one of them here." He gestured to Simon, still lounging around on the concrete floor.

I decided this wasn't a good time to mention Death punching her ticket for the Emerald Isle. I figured she could make her entrance on her own terms. Still, the druid had a point. What had Armaeus said was the reason for sending me and the Fool on this, well, Fool's errand? Because Temperance didn't know us? That had seemed to make so much sense at the time, but now…

"It's a simple enough question," I pressed. "Is the Green Knight a past Temperance reincarnated, yes or no?"

The druid sighed. "No. I will grant you, the Arcana Council has lost its share of members to the shadows of the In Between, its members and sometimes gifts far more precious. And yes, those who have returned to the light after their long walk in the tomb passages are never quite the same. But Conal McCarthy is no golem from another time. He's exactly what he seems to be: a druid whose abilities are outstripped only by his hubris. He seeks to bring the dawn of a new age of magic to an Earth that is not ready for it, nothing more. Though that's certainly enough."

"And are all the druids in agreement of that? That Conal is simply Seamus's son?"

"We've known both him and Niall since they were children. Believe me, Conal's spirit is far too fresh, too undisciplined to have tasted Council power before."

I peered at him. "You speak as if you've met a few Council members in the In Between before."

He shrugged. "You're not the first I've encountered in these passages, but in all truth, Conal is not Temperance. He's perhaps the absolute opposite of Temperance. Which introduces a bigger challenge. If he *had* been the incarnation of Temperance come back to lead the children of Earth on a quest to fully synthesize their magic, which is what Temperance is most skilled at doing, then you could rest assured that a spirit of coexistence would follow. Not a spirit of divisiveness. Not a spirit of anger and outrage and rebellion. That has never been what Temperance has stood for. But that is what we have with the Green Knight."

"Green Knight. Not the Hallowed Knight."

"Again, we sincerely hope not."

I sighed. "Fair enough. So who is he? Beyond the basics."

"The man who has dubbed himself the Green Knight came into his ministry only a few years ago, when he was no more than thirty years old. He's remained remarkably quiet, almost nondescript, until November of this past year."

"Of course." I lifted my fingers to squeeze the bridge of my nose. "That was a banner month for a lot of people."

"Since then, a crusade that would ordinarily take months, even years to build has now gained strength in the matter of only a few weeks. Through social media and the arcane web, McCarthy's followers have built their presence in every developed country and quite a few second- and third-tier nations as well. They are strong and they are eager. And they have no idea what they're doing."

"There's a lot of that going on all over the world by people far worse," I countered. "What makes the Neo-Celts such a threat?"

"The difference is, the Connected are a group without an advocate or an ambassador. Save for the Houses, who operate in secret mostly for their own private benefit, there is no consulate for the Connected in any corner of the world. So when they fly their flag, there is no one to defend them as they are struck down. That is the second danger we face with the Green Knight. That his actions will awaken the ire of the non-Connecteds who will react to what they fear as they have reacted throughout time. With chaos and bloodshed."

His words shimmered in the room around us, almost a living thing, because of course he was right. This was the same concern that'd been building in my own heart these past several weeks as the Connected of the world woke up to new and greater abilities. Fear had held them back so far, but that wouldn't last forever. The actions at the Vegas festival had already proven that. We were sitting on a powder keg of roiling, uncontrolled psychic power…

And the Green Knight wanted to light the fuse.

If he even got the chance. I had the feeling that the agenda of the Tuatha dé Danann wouldn't exactly match up with Conal's once they'd returned to Earth.

I sighed. "So what was your plan to handle this if I hadn't shown up?"

The druid's chuckle was soft and filled with compassion, and when he spoke, he sounded all too much like Seamus McCarthy, the man who'd started me down this twisted emerald path. "You *are* the plan, Justice Wilde. You had no choice but to show up."

CHAPTER TWENTY

A rock band started up above us, the sound transmitting into the room via high-fidelity speakers, saving me the trouble of informing this guy that he wasn't the boss of me. Instead, I glanced up. "Where are we, exactly?"

The druid nodded. "Directly below the Temple Bar district. One of the most highly trafficked areas in Dublin, and quite crowded, as it happens. You won't have any trouble blending in with the crowd."

I didn't have much trouble blending, period, but he didn't need to know that.

I looked down at the two prone figures. William was still out cold, but the Fool had awoken at some point during our conversation and was gazing up at me, his hands now positioned comfortably behind his head.

"You have a nice nap?" I asked.

Simon grinned. "I wondered when you'd get around to noticing me again." He sat up and crossed his legs, gazing around at the men standing there.

"Druids?" he guessed. "You people look way less interesting in real life than you do online, is all I got to say. You might want to check out some cosplay options if you want to get serious about your game."

"Noted," my druid guide murmured drily.

"You know, I was supposed to be protecting you down here," I put in.

"And I feel totally secure," Simon said, turning back to me. "I'm seriously stoked, for real. I managed to pull some data down about the In Between before William and I were hit with—something. Some*one*, maybe, but definitely more than just a force field or an overeager wall. It was a physical entity, and it was moving fast. I don't know enough about those passages to know what all is roaming through them, but I got the impression they extend way farther than we think they do."

I looked back to the druid. "How far do these go?"

"In Dublin itself, the passages start as catacombs that stretch well beyond the bar district and the college district and continue as subterranean passages all the way out to the suburbs. But the doors to the In Between are riddled throughout. Just as you found a doorway into the tomb passages, there are several doorways that lead out, only to open up at points far distant."

"Okay, so how distant?"

"Far enough that we have never fully mapped it," he said. Which was exactly the answer I'd most been dreading.

Simon, however, perked right up. "Are you serious? Like there's a whole Dungeons & Dragons game waiting to happen here? Do you have any idea how exciting that's going to be to a hell of lotta people?"

The druid stared quietly at him for a long moment before speaking again. "I suspect it would be interesting, if such information were ever to get out. However, since we have done an excellent job for three thousand years to make sure that that isn't the case, I feel certain we will be able to forestall such a terrible thing from occurring."

Simon scowled. He leaned over to grab his pack and drag it toward him, as if shielding himself from the Luddites harshing his mellow. "And why would that be so bad?"

"Perhaps because we don't know what those adventurers would find."

That answer did not seem at all satisfying to Simon, but that was an argument for another day. Instead, I helped him up.

"We've got to get going." I said, then glanced to the druids again. "I get that Conal isn't Temperance, but a past Temperance isn't hanging around waiting for us to find him, at least not down here, right? He would've shown up by now?"

The druid nodded. "The appearance of new Arcana Council members in the In Between would have been a beacon of brightest light to any former members. He — any of the former Council — would be inexorably drawn to seek you out."

"Or he's trying to avoid us," Simon offered up reasonably.

"Or that," the druid said. "But your journey has not been in vain. We have not been idle once we understood your plan to come to Ireland. At Seamus's suggestion, we've let word slip out that you had gained access to the In Between earlier today, and where you would most likely emerge. As you may imagine, that has attracted some attention."

I blinked. "Just how much time has passed with us down here? It's felt like only a few hours, but outside…?"

"To the outside world, mere minutes have passed since you entered the Long Hall of the Trinity College

Library. Fortunately, our expectation of your emergence at this time has allowed us to get all the players in place. You'll definitely be noted the moment you return to the world above."

I studied him skeptically. "And how is that a good thing?"

"The Neo-Celts are, above all, a people in search of signs, Conal first among them. Now they are as much, if not more, interested in finding you as you are in finding them. Beyond that, we've sent this information out along the very byways you have just traversed, and whispered it into the winds. If a past Temperance still walks this Earth, or roams the In Between, he will know that you are looking for him.

"And *that's* a good thing?"

The druid chuckled softly. "Everyone wants to be noticed, Justice Wilde. It's part of the human condition."

"Well, William's human condition needs to be addressed as well," I pointed to the poor guy still unconscious on the floor.

"We'll see to the librarian," the druid assured me. "We've been watching him for some time."

I lifted my brows. William had seen far more than he'd anticipated. Hopefully, the druids knew better than to mess with his memory, if they were even able to do that, which I suspected they were for them to have remained so unnoticed for all this time. However, I had bigger fish to fry, the Green Knight to track down, and Death's back to cover.

Looking remarkably satisfied with his sojourn through the In Between, Simon shouldered his pack and gave one last long look around before he and I set off with our druid guide. The doorway at the back of the chamber led to a narrow staircase, which emptied onto a landing with three other doors. The druid pointed to the one on the far left.

"That will let you out into a storage closet, which in turn will open onto a corridor leading to restrooms. It will be simple enough to affect that you don't know where you are, because in truth, you don't," he said. The man had a point.

We took our leave immediately after that, and the druid's words proved true. Within a minute or two, we found ourselves in the midst of a loud and boisterous pub crowd where the patrons stood packed cheek to jowl. I wasn't going to find anyone here, nor would they seek me out. We needed to get outside. I began pushing my way through the crowd, not trying to draw any attention by clearing it with magical means, and Simon quickly peeled away from me. I could only keep sight of him by tracking his enormous pack through the crowd. A few minutes later, he ended up back beside me again as I neared the front door, clutching two pints in his hands.

"There's a courtyard out back that looks promising," he said with a grin, waggling his brows.

I wasn't sure what promising looked like to a man holding two pints of Guinness, but I followed him out into the open and had to agree. The space was cool, well lit, and inviting, and had so few people milling about that it had to have been cordoned off for VIPs.

Simon unshouldered his pack, then took a long swig of his Guinness. "Look like you belong," he said, glancing around at the decidedly nontouristy group we'd just crashed. "Nine times out of ten, no one will bother you, and if they do, you can tell them you're waiting for the Green Knight. That's almost always how it goes down, I'm telling you."

A high, clear voice rang out. "Justice Wilde."

"Or, you can do that." Simon shrugged. He turned to take in the woman who stood a good ten feet away from me. Whether she was cognizant of my need for personal space or not sure if she was supposed to call security, I didn't know. I also didn't respond, and the woman's stern demeanor turned a little more hesitant.

"You *are* Justice Wilde, aren't you? My name is Patricia James, and I'm very glad to meet you. We were told to expect you."

"Out here? With a beer in hand?"

Now her face did crack into a smile. "Well, it seemed the most likely place, given your companion." She turned to Simon. "We have long been fans, Druid Simon. When you whispered of your new adventure, we could not stop talking about it."

I shot him a look. "You're kidding, right?"

"My outfit is so much better, you cannot *even* believe," he assured me. He grinned at the woman and raised his Guinness. "You're with the Green Knight?"

"I'm proud to serve." Patricia lifted one fist to her chest and tapped lightly, and I was struck by the familiarity of that gesture. Where I had seen that before, *Star Trek*? Sometime more recent?

"Is he here?" I asked.

"Soon. He wasn't at all sure that you would come. He has summoned you before now, to no avail."

"He has?" I'd only had this job since November. I was pretty sure I would've remembered somebody calling himself the Green Knight if he'd come shooting into my office via pneumatic tube. "Recently?"

She tilted her head. "Last summer solstice was the most recent attempt. He'd planned for a renewed request this winter solstice, but the Happening occurred instead."

I winced. The Happening. Great. "What exactly, ah, *happened* here in Dublin for that, anyway?"

"We were blessed to be standing in a circle of stones when the lights assaulted the heavens and the world was split wide and made whole again," Patricia said, her words almost hushed, reverent. I didn't know exactly what she meant, but I didn't need it to be spelled out any clearer. They'd been paying attention.

"And were you surprised? Or had you known it was coming?"

She smiled. "None of us knew it was coming, not even Conal. He proclaimed it both a miracle and a sign. And when reports came in from all over the world that those among us who were Connected had experienced a flowering of our abilities in many ways, we believed with him that the time to act was now. His ministry has been in place for years, but that moment was when it became real, you know?"

"Right." I took a long draught on my beer. "And what is your role in his, ah, ministry?"

"You could call me his chief of staff. I coordinate the online ministry, correspond with all members of the order, and recruit. It all equates to a lot of time online, some of which is spent waiting for people to get back to me." Patricia eyed Simon again, her cheeks coloring in the bright glow from the outdoor lights. "When the waiting gets to be too long, I've been known to explore the arcane web for rumors of the newest video games released by Arcon Entertainment."

Simon blushed, and I studied him with narrow eyes as the woman's attention was drawn back to the doorway.

"Does the Magician know you're doing this?" I asked, my words low.

"The Magician knows a lot, especially the stuff he doesn't want to know," Simon murmured back. "If he'd wanted me to stop, I suspect I would have stopped already on my own and thought it was my idea."

"Conal is here," the woman said abruptly. "You'll understand once you meet him."

Obligingly, I swung around to face the courtyard entryway to the bar. I didn't have to wait long. The door opened as if on cue, and a gaggle of humanity flowed through. Three tough-looking security-guard types, all in deceptively casual knit shirts and khaki pants, followed by two men who looked alike enough to be brothers, at least from a distance. Even if I hadn't seen him on Dixie's camera feed, though, I'd have known at a glance which one was Conal.

The man who'd become the Green Knight would've been attractive in nearly any setting, but in the lush, luminous glow of a humid Irish evening, he was almost transcendent. Tall and moderately built, he wore a dark knit shirt and dark pants, which seemed to set off his fair good looks. His hair curled around his face in a short choppy blond mop, and his blue eyes twinkled with a fire I could see all the way across the courtyard. But it was his smile that was truly captivating, bright and engaging and so full of repressed excitement he seemed to draw those around him closer to him just by turning on the charm.

Speaking of charm, I flicked my third eye into motion and nearly flinched at the cacophony of energy that swirled around the man. It was the same tangled weave I'd seen earlier in the chapel and to a lesser extent in the heart of the festival, when the Neo-Celts and spectral opposition warriors squared off. I looked closer, trying to penetrate that power, and instantly, I was put in mind of the magic that swirled around the Magician.

Armaeus's magic was elegant in its symmetry in form, carefully studied and mastered, a true art. This, however, was a wild frenzy. But was that simply because I wasn't seeing a natural, organic pattern to the chaos? Was I looking for the elegance of the Magician and getting instead the raw power of the man who could be Temperance?

Either way, it was too much. I clamped my third eye closed and waited for Conal to turn our way.

"Who's the guy with him?" asked Simon, and my gaze flipped to the man beside Conal, who I assumed was his brother, Niall. Though I knew they were several years apart in age, they were close enough in looks to almost be twins. As they got nearer, I could tell more differences between the two, though their features seemed weirdly less distinctive, not more, as they came closer, glad-handing all their cronies. My head was already starting to hurt with these two.

"That's Niall, Conal's older brother," Patricia confirmed. "Given his druthers, Niall would rather close himself up in a cottage and read books all day, but Conal has become so used to having him around that he doesn't like to make a move without him. Niall is a good brother and he works hard to support Conal. It isn't easy running a global ministry when you're only thirty-three years old."

I winced, not missing the subtle Christ allusion that these people seemed eager to be pushing here. "How's that ministry going, anyway?"

At that moment, however, Conal turned to us, stepping away from his brother, who stood back even as Conal moved forward. Conal strode toward Simon and me with a broad smile, extending his arms wide—not to hug us, but to include us both in his greeting.

"Justice Wilde, Trickster Simon," he said, stopping a few feet short of us to execute a brief bow. "I am Conal McCarthy. You honor me with your presence. You honor us all. I have long wondered when the Arcana Council would take note of our order's growing strength. I'm happy that time is come."

There was something about the guy that nagged at me, but I was pretty sure I was being churlish. He really was devastatingly good-looking, and the addition of the Irish brogue did nothing to take away from that. Quite the opposite.

"I understand you reached out to the Council before," I said.

"I did! I didn't quite understand that Justice was not in office, until suddenly she was. I had a sense I needed to contact you, though I confess even as I did it, I wasn't sure what I was looking for. And now you're here, so perhaps we can figure that out together."

There was the slightest hint of flirtation to his voice, but I didn't take it personally. Conal McCarthy seemed to be the type of man who would flirt with a stone and not mean anything by it. It was simply the way he interacted with the world. Once again, I suspected it was part of his charm.

"Are you all gathering tonight for our benefit, or do you have a base of operations near here?" I asked.

"We did, but we do." He grinned. "We've purchased several buildings in the city center, expanding as we go. We thought first a more remote location, given the noise and hustle of Dublin, but there's no denying the energy of this place. It draws our people from all over the world. I can meet you at my headquarters tomorrow if you like." He rattled off an address. "Or, if you prefer, we'll be gathering in St. Stephen's Green around noon."

"What's wrong with tonight?"

"Because tonight we are friends." He smiled. "Tomorrow, who's to say?"

I tilted my head, taking in the magic of his person — the magic and the undeniable youth. I decided not to beat around the bush. "There are those members of the Council who believe you're Temperance reborn."

"Reborn?" Conal laughed, shaking his head. "I am no one but me. The role of Temperance on your exalted Council is a noble one, to be sure, but I don't seek to marry up the elements or even the disparate spirits in this world. No. I wish to light a great fire for the Connecteds, that all might see the truth of who and what we are."

"You believe the world is ready for that?"

It was a softball of a question, and as I expected, Conal hit it out of the park.

"It no longer matters if the world is ready for it," he said with a resonance that seemed to lift his voice and extend its reach. Everyone in the courtyard took note, and even I settled back a little on my feet. The guy could have been in the opera, with the kind of vocal projection he was rocking. Was he, in truth, the Hallowed Knight? "What matters is that we are ready for it. There is no more time to lose. Beltane is scarcely more than a day away. When those sacred fires are lit — nothing will be the same."

I watched his energy build and twist as he spoke, the charisma of a true zealot layered over a very real web of power. This wasn't someone who was going to listen to reason, I knew in an instant. *Note to self, wrap this up before Beltane.*

"*It would be advisable, Miss Wilde.*" The Magician murmured in my ear, teasing a smile from me. It was good to know he was paying attention.

211

I managed to keep my expression neutral as I studied Conal. "Tell me, why the Green Knight? It's been a while since my English lit class."

"Believe it or not, it wasn't the moldering old tales of the druids that inspired it, the name just sort of came to me." Conal laughed, spreading his hands in a "what're you gonna do, I'm a genius" gesture. "The Green Man has long been a fixture in Irish mythology, and the Green Knight was all about the symbology of a true code, not one that weak fools paid lip service to. A code of the earth and sky and mortal grace. That's what I wish to put forth to guide the Connecteds of this world. And that's what I will do. You'll find that most of my presence online and in person is created to get people to pay attention, Justice Wilde. My motives are pure, my intentions true. But if the more outrageous things I suggest gain us the attention that we desperately need to get our messages heard? Well, I'm not about to let the moment pass me by. We need eyes upon us — all eyes — to launch the era of the Connected as powerfully as possible."

"Uh-huh." I crossed my arms, not knowing if anything that came out of this man's mouth was the truth, the truth as he firmly believed it, or a bald-faced lie. I definitely wasn't going to tip him off about the Hallowed Knight concerns of the druids — or the whispers of the In Between. "And the women in Las Vegas who thought they were marrying you and got a face full of Fomorians for their trouble? They died, Conal. Badly."

"They *lived*," he countered. "The Fomorians needed a human host to serve as their gateway to this world, and both Lenora and Alison eagerly volunteered. They knew their path would be one of passion and surrender, and it was. They got to experience a purpose, a power

212

most mortals only dream about. They were also consenting adults and able to make their own choices."

The way he said the last bit made me think he had a phalanx of green-jacketed lawyers huddling over hold-harmless agreements somewhere, which pissed me off. This guy was way too smooth for his own good. But now he'd attracted the wrong attention.

Then again, maybe that had been his goal all along.

I narrowed my eyes at him. "And that bit about the fae coming back to rule in their rightful place, taking dominion over Earth once more? You have to know the Council has heard about that."

To my surprise, Conal merely winked. "Made you look."

Yup.

CHAPTER TWENTY-ONE

I was in the same pub the next morning, waiting for my coffee despite the owner urging tea on me like it was the elixir of the gods, when Simon joined me. He looked absolutely awful as he staggered toward me, gratefully accepting a mug from an industrious barmaid on her way to my table. She was my barmaid, as it happened, which meant it was my coffee Simon was now drinking. In this case, I didn't mind. Simon clearly needed the brew more than I did.

The woman scurried off for more, and Simon slunk into my booth.

"What happened to you?" I asked. "We didn't stay out that late."

I'd bailed on the fawning gathering after enduring a few more rounds of Conal's cryptic pronouncements. I'd decided I'd had enough. No way was this guy a former Temperance, but he *was* a budding megalomaniac. That was reason enough for me to deliver him to Judgment at least long enough to get us past Beltane. After that, we could all discuss the coming surge of Connected strength in a slightly saner and more rational way. I hoped. I'd managed to use the time in my room to go over Mrs. French's files, which was time much better spent. This wasn't the first time the ancient gods of Ireland had been summoned, and it had never gone well.

"We didn't stay out late," Simon agreed. "But when I got up to my room last night, I decided to check the Internet. There's been an explosion of activity on the arcane web. Conal's chief of staff Patricia she said was online a lot? You have no idea. I fell asleep three different times, but she never seemed to stop posting."

"Could've been a bot," I suggested.

"Could've, but I don't think so. There was an earnestness to it that's hard to fake. She also changed her primary talking points too many times, but not so many times that it appeared to be a truly randomized sequence. And then she messaged me directly about game play."

I looked more sharply at him, and he immediately clarified. "As in MPG. Online games. She wanted to play, and she was good. Too good. We decided to team up and play a game we'd never tried before, and…hours passed. Now I'm here."

"You certainly are that." Not knowing what would help him best, I ordered a traditional Irish breakfast. The Irish apparently ate a lot of meat for breakfast, but Simon fell on the plate as if his life depended on it, and maybe it did. The combination of savory meat, eggs, beans, and potatoes called to me as well, which surprised me, but when in Dublin…

While we ate, I pulled out my phone and engaged the map app, pointing at the district that Conal had mentioned the previous evening. "Can you program that into your little spy toy and let me know if we're running into a trap?"

"Absolutely." Simon pulled a much smaller daypack from his shoulder and unzipped it, reaching in to pull out a slender laptop. "Left the rest of everything in the room, warded to the gills. Uploaded everything I could to the Arcana Council servers before I did so."

I lifted my brows. "I thought you didn't have Wi-Fi access in the In Between."

"I didn't. But I did have recording capability, and Armaeus sounded like he might cry when I uploaded the feed."

I had no response to that and pushed my eggs around on my plate as Simon finished tapping on the device.

"Here we are. Nice little area of homes near St. Stephen's Green. That entire area is old, old, old, but nothing untoward, and nothing hyperpowerful except right here." He tapped the address Conal had given me. "Which I assume is because that's where Conal is located."

"Any other activity we need to be aware of? Witch, demon, revenant, Connected, non-Connected, anything?"

"Not a ton of Connected activity of note, except for here," he said, pointing at a collection of buildings near the southwest quadrant of the green. "There's definitely something cooking there, though it has the sense of being muted. More like there's some sort of shield or whatnot going on."

"A shield?" That was interesting. "Someone trying to use their abilities on the sly that close to the Green Knight's headquarters? Why?"

"Don't know, but remember, this device I have is pretty sweet. It's not like any rando Connected would be able to pick up on this, given the quality of the shield they've got going on. They're good."

"Well, Conal doesn't need to know where we are until we show up on his doorstep. Let's see how good."

It took another thirty minutes of stout Irish coffee, spicy sausage, and eggs before Simon began looking more himself, then we headed for St. Stephen's Green. The walk was easy and surprisingly pretty, with a bright sun streaming down on a city that appeared freshly scrubbed. As we approached the park, however, I began to get decidedly uneasy, my right fist clenching and unclenching involuntarily. "You sure you didn't pick up any activity in the park itself?" I asked.

"Nada," Simon said. He pulled the device out of his pack again and scooted over into the shade so he could read the screen more easily. "Cancel that. There's definitely something going on now, something on the darkish side. But also a signature I recognize." He squinted at the park, then back at me. "Would it make any sense for Death to be in there?"

"Maybe," I allowed. I knew she was going to be in the area, and I knew she wanted to be on hand when things got real with the Green Knight and his little troupe of leprechauns. But what she was doing to keep herself busy before the confrontation happened, I had no clue. I'd only worked with Death directly a few times, so I was in completely uncharted territory.

"How much do you know about Death?" I asked Simon as we resumed our trek. I'd heard Jimmy's take on his employer, but I'd also seen firsthand Simon's ability to collect and parse information. I suspected he had a file on each of us, and I was looking for a deeper dive into the data.

"Not as much as I'd like, of course, but I've got the basics," Simon said. "Second-longest tenured council member after the Archangel, who shouldn't really count since he was around before the Council even got started.

Druid priestess before she ascended, timeline super fuzzy on that. Could've been right around the start of the Common Era, or it could've been several hundred years earlier, or as much as three thousand years. She's given all three answers at different times. And too, they counted time differently than they do now."

"Fair enough."

"A few things that she has been consistent on, though," Simon continued, ticking off the points on his fingers. "Daughter of a high chieftain. Never was married, but she'd been promised in marriage several times, sort of the nature of the beast back then."

"Really." I tried to imagine Death even entertaining the idea of being married off, but then again, she hadn't always been a demigoddess. Once upon a time, she was simply your ordinary, average druid high priestess.

No. I still couldn't imagine her entertaining the idea of being married off.

"Her time as priestess did not go completely without note, despite her best efforts. The oral tradition was still alive and well for several hundred years before that eventually got scuttled, but when I first ascended, one of the top non-Council Connecteds I was friendly with was a channeler. I managed to find people who'd been alive around the time of every Council member when they ascended and pumped them for information."

I stared at him. "Please tell me you're joking."

"Nope." He grinned. "I was a little messed up at the time, strung out on drugs before I ascended, and then seriously mind-fucked by the Emperor afterward, but I wasn't a complete wasteoid. I figured out pretty quickly that if I wanted to understand who was on the team with me, I needed to do my own digging. Nobody was giving up any information, so I went out and found it myself."

"And you seriously were able to call up contemporaries of people like Death."

"Death, Eshe, Viktor—yep. The Devil too. I tried Armaeus, of course, but he knew what I was doing and hadn't cared up to that point. He drew the line at his own 'This is Your Life' rundown. He said if I needed to know any information for something other than my own idle curiosity, he was happy to share."

I snorted. "Right."

"Agreed." Simon grinned. "But I let it alone at that point. No point in setting him off, and I had enough data on the other members to at least get my footing. Anyway, my contact for Death was another priestess in her tribe, or whatever they called it back then. Not a very successful priestess, either, and bitter about that. Those always make the best informants. She said Death was a pain in the ass."

Simon stumbled abruptly, then swung his gaze to the park. When he spoke again, his voice was a little higher, a little threadier. "You know, maybe we should wait until we know exactly where Death is before we have this conversation."

I glanced over to the park as well, then scanned the street ahead of us. "Probably not a bad idea. And look there. I think that's our stop anyway."

Simon refocused on his device and nodded. "That's definitely it. Pub, pub, pub, shop. It's the shop, most definitely."

I took in the hand-painted sandwich board sign sitting on the sidewalk outside the quaint little store. *Faery Readings! Crystals! Lucky Clovers!*

"Color me surprised."

Miranda's Faery Garden Shoppe boasted a cheerfully painted storefront that could easily have passed for a bookshop, and when we stepped inside, it smelled like a bookshop too—more old leather and polished wood than the typical overwhelming aroma of patchouli. A cheerful set of bells rang as we swung the door open, and a young blonde with gossamer fairy wings perched high on her back popped up from behind the counter, where she'd either been putting something away or playing jacks with pixies.

"Hello there," she chirped, waving us in. "Please take your time and look around. We've got tea in the back if you'd like to sit a spell in the courtyard, and if you have any questions, don't hesitate to ask."

I poked at a jewelry tree from which were suspended two dozen pendulums in various hues of crystal, drifting my finger along chakra trees and selenite wands. There was an entire table given over to leprechaun statuary, and four full stacks of books on every metaphysical topic I could imagine. And I could imagine an awful lot. The shop extended farther back from the street than I expected it to, with kiosks and shelving and hints of other rooms.

"Is there someone doing readings right now?" Simon asked. "Like a psychic?"

"Oh! That would be Miranda. She's out in the courtyard, but she's meditating. If you could tarry another fifteen minutes, though, she could see you then."

I checked my watch. "She takes clients at ten a.m.? Every day?"

"Every day she's here, which is most days." The cashier nodded cheerfully, her broad Midwestern American accent coming through more strongly now. "It's her store, actually, and she lives right above it, always has. She says the place has good energy."

"It definitely does that," Simon muttered, once more looking at his device. "And a whole lot more of it now that we're inside. What the…"

He turned away from me and wandered down an aisle that led to a short staircase, taking him deeper into the store.

"What's back there?" I asked the cashier, my gaze dropping to the little pin on her shirt. "Ah…your name is Lily?"

"It is." She beamed. "Actually, this entire store is cut up into lots of little sections so that you have the impression you're here all by yourself, even if there's a crowd. Miranda's always trying to make each space its own special oasis. I don't know what your friend is looking for, but I know he'll find it. I truly do."

I eyed her curiously. Lily didn't have any Connected ability, yet there was an effervescence to her spirit that still projected strongly. "How long have you worked here?"

"I'm in my third year. Unfortunately, I'm only allowed three years. House rules."

"Whose house?"

"Well, Miranda's, silly. Oh!" She clapped her hand over her mouth, glittery painted fingernails flashing. "I'm so sorry, that was completely rude. I'm a student at Trinity College, and Miranda hires almost exclusively from there. She won't let any students stay longer than three school years, though."

"That seems…oddly specific."

"Right? And she only hires non-Irish students, at least so far as I know. She says she's doing her part to help tourism, but I've always found it cooler to go in shops that have people who have the whole Irish-accent thing going on. It's just so pretty and different."

"You never asked her why she didn't hire locals?"

Lily's eyes widened. "Well, gosh, no. I mean, I'm happy for the job. And if she likes to hire exchange students, then so much the better. I'm a little different because I came to Trinity and stayed, which most students don't. But it seemed like my place, you know?"

"Yeah," I said, flicking my third eye open again. This time, with my focus more attuned, I could see it, the smallest bud of Connected ability blossoming deep within Lily's heart. It was hardly recognizable, but it was definitely there, and I suspected made all the stronger by her open and accepting demeanor.

"Have you ever done readings like Miranda?"

"Oh my, no," she said again, blushing. "I'm not psychic or anything."

Because I was watching closely, I noticed the tightening up of that little bud of Connected power, the flinching back of delicate petals.

Once again, I was keenly aware that I was about to overreach, and I knew I should be keeping my psychic hands to myself. But this young woman was already on the path, already had within her the power to do and be so much more than what she was. I didn't need to shove her sprawling down the Connected path, but would it hurt anything to let her know that path existed for her? Would that be so awful?

And was this how Conal McCarthy had started down his road of rationalization too?

The tinkling of bells sounded behind me, and the moment was broken. Lily looked up, her face stretching into an even wider smile.

"Oh, hello," she said. "I've got your package from County Fermanagh right here. It came just this morning."

I turned as well, blinking as I recognized the man who stood just inside the doorway, half expecting the Green Knight himself.

It wasn't, but I was close.

Conal's brother, Niall, was built to a slightly smaller scale than his more outgoing counterpart, and quite a few years older. His hair was more ginger than his brother's, and his face slightly more weathered, green eyes bright and inquisitive. Despite the relative chill of the morning, he wore only a light sweater of sage green buttoned at the front over a worn checked shirt. His khakis were a deep loden green, and his shoes were hardy but basic. The man couldn't look any more Irish if he were walking in a field of clover.

"Justice Wilde," he said easily, stepping forward. He didn't reach out to shake my hand, but I didn't mind that so much. Anyone who'd done any research on me at all knew what my hands could do. I was disappointed to realize that Niall's Connectedness hadn't improved overnight, though. I'd assumed he had simply been overshadowed by his brother, but in truth, he didn't burn with much light at all.

"Just out for a stroll?" I asked. "Or did Conal want our meetup to happen a little earlier?"

"Time does seem to be of the essence, doesn't it?" Niall smiled, his lined face creasing with a wry merriment that had long since been etched into his skin. "But no, come when you wish to come, we'll be ready. I merely wanted to tell you about the package Lily has behind the desk. It's actually for you. Compliments of the house, as it were."

CHAPTER TWENTY-TWO

That's great," I said, casting a glance behind the desk, but I wasn't about to let Niall off that easy. Besides, the glass jelly jar that Lily was removing from its packaging looked like it held, well, dirt. It wasn't going to go anywhere. Lily set the small jar on the desk and scuttled away, doubtless looking for some thirsty pixies eager for tea. "You order it up for me, or did your brother?"

Niall put his hands in his pockets, and rocked forward on the toes of his thick-soled shoes. "My brother isn't the fiend you would make him out to be."

"No? This is the same guy that tried to take you out some years back, according to your dad."

"Oh, tosh," he scoffed. "My da means well, he truly does, but he oversteps, like most parents. Conal is doing what so many of us can't—or won't. Nothing more or less." Another rocking motion on his feet, and I sighed. Niall McCarthy seemed like a gentle enough soul, the opposite of his more hard-driving sibling, and I almost got the impression I'd like him if it wasn't for his association with a group of Connecteds who wanted to take over the world. Little details like that tended to stick in my craw a little bit.

"How long have you guys been all Lords of the Dance here? I've been told Conal had only started his ministry in earnest late last year, but I'm not buying it. It's all too organized for that."

Niall's smile equal parts gentle and, increasingly, irritating, as I picked up my first hint of entitlement. "That's not what you really want to ask."

"Oh? And what do I want to ask?"

"If Conal's the Hallowed Knight, the ancient bogeyman of the druids. I'm sorry to say, he's not. Which is a shame. It wouldn't be a bad thing to have captured the interest of Justice Wilde. Alas, he's just a man who, again, is doing what most won't."

I felt my fingers tingle. This guy was about two sentences shy of getting a fireball to the mouth. "Okay, then tell me this. How long have you and Brother Zealot been crafting your plan for global domination? Because you're playing a very dangerous game."

"You think so?"

That was sentence one.

"I know so. You guys are doing a great job riding the #FaeToo movement, but you have to know you're drawing the attention of people who have the ability to shut you down."

"Ah, but you see, that's the beauty of it. No one can—"

"I'm going to go ahead and stop you before you complete sentence two. When I say shut you down, I don't mean you guys here at Dublin central. I mean the acolytes you've got logging in to your Celtic Faedom website and pledging their support. The Internet is forever, and it's hackable like you would not believe by people who are way better at this than you are. It's the little people—and not the wee folk little people—who are going to be hunted down if you cross the wrong mob. It's your followers who are going to be tried and imprisoned in the court of public fear. If you gave a crap about them, you'd be a little more careful."

Something had changed in Niall's demeanor as I spoke, but when he stiffened at the end, it wasn't in reaction to my pithy little speech. He turned slightly. "I need to leave."

"You need to do a hell of a lot more than that."

The bell jingled, and the chill that slid into the gift shop was so profound that I turned despite myself. In that moment, Niall darted past me, nothing but the patter of his thick-soled shoes sounding on the steps as he fled deeper into the shop. Presumably he knew a back way out of the place, away from the newest patron of Miranda's store.

Only, there was no one standing in the doorway. "Did someone just come in?" I asked aloud.

"Oh, that happens from time to time," Lily the cashier said cheerfully, scuttling back up a different set of stairs. "You never can tell when it's just a breeze or if there's a playful spirit wandering about."

"Yeah." That chill didn't exactly remind me of a playful spirit, but when Lily held up my special jar of dirt, I scowled at it. "That was shipped to you? How long ago?"

"Special delivery this morning, but Mr. McCarthy asked for it last week, he surely did. Said he might have need of it, and here you are. It's come direct from County Fermanagh, itself—and it looks hand packed too. That's important."

I eyed the small jar. "It looks like dirt."

"That it is. But finer dirt than you ever did see, and that's the truth." She mimicked an Irish brogue, bubbling over in laughter. I got the feeling she bubbled over in laughter a lot.

"You know..." I lifted my hands slightly, the tingling in my fingers growing stronger, and it was everything I could do not to tease the magic forth. "You, ah, have a really bright spirit."

"You think so?" she asked, blushing to the roots of her hair. "I've always wondered but, you know, how can you not when you're surrounded by so much of — this." She gestured to the whimsical displays of crystals and fairy wings. "It makes you almost believe."

As she spoke, I watched her energy. While it jumped a little as she began, it dipped just as quickly. Her own beliefs were both pushing her to accept her nascent psychic abilities and discount them at the same time. It must be exhausting. I had a feeling she'd be forced to face the truth soon.

I tucked the jar into my jacket and glanced at the clock. "It's after ten o'clock," I said. "When my friend pops up again, send him out into the courtyard, okay?"

Without waiting for the woman to respond, I headed toward the back of the shop, aiming for the big sign that said "Faery Garden." I figured I was on the right track.

I pushed open the heavy door and was pleasantly surprised to see a cute courtyard in the space beyond, overflowing with flowers, ornamental trees, and babbling fountains. In the center was a setup of several tables and chairs, one of which was occupied by a plump, dark-eyed, curly-haired woman chattering merrily...to no one at all.

"Excuse me?" I followed the most direct cobblestone pathway, glancing around. Yup, sure enough, there was no one sitting opposite the person I assumed was Miranda. We were alone in the garden.

"Ah!" she exclaimed, beckoning me forward with hands glittering with several delicate rings. "You've quite chased them all away, but rest assured they are listening, so do be kind."

I knew I wouldn't like the answer to my next question, but I asked it anyway. "Who's listening?"

She beamed at me. She wasn't a young woman—gray shot through her dark curls and soft lines bracketed her mouth and eyes, but she had an effervescence that belied her lack of cosmetics, making her cheeks bright and her lips full and glossy. She was quite attractive, actually, in a woodsy, flowers-in-her-hair sort of way, and when she moved, her long, silky caftan fluttered in the sunlight. "Why, the brownies of course. Or the wee ones, the little people, and yes, even the fairies, if you'd like to call them that. They answer to anyone seeking them with a pure heart."

"I'm sure they do." I didn't bother hiding the skepticism in my voice, but I did stop short calling her a liar. Progress.

"Ah, now there you go. They can pick it up in your tone just as easily as your words, though, to be sure, words matter more."

"Than actions?"

"No, not that, to be true. But what you're willing to say aloud carries more weight, it surely does. It codifies your thoughts, solidifies them. There are many of us who walk around wondering if we're good people, feeling poorly for our weaknesses and our petty thoughts. But far worse are those who give those thoughts wings and claws and teeth when they know better, when they know that what they say is purely designed to harm another soul. I don't think you're that kind of person, Justice Wilde. I don't think you'd be here in my garden if you were."

I smiled a touch wearily. "Well, thank you, but let me be clear. I don't believe that brownies dance on the head of a pin."

"Oh, of course not," Miranda scoffed. "They're far too bossy for that. But, really, Justice Wilde. You've gotten so far in your life by being willing to believe so much. You believed in your own resourcefulness, you believed in your ability to make magic even when you didn't want to believe. You believed in things, and people, and in even the gods themselves."

"They sort of kept showing up. It made them tough to ignore."

"And yet you're not willing to cultivate an air of *general* belief, and that is what is holding you back."

Something in Miranda's delivery made me stiffen a little, a strange tremor lighting along my nerves. For once, I didn't have a snappy comeback. "Meaning?"

"Meaning, if you could only accept that which is unacceptable, you could do everything you think you can't do. It's all right there, but you're stopping yourself before you get — oh!"

With as closely as I was paying attention, Miranda's sudden, startled near scream completely unnerved me. I whirled around, fire springing to life along my fingertips, while Miranda stood up so quickly, she nearly knocked over her chair.

"Annwn!" she spluttered, the name so lyrical and right that another chill swept through me, exactly as it had in the front of the shop. Only it was Death standing there, looking like she was fresh off a reaping season and in no mood for fools.

"Onórach Annwn, you've returned," Miranda continued. "I knew you would, they've been telling me for so long that the time was nigh, and we've made everything ready, we truly have."

Death stalked into the courtyard, her face so stony, I was surprised the blossoms didn't fall right off the trees. "There was nothing to get ready," she said.

Another shiver swept over me, but now the sensation felt cooler, more effervescent. All I wanted to do was to hear Death talk. The flowers on the trees did move this time, but only to wiggle and expand, as if trying to blossom more fully.

"But of course there is," Miranda exclaimed. "I have your harp—"

"No." Death's voice cracked like a whip, and despite myself, I quailed right along with Miranda. "I ordered that instrument destroyed a long time ago. It isn't safe for this world."

To my surprise, Miranda didn't back down. "You did, Onórach Annwn. But Scáil An Bháis isn't any old harp now, is it? It's special, like you are special. And the two of you together…"

"Had our run," Death said. "Scáil An Bháis exacts its price eventually, and that price won't only be mine to pay."

Miranda waved her off. "That's as may be. But you cannot deny the power you wield. And humanity has needs that the Council cannot deny either, no matter how much they may want to."

"Humans can't be trusted," Death countered, looking at her meaningfully. "Case in point."

"Perhaps and perhaps not," Miranda said staunchly. "Not all humans are able to be trusted and that's also as may be, but as you know more than anyone, Connecteds are not all humans. They're special humans, they're gifted, and they should be allowed and expected to use their gifts to keep the magic flowing through the world, not to pound it into nothingness."

I stared at the shopkeeper, trying to decide which surprised me more. That she was willing to argue with Death, or that she was actually making sense. She winked at me. "Just as not everybody can be special, because if *everyone* is special, then nobody is."

"You did not just quote *The Incredibles*," I broke in as the earth began spinning on its axis again and I recovered my snark.

Miranda shrugged one shoulder, as coy as a teenager at her first dance. "There's more truth in our fairy tales than we ever would dare to admit to ourselves. But just as that holds true, so too does this: if those who are special act like they are *not* special, eventually they will become not special. And that's as great a tragedy as anything in this world, wouldn't you say?"

Once again, the woman had a point, but Death regarded her with flat disapproval. "Are you done yet, Bartholomew?"

My eyes popped wide. If I'd had a teacup in my hand, I would have dropped it. Instead, I had to settle for my jaw falling open.

"Bartholomew?" I gasped, my gaze going from an offended-looking Miranda back to Death. "Bartholomew *Simms*?"

"Hush, hush, hush!" Miranda/Bartholomew hissed, flapping her hands. "The girl is coming!"

"Mistress Miranda?"

Lily the cashier stepped out into the courtyard, Simon right behind her, and the combined intense focus she drew from all of us was apparently too much for her body to handle. Lily's skin suddenly started to glow, a rosy hue billowing out from her a good three feet. She lifted up her hands, issuing a startled "Oh!"

Miranda/Bartholomew groaned. "Ah, for the love of the saints, look what you've done, Lily. I knew I'd kept you on too long. Back into the shop with you."

"But…what's happening to me?" the cashier asked, staring at her glowing fingers.

I caught Simon's eye, and he nodded. "It's okay, you'll get used to it," he said, ushering Lily back inside the building.

"Always the same damned problem," Miranda/Bartholomew said, her Irish brogue thick with dismay. "If they stay here too long, I can't seem to keep them from blossoming where they're planted."

Death smirked. "I thought you were the one who thought everyone should be special."

"It's different when they've no blessed idea what they're in for," Miranda/Bartholomew snapped back. "I try to recruit the magic curious, not a nascent Connected. But they all become Connected in time."

"Let's all back up a second," I interjected, barely able to keep from spluttering. "You—you're Bartholomew Simms. As in the Bartholomew Simms who was Temperance of the Arcana Council for, like, five hundred years, up through the 1850s. You knew Abigail Strand."

Miranda/Bartholomew stopped her hand-flapping and sighed. "I am," she said, executing a short bow. "I did. Abigail…shouldn't have died so young, and that's the truth. When she did, I found I just couldn't stand to remain on the Council any longer. And I knew a little about the In Between. Specifically, I knew the Magician couldn't travel parts of it, especially those bits that extended over Ireland. It wasn't so difficult to slip in and…well, not slip out again. I suspected Death knew, of course. But I used my time well, I well and truly did."

She pointed a heavily ringed finger at Death. "And I'm *Temperance*, after all. I found the things that were hidden in the In Between, hidden away for millennia, in some cases, so well, even you couldn't find it. Like an ancient, powerful harp that humans were too god-struck to destroy, despite your haughty demands. And it looks like you'll be needing that harp now, won't you? So I helped."

"You meddled," Death countered. "Totally different."

"Only to you. I did what needed to be done. I took on another identity, and then another, and eventually, well—" She fluttered her hand at the garden. "Here I am. With workers who can't seem to help but bloom into Connecteds despite my best efforts to keep them safe."

"I'm not sure how much you can help anyone keep from growing when they're meant to grow," I put in. I was familiar enough with contact-high Connectedness, so Lily's transformation didn't surprise me. "Like it or not, we're in a brave new world here."

"You should talk," Miranda sniped. "You went toe to toe with Seamus and his spectral opposition warriors, but you didn't raise a hand to stop them—*or* to help them. You simply walked away."

I blinked. First Niall with his dig about the Hallowed Knight, and now Miranda? Did everyone on this island know my business? "Why should I stop them? They're entitled to their beliefs."

"Not when their beliefs are wrong," sniffed Miranda/Bartholomew, every inch the stubborn Irishwoman. In this incarnation, I decided, it was simply easier to think of her as Miranda. I'd have to open the box of Bartholomew crazy sometime soon, I knew. But not today.

233

Today, I merely needed to shut down her judginess. "Whoa, whoa, whoa. You're an advocate for the Neo-Celts and free expression of magical abilities, and that's great. But what about the beliefs of the spectral opposition warriors? Should they be repressed just because they don't want to be attacked by those who wield magic?"

"*You* wield magic," Miranda protested. "And you're on their side?"

"Nope, I'm on the side of people not killing each other while they work out how to coexist. Once you start appointing who's right and who's wrong, it leads to a very slippery slope."

"I disagree," Miranda said, folding her arms over her chest. "The forces allied against magic have had their time for all these millennia. Why shouldn't it be the time of magic?"

Death took this one. "Because, *Temperance*, any power in the wrong hands is too much power. And by definition, hands that would seek to oppress or overcome by force are the wrong hands. That kind of power given too much sway is dangerous."

"Dangerous to whom?" Miranda countered. I had to hand it to her, she had plenty of starch in her skirts.

"Dangerous to this precious, fragile planet and the precious, fragile beings who live upon it. Magic is not a static force. It grows when it is used." Death turned her gaze upon me, her pale eyes suddenly fierce. "You know this to be true too. You've used your magic more actively of late, no doubt assuming that you'll eventually reach the limits of your power. But you haven't. You won't."

I lifted a brow, unnerved by her focus on me. "Everybody reaches the limits of their power eventually."

"In this case, Justice, you're wrong," Death said. "The body is a physical construct, while magic is a metaphysical construct. The body has limits. Magic does not have limits. It can stretch your sinews and break your bones, overtax your heart and explode your blood vessels, and yes, it can kill you. Because your vessel defines your limits. But if you learn how to transcend the vessel, there is no limit. Eventually someone is going to figure that out. Might as well be you."

"Oh, great," I muttered. "I'm back to Jean Gray, eater of worlds."

"Or maybe just Sara Wilde, stubborn—" Death broke off abruptly as a dark shadow passed over her face. When she spoke again, her eyes were troubled.

"Blue?" I whispered as my gut clenched. I didn't know the name Miranda had called her, and I rarely used Death's current name. But now I stared at her in quickly mounting fear.

"Nikki is failing," she said without preamble.

All the blood left my head in a rush, leaving me swaying on my feet. "What? Armaeus said she was fine."

"She was fine, but she's not anymore. She's gone into a coma, and she's sinking fast. You've got to go to her."

I could already feel my body starting to destabilize, flame licking along my skin. "Yes. Yes, of course. She's with Sells?"

"Not to her body, Sara," Death snapped. "She's already slipping away from that."

"But how…" My arm suddenly flared. I knew how to reach Nikki, Death had seen to that a long time ago, but that wasn't my only problem. "But how can I help her heal? I *tried* once. I failed."

"And you'll fail again if, as Miranda says, you don't believe." Death pointed at my pocket. "You've got all you need right there."

I shoved my hand into my pocket and pulled out the jar of dirt. "Please tell me you're *joking*."

But Miranda had her hands up to her cheeks, her eyes wide. "The soil of Fermanagh," she breathed. "Do you know what that is — what you have? Though I don't know how you came by it. Since all the publicity, they're treating that sacred earth like the crown jewels."

I stared down at the small jar, my heart pounding with panic. "It's *dirt*."

"No, sweet Justice Wilde," Miranda said, her smile a little sad. "It's magic."

"You don't have time to argue, Sara." Death's voice cracked between us. "Go. Now."

"You have got to be *kidding* me!" I wailed, wrapping my hand around the jar as flames burst around me.

I went.

CHAPTER TWENTY-THREE

Despite Death's admonition, I fully expected to arrive at Nikki's hospital room once I focused on the tattoo that Death had inked on me months earlier, the design crafted to ensure I'd be able to find my best friend no matter where she went or what befell her.

Of course, it didn't quite work out that way.

In fact, there was no building, no hospital bed, and nobody in sight. Instead, I was lost in a tumbling murk of gray mist, thick and unguent and intrusive. It slapped and poked at me, brushing up against me like a living thing, chittering and moaning. It *was* a living thing, I decided, or at least there were living things in it. I shoved the jar of dirt into my pocket, then snapped my fingers out, but my hands emitted only the barest crackle, like they had deep in the catacombs beneath Trinity College. I flickered my third eye open, and saw — exactly nothing.

"Nikki," I shouted, and was rewarded with a panicked gasp to my right. With no other option, I blundered forward, slipping over the wet rock surface — what I hoped was a rock surface anyway — my hands flailing as I tried to make sense of my surroundings. "Nikki?"

"Doll—" Nikki's familiar sobriquet was cut off beneath the sudden stamping of many tiny feet that rushed past me into the gloom. I got the impression of short, long-armed bodies covered in fur, like chimps on a rampage, then they were gone. A second later, though, Nikki gave a startled, agonized yelp of pain, and I jerked at the desperation in it. This was someone desperately trying not to make any noise at all, but she couldn't help herself, because she'd been hurt.

Something inside me snapped. "Fuck *this*."

All of Death's words came back to me, Death's and the other Council Members' as well, Miranda's, even the chiding disapproval of a brilliant human sensei who'd tried and failed to get me to connect to my inner Connected power—so many words, so many ways to access that which lurked deep within me, a jack-in-the-box of ability ready and waiting to spring out. I'd never tried to turn that crank too hard, though. I'd always been scrambling to catch up to the powers I already had, with no desire to add to the mix of crazy. But now I ignored the lever completely and reached out for the box of my magic in blind rage, wrenching off its top with a roar of fear and pain.

My hands lit up with fire all the way to my elbows, and more flame gushed out my back, soaring up in arcs of light that spread like wings behind me, knifing through the shroud of gloom and chasing it back.

And with the added light, I saw Nikki. And the things that were feasting on her.

I raced forward with the speed of teleportation, though I could feel my feet moving to eat up the twenty yards that separated me from Nikki. The short, squat imps of the In Between caught wind of their imminent destruction a nanosecond too late. I swept them off Nikki's body, blasting them into nothingness as Nikki flinched away from the swath of blue fire.

Then I fell to my knees, dousing the flames that burned along my arms but not the arching barrier behind me.

"Nikki!" I gasped again.

She turned to me with a blighted face. If she wasn't my best friend in any world, I would have flinched away. I wanted to flinch away. Her beautiful strong features had been ruined—eyes gouged out, mouth sliced away on one side, as if she'd been caught by an errant claw.

"Dollface." Her words were only slightly slurred.

I rammed my third eye open, pain exploding at my temples. Nikki's energy circuits were overloaded to a white-hot degree, and I realized her eyes hadn't been gouged out, they'd been burnt in their sockets. A seer who'd seen too much.

"Nikki, my God." Instinctively, I lifted my hands to her, feeling my energy scorching me from the inside out as well. It seemed incongruous to add fire to what was already burnt, though. "What do I need to do?"

"Just touch me, dollface," Nikki whimpered, her soft voice bringing a rush of tears to my eyes for no good goddamned reason. Then her mouth worked, and her next words were broken, agonized. "I want to be held again."

My heart shattering, I moved my hands forward and then, a heartbeat later, I remembered the jar of soil. I twisted away, plunging my hand in my pocket as Nikki tried not to sob, and pulled the jar free. Not knowing what else to do, I poured the soft, wet loam over my palms and pressed it into my skin, coating it with a thick black layer. Then I turned back to Nikki.

Without hesitating further, I placed my palms on her face, not knowing what this new magic coiled inside me would do when it broke free, but praying to whatever pantheons who would hear me to guide this precious flame and dirt and magic to its highest purpose—

Crimson light exploded from my hands. Not the blue light I was used to, but the urgent, vital color of life's blood. It set the soft earth of Ireland aglow, and it flowed over Nikki's face, sealing it, penetrating it, pouring into her. Where my healing fire in the past had traced circuitries of energy, rekindling that which had been frayed, broken, or burnt away, this fire was more like a molten tide, cascading in a full wash of healing— bone and sinew, thought and mind, heart and emotion. Nikki's body didn't jerk with the agony of being jammed back together again, she simply collapsed in full surrender, going boneless in the little crack of rock into which she'd wedged herself, which had left only her face and torso exposed, her legs protected so she could run back to the light when it appeared again.

So she could run…

How did I know that?

I tried to grab at that tiny thread of awareness, but Nikki's face began contorting again, shimmering in front of me, and I ripped my hands away, the crust of soil coming with me like peeling a sheet off a sleeping person. Only this person was wide awake and staring now, her eyes returned to their full, startled glory.

"Sara," she whispered, bringing her hands to her face, her mouth, gently probing her eyes. "You *came*."

My arm flared with cold heat where Death had inked me, deep and true, and I didn't need to glance down to see the crisscrossing blue coils of Celtic artwork, symbolizing the eternal path back to Nikki, wherever she might find herself. "I came."

She blinked several times, as if trying to fully understand what she was seeing. "So what the *hell* is that on your back?"

I stumbled back away from her then, getting my own bearings. We were in a large, irregularly sized room, ancient in its angles and worn rock. The fissure where Nikki had shoved herself appeared to be part of a series of passages that roamed off into nowhere, and some, I realized, that disappeared into darkness where gloom and danger lurked, out of the range of my fiery…wings, for lack of a better word.

"Where are we?" I demanded. "How do you feel?" At this point, I didn't know which question was more important, so I was okay with whatever she answered, but as Nikki braced her hands on either side of the crevice and pushed herself forward, there was no hesitation, no wince of pain.

"Well, I feel a damned sight better than I did a short while ago." She placed a trembling hand on her chest. "Ticker is beating normally again too. There was a bad stretch when it seemed like it was going to pound right out of my chest. I figured it was some sort of adrenaline reaction, but I couldn't get my Zen on with my eyeballs burned out."

I reached out a hand, making sure it didn't glow with any sort of fire before I did so, and she took it, her grip certain and strong. I pulled her out of the crevice and realized she was wearing a hospital gown. Sort of.

"*That's* what Dr. Sells allowed you to wear in her ICU?"

Nikki half smiled with a trace of her old energy, glancing down to the custom-made mini shift of light blue cotton, the neckline a deep V and the waist bound in a surplice style—easily undone with a quick tug, but not a shapeless muumuu. "Dr. Sells didn't have much of a choice when I hyperventilated at her sartorial options. But we managed well enough until I..." She frowned, looking around. "I don't actually know how I got here, you want to know the truth. I was doing fine. All my vitals were registering, there was no sign of the toxin, I'd recovered my ability to read memories— handier than hell in a hospital, I will tell you that, at least if you can get the person to focus on what you want to know."

"Yeah, I suspect any of those nurses or docs have a dozen different cases running in their minds at all times, only one of which is you."

"I wasn't the problem they were flipping out over, though," Nikki said, narrowing her eyes at the memory. "You were."

"Really?" I shifted back as she came forward, careful not to singe her with my wings. "I recovered more quickly from whatever hurt us, though."

"You did, but that's not what I mean. What I got from the lab weenies who were tapping my bloodstream like a champagne fountain on New Year's Eve was that the formulation of the poison had a target, and that target was Nikki Dawes. You were always supposed to be the carrier. For you to be damaged makes them think we have some sort of weird connection between us, and they're all atwitter about it."

"We do have a connection." The fact that Nikki had gotten poisoned because she was with me made me feel far worse than the fact that someone out there had enough of my DNA that they could formulate the toxin specifically for me. Still, it wasn't completely unreasonable. I'd spilled enough blood over the course of the past decade that someone paying attention could easily have taken advantage of it. And it wasn't the main issue now.

I refocused on Nikki. "How in the hell did you manage to get sucked into the In Between?"

"Honestly, I've no idea. Brody told me that's where you were heading off to, and I suppose I had it on the brain. I was drifting in and out of a half slumber, listening to the chirp of the monitors, when something took a turn. It was like I was trying to wake up but couldn't, and every attempt I made to get closer to the light…"

"Nikki, never run toward the light. I thought you knew that," I cracked, even as my voice wobbled.

She wasn't listening to me anymore, however. "There was a light coming in from the doorway, I think…" Her voice grew softer, more indistinct as she tried to remember. "There was definitely a doorway, and it was filled with light, not just a sliver, but as if someone had pushed it wide. And I knew I had to get back to it, but like I said, I couldn't. There was something in the way. First it felt like a sort of thick air and then it was bodies. Short and scrubby bodies with claws." She shuddered. "Teeth too, I suppose. I flailed out and caught one of them, and the moment I felt the skin beneath my hand, I attempted to read its memories, and boom. There went my eyes."

My own eyes recoiled in their sockets in sympathy. "That must've hurt."

"It didn't." She shook her head. "Nothing hurts here, except the knowledge that you're *being* hurt, if that makes sense. Because if you're hurt, if you're wounded, if you're weak, you can't get out."

"Holy crap," I muttered, trying to put together pieces of lore versus my own experiences in this nightmare called the In Between. "What kind of rule is that?"

She turned toward me, looking surprised. "I think that was something I managed to parse out from the garbled thoughts of the...whatever the hell those things were that were on me. Monkeys. They were like really fat, furry monkeys. Long arms, long fingers. And teeth. Definitely teeth."

"Imps. They're called imps." I shivered, looking around. The chittering noise in the gloom, beyond the reach of my wings or whatever I was going to call them, had started getting...louder. "Magic is suppressed here, but I was able to call mine if I went deep enough. You managed to survive because you also dove down deep and didn't give up. Both of us are pretty special people, but—"

"But we're not the only ones who've ever figured that out. I don't remember any near-death experiences that involved death monkeys, though. Everyone always seem to focus on the bright light. So we clearly took a wrong turn in here."

"We definitely did." I thought of the surging rock wall in the section of the In Between we'd raced through in Dublin. Clearly, there were a lot of creatures lurking in the darkness of the In Between that weren't friendly toward humans. I'd need to be a lot more careful in the tomb passages, if I ever got back there. Which, given what I now knew about Miranda/Bartholomew, I expected I would.

Nikki swung her head as if seeing something that wasn't there. "The light is important, though. It's like— I mean, it's obviously a doorway, but I couldn't quite work out whether I only could go through that door, or if there were other doorways I could try, and then I thought I saw, I had to have seen..."

"More doors? More passages?" I'd run parts of this maze when trying to get to Simon and William. I understood her confusion all too well.

She nodded. "There were more. There were definitely more ways out, but where those ways led, I have no idea. And then the monkeys came. Which sort of took precedence."

"They chased you deeper into these caves?"

"I didn't want to go, I remember that now. I wanted you to find my doorway, if that makes sense. But once my sight went..." She shuddered. "I don't even know how long I've been down here. It seems like a long time."

"Yeah. I'm pretty sure time passes differently down here or up here or wherever the hell we are. But we need another of those doorways now." I narrowed my eyes, staring around the gloom, my spiffy new wings twitching on my back. "Or do we?"

Nikki snorted. "Unless you want to deal with another attack of zombie monkeys, yeah. I'm pretty sure we do."

"I don't think so." I held out my hand for Nikki, and she grasped me by the forearm. I drew her closer to me, under the canopy of my crackling wings. "Not anymore."

"You realize you burn my clothes off me. I'm going to be showing up wherever the hell it is we're going without proper attire."

"I don't think that's going to be a problem," I said. "As long as you're good rocking Celtic caftans."

"Darling, I've done some of my best work in Celtic caftans."

Grinning into Nikki's beautiful, restored eyes, I destabilized.

Crackling out of the In Between was surprisingly successful, with a few caveats. Unfortunately, I'd forgotten about the enormous wings growing out of my back, which resulted in the process having far more of a sense of self-immolation as Nikki yelped in alarm until I managed to tuck them away, wincing as they melted back into my back. I didn't know if they'd pop back out if I ever had need of them again, but, something else to add to the list of "what new fresh crazy is this?" It was getting to be a long list. We sizzled out of existence, then emerged once more in the middle of Miranda's garden — accompanied by the sound of falling crockery.

"You…" Lily the cashier stood in front of a shattered teacup, her eyes bugging wide. I winced as I turned to Nikki — and yup. Totally naked, her hair a corona of short chestnut-red locks: Nikki's real hair, wild and wonderful and free.

"We need some clothes," I ordered, as if showing up in a Dublin shop with my shoulders on fire was completely normal. "Like, right now."

Lily squeaked. "Of course, but — "

"No buts." I turned to the door back into the shop, shoving it open. As I recalled, there was a complete side room filled with long, flowing shifts, hair accessories — even the obligatory fairy wings. "No wings," I said, pushing Nikki inside.

"You suck the fun out of everything," Nikki shot back before I closed the door on her.

I grinned and shook my head, then stepped back out into the courtyard. I looked back at Lily, who was still swiveling her head back and forth. "What?" I pressed. "What is it, what's wrong?"

"Ah…Miss Wilde?"

Two members of the Irish police stood in the center of Miranda's quaint little garden, staring at me.

CHAPTER TWENTY-FOUR

A h...hi there," I said as I turned to face them more fully. "Any of you happen to know the time?"

They gaped at me another long moment, then the officer on the left, a tall, slender man with a hangdog expression and coal black hair, glanced at his watch. "Eleven thirty," he said in a rough brogue. "What exactly did we just see?"

"Me crashing my own tea party?" I asked brightly. I eyed the shattered teacups. "I don't suppose you have extra?"

"I'll get more," Lily chirped, desperate to make her escape. She vanished back inside before anyone could stop her. I wondered if she knew where Simon was, and I secretly hoped he'd managed to escape before the Garda had shown up. I knew Death had. You rarely caught Death unawares; she'd sort of cornered the market on that little trick.

Speaking of tricks, I *had* just left the In Between. "And the day? If you would?"

"April thirtieth," the second Garda officer said, this one a stern, willowy blonde. At least she'd managed to keep hold of her teacup.

"Good, good," I said. No time at all had passed, apparently. That meant I still had more than twelve hours before Beltane started…plenty of time. No, really.

I gestured to the tables at the center of the garden. "You guys expecting other company, or do we have time to talk?"

"We have time," the male Garda officer said curtly, and his sudden, unexpected animosity brought me up short, fraying the last of my nerves. "You don't. We've just gotten word from Interpol that you're in town, involved with Conal McCarthy's proposed demonstration on St. Stephen's Green. We'll not tolerate any foolishness, and that's a fact. We know your history, we know your organization, and we're prepared to restrain you forcibly, if necessary. You should know—"

I didn't mean to do it. I wanted to work with these people, and I wanted them to want to work with me. But the adrenaline of finding Nikki where I'd found her—looking as she had—was still sluicing off me like a waterfall, and my pulse was still jacked way too high.

Adding to that, I was tired of being treated like the ball boy of the Arcana Council, when I was arguably the whole damned team wrapped up in one.

I lifted a hand almost casually, overcome with the need to flick his words away like flies, and two things happened almost at once. Instead of my hand exploding with blue fire, it glowed once more with a steamy, rich crimson flame that undulated and whispered and scurried across the space between us. With a playful slap, it knocked the male officer's cup out of his hand as he stood, transfixed. The cup toppled to the cobblestone path, shattering to bits. Neither officer moved for a moment…and then another moment…and then I realized they weren't moving at all. I'd frozen them, exactly like I'd frozen the Emperor at the Council meeting. I couldn't stop time, exactly, but I could stop a person or two. That was good to know.

I strolled past them, taking a seat at the table and leaning back, before I waved the smoky red flame away.

"Bill!" The female officer stared at her partner, then at the ground, then back at the space where I'd been. The male officer, presumably Bill, still stood frozen, but no longer through any effect I'd cast. Then he also snapped his gaze first to where I'd been, then to where I now sat, his face mottling with fury.

"It would seem that I do have time you don't," I said, patting the table. "Now, why don't you sit down before we break more of Miranda's tea set?"

As if drawn toward me on a string, the two officers made their way to the little table and perched gingerly in the chairs. "What the bloody hell is going on?" Bill demanded. "What sort of trick was that?"

"It's not a trick, at least not in the traditional sense of the word. I don't mind going open kimono here, and there is a *lot* of information I can provide you in a very short period of time, but I want some assurances in return."

He straightened, because I was finally speaking in a language he understood. "What sort of assurances?"

"You don't persecute the Connected unless they harm someone else."

"Connected," he repeated with a sneer. "Now you sound like one of them."

"I am one of them."

"No—I mean the Neo-Celts and their acolytes, that's what I'm talking about. Not you. You're something else entirely, but we know that. We've been notified by Interpol about you, and we're watching. We may not understand quite what to do with you yet, but we are aware that you exist. But you are an anomaly, Ms.

Wilde, and anomalies can be compartmentalized. What we're dealing with in McCarthy's organization is far more dangerous."

"You think so," I deadpanned, but Bill was on a roll.

"The idea that there are more people like you, lots more, the kind of people who can take over a place with specific skills that no one else has? That's not going to go well. Because those are also the kind of people who get other people killed."

"A couple of key notes here," I said, reasonably enough. Despite my little temper tantrum, I needed to keep myself reined in. Again, I didn't have to like the Garda, but I did need to work with them, at least for another several hours. "There are more of us than you think there are, although arguably there aren't more than a handful with my kind of abilities."

A strange, dangerous light flickered in the Garda officer's eyes, and maybe because I'd had a recent jolt of Nikki, I knew what he was thinking. Not in the sense of reading his memories, but knowing the language that was running through his mind. I speak fluent asshat.

"The trouble with the idea that you're forming in your brain, Officer, is that there *is* that handful. And I can assure you, this handful of people, properly motivated, could blast the crap out of most of the developed world. Which will leave you with a much bigger problem. So *you* should know, you can't neutralize me. You can't simply take down the people you think are the mightiest Connected in a surgical strike. You can't even launch a campaign of suppression, because your biggest nightmare happens to be the Neo-Celts' fondest dream: waking up the Connecteds who don't realize what lies within them. So the more attention you place on the viability of ordinary humans being special, the more you open a Pandora's box you're not going to be able to shut again."

"Interpol isn't the only government agency tracking this," Bill said, changing tacks. "We're all watching you — you and these Connected types. You can't just go around waving your hands and claiming you have powers. It doesn't work like that."

"You're right, it doesn't," I acknowledged. "But we don't have time to discuss exactly how it does work. Right now, I mainly need for you to stay out of my way while I neutralize the very real threat that the Neo-Celts represent in the next twenty-four hours."

"Just because you can toss a little crockery around doesn't make you God," the female Garda interjected, clearly still frosty over my display of psychic abilities. I shot her a glance.

"The trouble with that, ma'am, is that you have no idea what I'm capable of, because news flash, I don't either. And while that makes for a somewhat fraught situation on my own part, it should make you very scared."

She stared levelly back at me. "Are you threatening us?"

"Not at all. You'd both already be dead if I swung that way."

"I think this little conference is at an end," Bill said, his tone icing up. "You insist we cannot tell you what to do, but neither can you go around telling us what to do."

I sighed. This was why I should never be involved in negotiations. "I'm not telling you to do anything, I'm suggesting you reconsider your stance on McCarthy's group. Until they prove otherwise, maybe treat them like ordinary citizens. Good people trying to figure out who and what they are, which you could say about most of us."

"Those good people are currently preparing demonstrations this very day that could easily turn violent and could become a rallying cry for similar demonstrations around the world," Bill responded flatly. "We need that like a hole in the head."

I lifted my brows. "Today? Beltane isn't until tonight."

"I'm aware of that, Ms. Wilde. But we've been hearing from Interpol that movement has already started in the streets of a dozen major cities. It looks like they're starting early."

Conal, you sneaky bastard. "Well then, let me do my job," I said. "My job is to remove threats to the Connected community. What Conal is planning—today, apparently—could present a viable threat. Or it could be a peaceful self-help movement that sputters out almost before it gets started. Do you really want to exhaust your people chasing down a pipe dream that might never prove to be more than just words?"

Bill dismissed my words with a wave of his hand. "You're talking in circles. First you say the Neo-Celts represent the risk of inciting a global community of psychics, next you're saying Conal McCarthy is no more dangerous than a Girl Scout leader urging her troop to sell cookies. Which is it?"

"I don't know," I protested, as reasonably as I could. "Because I haven't confronted the man. I need to do that, first. Pretty much today, it would seem. But I'd like to do it without staring down the barrel of one of your guns."

We argued back and forth like that for another ten minutes, and it was all I could do not to pressure the man's mind magically. I wasn't sure how that attempt would go, but I could definitely understand the temptation. It was that temptation that scared me more than anything else that'd happened today. I didn't know where this curious path would lead, but I already wasn't liking it.

Finally, Bill pushed back from the table a second time. "We have to go."

"We haven't resolved anything."

"We won't resolve anything. We will watch Conal and his people, and we will wait, and the moment we decide they're a threat, we will act. Whether that is on your timetable or ours is irrelevant to us. What matters is that the threat is neutralized before it gets out of control."

"Of course," I murmured. I didn't have the heart to tell him it likely was already out of control.

"Where will you be?" Bill asked me abruptly. "You should know we have surveillance on you."

In an epic effort of maturity, I didn't snap back the first thought that came into my mind. Or the fourth or fifth or even the ninth. The tenth one, however, managed to slip through. "I'll be sure to say hello as I lose them."

The door to the courtyard opened, and Lily finally emerged again, distinctly tea-free. "Sir?" she asked tremulously. "There are some people here who need to see you. They say it's urgent."

"Of course." Bill nodded at me, and together, he and his partner made their way to the door. I sincerely hoped Nikki had fully clothed herself by now, but given that she hadn't made another appearance, I suspected she was availing herself of all the woo Miranda had to offer. I started after the officers as they disappeared through the front door, but hesitated, letting it swing shut instead. That way lay surveillance I would need to evade, and even though I'd be able to accomplish that in short order, it still was a tedium I didn't mind putting off for a moment. And the garden seemed unreasonably serene, the very air fluttering with promise.

I frowned, looking around. Since when did air flutter with promise?

"Miss Wilde."

I turned as Armaeus stepped out of the shadows. How the shadows in this tiny garden managed to obscure a full-grown Magician was something I didn't even bother wondering about. It was one of his many charms.

"How much of that did you hear?" I asked, feeling slightly abashed. Nobody would ever say negotiations were my strong suit, but I'd need to get better at them.

"Enough," he said. "Enough to know you do understand the balance we have sought to walk all these centuries. That balance has never been more imperiled."

"I...yeah." For a full five seconds, I debated telling him about what I had learned about Miranda/Bartholomew. In the end, I decided against it for purely selfish reasons. I loved the Magician more than any man on this earth, but I understood him well. If he knew there was a Temperance still extant in the world, he would not rest until he brought him back to the Council. I needed to speak to Bartholomew first. About Abigail, about the In Between. About...so many things.

"What are you thinking about?" murmured Armaeus. Without the aid of magic or time disruption, the Magician moved toward me, until we were close enough to touch.

I instantly lifted my hands, more than happy to redirect him. "What do you know about steaming red flame?" I placed my hands in his, stretching the fingers wide as Armaeus's eyes drifted shut and I felt the touch of his presence in my mind, along my nerves, and pulsing through my blood vessels.

"You healed Nikki," he murmured. "With…dirt?"

"It's sort of a long story."

He laughed, drawing me deeper into the shadows. "As it happens, we have time."

Tugging me close, Armaeus leaned in for a kiss. The moment his lips touched mine, however, I was beset with a terrifying spike of power. A panic of the kind I had not experienced with him in months. It surged up, bright and terrible, and I gasped, jerking back. Armaeus didn't let me pull away from him, however, didn't fully let me go.

"What is it, Miss Wilde?" he whispered, searching my face. "What is it you learned in the In Between that I have forgotten?"

CHAPTER TWENTY-FIVE

I blinked, transfixed, my mouth moving but no sound coming out. Then the panic passed.

"What the hell was *that*?" I gasped, sinking against him. "That panic…that was for *you*, Armaeus. Not for me. I'm not afraid of you anymore. I trust you. I love you. You wouldn't hurt me."

"I wouldn't hurt you," Armaeus agreed, holding me tight. "Not intentionally, not directly. Not—"

"No," I said, looking up at him. "You don't need to make qualifiers. Not anymore. You don't need to cover yourself against some action in the future that you can't predict or control because there are too many variables to consider. Because the reality is, *you love me*. And not simply because you find me an intriguing experiment, no matter how much you would like me to believe that, and no matter how much I was willing to believe that for far too long."

"This is what you've decided?" he asked with a slight smile, his face otherwise unreadable.

"This is what I finally understand. I mean, come on, Armaeus. You split yourself into *multiple entities* to find a way to protect me. You drowned yourself in a *pit of dark magic* to find some way to protect me. You sacrificed control over me and even allowed me to accelerate in my abilities to the point of temporarily being stronger than you are in an effort to protect me. There are a couple of common denominators here. One, it appears you have an endless supply of avenues to explore to protect me, and two...you seem to be unreasonably willing to go down every single one of those avenues, the worst of them — first."

My voice had started wavering at the beginning of this explanation, but by the end, my words were little more than a halting sob. I tightened my fingers on Armaeus's shirt and clung there, the most potentially powerful woman in the world unable to meet the gaze of the man she loved.

"You have to take better care of yourself," I whispered. "I won't be able to survive this world without you. I won't."

"Sara," Armaeus spoke, his voice filled with such resonant emotion I blinked away tears I hadn't realized had been forming. I lifted my gaze to his. His eyes were black, rimmed with red and gold, a holdover from the intense magic he had accessed to find ways to protect me, ways to deepen his own abilities so that he would be enough against whatever my burgeoning abilities summoned. "You can't be afraid *for* me. It will render everything I'm doing moot."

"Then you have to find a way to — ah!"

This time, the pain to my temples was so intense that I wrenched away from Armaeus and staggered to the side, nearly falling. I slapped my hands to either side of my head, flame billowing out around me, both the cool blue fire I was used to and the red, smoking liquid heat I wasn't. Just as quickly as it had come, the pain disappeared again and Armaeus was at my side, drawing me down to the ground, cushioning me as my legs gave out from under me, my body completely spent.

"What's happening?" I whimpered, and once again, Armaeus's arms went around me. His voice was steady and sure, the voice of a trained master comforting a bewildered student.

When had I become the student again?

"You increased your abilities when you were driven to the point of extremity in healing Nikki in the In Between," Armaeus said, his lips soft against my hair. "From all I've read, that is a wild and untrammeled space, shrouded by a veil that not even the gods can easily navigate. Mortals have managed it, but not gods. And not demigods either, until now. But its passage comes with a price, it would seem."

"I wasn't in there that long," I protested. "How could it be affecting me so much?"

"Because while you were in there, you blended disparate elements from two very different planes. Three, if you want to count the In Between itself. You brought with you the very dirt of earth as well as skills both inherited from the spectral plane and evolved within you. You are a complete rarity. Did anyone speak to you other than Nikki?"

"What? No," I said, my heart gradually slowing its frantic flutter. "I got in, I got lost, I got angry, I found Nikki, I used the dirt to heal her...or I did that—I don't even know. Regardless, she was healed. And then we left. It's not like I was there for a networking meeting."

"There was no sound at all?"

"Well, there was sound, but it wasn't like it was conversation. I heard the word *Hallowed* over and over again, but that could have been my mind playing tricks on me."

"Or the fairies."

I grimaced. "Or them." As for the rest, it wasn't like I could translate the chattering of wild monkeys and understand what they're saying other than 'eat her.'"

"Monkeys?"

"Imps, whatever. But they look exactly like monkeys, only squatter, fatter, and with much sharper teeth and really sharp claws." I paused, considering the image I recalled. "Okay, maybe not exactly like monkeys. But close."

"And why do you think they weren't talking to you when they were chattering, as you call it?"

"Maybe because I can translate any language known to man, even the languages I don't personally know." Even as I spoke the words, I understood their inherent flaw. "Well, it does me no *good* if it's not a language known to man. So, see? I do have limits to my abilities."

To my surprise, Armaeus only chuckled. "You are a wonder and a magic to behold."

He dropped his lips to mine, capturing my mouth with a soft, searching kiss. As he did, I felt the touch of his presence skip through my mind.

"What are you looking for?" I whispered. I didn't try to block him, beyond the natural defenses my system invariably raised. There apparently were certain things I wouldn't share even with the Magician, as much as I'd come to love him. Some of those things I understood, some I didn't know existed.

"What was said to — no." Armaeus's arms tightened around me as another flicker of panic woke to life. "I don't like you being afraid. Of anything."

He tightened his grip on me, and we both disintegrated into a rush of smoke. A second later, we materialized in a bedroom surrounded by a sea of white. White sheets, white pillows, white coverlet, white curtains draping snow-white walls and pale gray floors. It was like he'd transported us into a cloud sponsored by Restoration Hardware. There was a clock on a pale gray side table that glowed with ice-white numbers. As I watched, they shifted: 11:43 a.m. Otherwise, there was no movement in the room at all, no sound at all except our own hearts thudding in frantic time, our own limbs stretching on the luxurious bed.

I laughed softly. "I wonder how long you would last lying in the dirt."

"I spent a good portion of my mortal life scrabbling in the dirt," Armaeus said, his warm body as naked as mine. As he spoke, he trailed his mouth along the curve of my neck, pressing his lips against my collarbone before angling farther south, drawing one smooth cheek along the fullness of my left breast. "While I would not exchange those experiences for anything, it's not necessarily a time I seek to revisit."

I saw no reason to argue with him as he continued to explore my body with his hands, his mouth, his tongue. With every touch, he awakened in me a heat that had nothing to do with my spectral fire and yet everything to do with a profound sense of healing. I caught on almost too late, but by then, I no longer cared so much.

"I wasn't hurt in the In Between, Armaeus." I moaned as he scorched a trail of kisses up my thigh, pausing at the junction between my legs. His tongue slid along the sensitive skin, coiling me tight. "I would've remembered that."

"Perhaps," he said. "But it won't do either of us any harm to make sure."

My body arched beneath his in a jolt of pure electricity as he gripped my hips and lifted me, his breath and tongue and lips hot and urgent, creating an answering urgency within me that made me cry out with frustration when he didn't move quickly enough. I reached for Armaeus's shoulders, pulling him roughly up my body until his face was even with mine, our bodies hot and tightly entwined. The moment he filled me, my sight blacked out, and I existed in a space of pure light, pure energy, every one of my circuits exploding into brilliant life. This was the recreative force that Armaeus had given himself over to. This was the regenerating fire he was pouring into me. This was the spark of life that could be found in no other act so profound—

But this time, it was something more as well.

Armaeus wrapped his arms around me, flipping me until I straddled him and his face was a mask of emotion I couldn't understand, his eyes no longer the deep black and gold I knew so well, nor even the crimson fire I'd seen more recently. No—the hue that raged deep within the fiery depths of his eyes was a cold and merciless white, like smoke on the verge of turning to pure ice. It was ancient and primal—far more ancient than even Armaeus—and it opened before me, sucking me deep before I had any chance of resisting it. It was the deepest force of creation, and it was mine—*mine*. It had always been mine to grasp, to hold, to have, to use—

"Sara." Armaeus's exultant voice drew me back from the brink, barely, and I realized his body was bucking with the storm of sensation jolting through him, so violently he was passing in and out of corporeal form—only each time he returned, he was larger, more powerful, and—

"*Armaeus.*" My own body reacted to the sudden surge of his shaft thickening within me, every inch of me mapped for a dance of pleasure and pain so exquisite, I couldn't stop the climax from rushing up and over me, shattering me into a hundred million pieces. Armaeus cried out in a language I didn't know, whether a curse or a blessing or a cry against the heavens I couldn't guess, but his energy surged out of us, blanketing the room, the inn, the countryside, the sky, space, and reaching for the veil itself for the barest heartbeat— before plummeting just as quickly and pounding us flat against each other, an avalanche of power we could no more understand than we could fend off.

We collapsed, boneless, until the eddies of fire sluiced off our bodies and sizzled into nothingness.

For a long, long moment, we simply breathed.

Then the clock on the side table shifted, clicking over the time: 11:43 a.m. Not a single second had passed.

I stared at the glowing numbers, unable to do much more than sigh against Armaeus's chest.

"Time was away and somewhere else," Armaeus murmured, the phrase catching at me.

"What's that from?"

He glanced at me. "A poet from the mid-1900s, born in Belfast, as it happens. I never thought much about that until this moment. His work will bear some new review. But more to the point, it would appear our idyll is at an end."

He handed me my phone, opened to my text stream. There was a link repeated over and over again, all coming within the last ten minutes, but from different numbers.

"What's this about?" I asked, trying to refocus.

"When I decided to come to Dublin to see the situation firsthand, my projections indicated my arrival here would accelerate the timetable for action. Currently, that probability sits at—"

"I don't want to know," I said sharply. "Probabilities make me sad."

Armaeus smiled. "Very well. But the empirical evidence also holds. Beltane doesn't officially begin until tonight at midnight, yet your phone is currently being flooded by texts of an increasingly urgent nature. It can't be a coincidence."

I waved the phone at him. "I need to click this link, don't I?"

"It seems a lot of people think so—"

Another text popped up, this one also from an unknown number, but the message was far more succinct. *Sara! This is Simon click the goddamned link.*

I did, and a web page opened up on my phone that immediately made me sit up in bed. Because a full-bodied representation of me was at the top of it, swathed in a cloak of midnight blue, with a crown of stars above me, the scales of justice in one hand, a sword in the other. And alongside this goddess-like portrait was an exhortation to arms to all Spectral Opposition Warriors.

"Heed me and know that I will fight to the death to protect you against the criminal acts of magic levied against you, rousting you from your homes, striking you down in the streets. I am committed to protecting all from the tyranny of the few, no matter their strength or force of will. The right of magic is the right of coexistence, and the choice to believe and be that which you will—but not to be forced to abide in a world of anarchy."

"These guys are out of control," I muttered.

"These guys know that help is needed to maintain the balance of magic. They simply don't know how to render that help."

"How about not at all? How'd they even find me? It's not like I put an ad out."

"Seamus," Armaeus said. "Who remains in the wind, though the Fomorians have been returned In Between."

That stopped me. "You got them?"

"We didn't get them. We were able to identify their energy signature and close in, but they opened a portal—or found one—and returned to the In Between before we could confront them. Where, as I may have mentioned, I can't go."

I made a face. "Well, you're not missing much."

"Anything denied becomes desired eventually," Armaeus countered, a ghost of a smile tugging at his lips. "Seamus hasn't come out of hiding, but his troops remain at the ready, awaiting your command, it would seem. Spectral opposition warriors. It has a nice ring."

"Well, I didn't ask for them. How do you return an army?"

"You don't. So you better find a way for them to work for you and with you, because in the absence of that, they will eventually work against you."

I winced, but I knew he was right. "How do I tell them to just—stop? I need to get out ahead of this, but I feel like I'm already too late."

"You're not too late. The Council's exhortation for balance has not always been for the sake of people, but for the sake of the Council as well. That said, there has never been anyone on the Council quite like you, Miss Wilde. Command your warriors to stop when the time comes. Or to protect but not strike. You have led Connecteds before. You can lead these Connecteds too."

"Really not the best use of my time."

Armaeus chuckled again. "You will know what to say and how to say it when the time comes."

"Yeah, yeah."

As I focused more fiercely on the website, wondering how to connect with a group of highly charged humans spread all over the globe, the Magician's words grew softer, almost indistinct. "If anyone can rally a vengeful army to rational thought, I believe it's you."

I rolled my eyes, turning on him. "Dude, have you *met* me?"

But it was too late. Armaeus was gone.

CHAPTER TWENTY-SIX

My phone buzzed again, and I swiped at it, realizing that Simon was phoning me now, not texting.

I sprang out of my now-empty bed, yanking my clothes on. "What?" I demanded, moving toward the window.

"Where are you?" he demanded in turn.

"I'm in some sort of hotel room, maybe?" I scanned the room, trying to find anything that looked like a typical hotel, but of course the Magician would never stay in a typical hotel. "Or maybe it's someone's private home? I really don't know."

"Pinging your phone."

My brows lifted as I moved to the window, fighting my way through the gauzy curtains. "You can do that?"

"Not usually, but if a Council member wanted to leave her phone lying around while we were eating breakfast in an Irish pub, I'm only so strong." A second later, Simon chuckled. "Why the hell does Armaeus have property in Dublin? I didn't think he ever came here."

"Simon—"

"Well, you're practically on top of us. And this house is definitely one of the Magician's ghost aliases, right here at St. Stephen's Green. And, yo, everyone's here, so you might as well come join the party."

I stared at the proof of his words—the beautiful park of St. Stephen's Green, with way too many people milling through it. "Everyone, who? It's a public park in the middle of downtown Dublin. It's not exactly where I would go to stage a confrontation with spectral forces. Especially since it's not even Beltane yet."

Even as I said the words, I realized that no, in fact, a public park in the heart of Dublin was *exactly* where I would go to stage a confrontation of spectral forces. Even if he couldn't leverage the ancient holiday completely, Conal still wanted a show, and this was the quickest way for him to get one. That show could be calm and orderly, or it could turn into a nightmare, but either way, he would have the audience he wanted. And he would do it in broad daylight, on the eve of Beltane.

"Son of a bitch," I muttered.

"Pretty much," Simon said. "You remember where we stepped away from the park, the entrance where we headed across the street to Miranda's? I'm there…and, oh. So are you."

Simon stepped back a little as I pocketed my phone, with barely a fried split end to show for my astral traveling adventure. We headed through the park's entrance.

"There are cameras all over this park." Simon tipped his head toward a conspicuous gray box with a flashing red light. "I think everyone's playing it cool for now until they get their assemblage together. I figure they're going to emerge into the center of the garden at what's called the common green."

"Are they armed?"

267

"Ceremonially so only, from what I could see, but that actually makes me even more nervous. If they think that they have enough magical abilities at their disposal they don't need to have conventional weapons, they might be a bigger deal than we suspect."

"Or they might be really good at bluffing."

Simon nodded. "Or that."

We strode deeper into the park, and I noticed something else along the way. Namely, there were a fair number of decidedly non-touristy folk in the park as well, looking ever so slightly not casual. Not paramilitary, and there were no weapons in evidence, but they walked with a purpose that seemed pitched at a higher level than taking their midday constitutional.

Simon noticed it too. "Is that your personal army?"

"Will you stop *calling* them that? I didn't ask for an entourage."

"Which is funny, because you seem uniquely qualified to draw one to you." I couldn't argue the point. Simon had seen firsthand my ability to attract unwanted attention. And I did sort of understand the concept of guru attachment. I just didn't like it being attached to me.

I sighed. "People want to belong to something larger than themselves, especially when they start to believe that they're also bigger than they thought they were."

"See? You can do this. I bet there's an online training program for it. You'd be great."

I sent him a withering stare that seemed to have absolutely no impact, but we kept walking. It didn't take long to identify where Conal and his group of Neo-Celts had set up camp. A small gathering had assembled in an open amphitheater that I suspected was used for improv acting during happier times. Conal certainly seemed willing to command the show.

"Justice Wilde, you honor us with your presence," he announced the moment he caught sight of me.

"Here we go," Simon muttered.

I approached the Neo-Celts slowly, but not too slowly, like they were a skittish horse about to bolt, and focused on them with my third eye. About a quarter of them were true Connecteds, but the others had only sparks and sputters of ability, nothing cohesive. Was that why so many of them had fallen in line with Conal? They wanted to believe they were something more, or that they could become something more? And once again, was that so wrong?

I guess the answer to that depended largely on what Conal had planned.

Around me, I could feel the net of spectral opposition warriors draw closer. A quick scan of the green with my third eye showed me something else too. While the other mortals in the space, Connected and Unconnected alike, vibrated on typical frequencies, my personal army, as Simon had called them, kicked it up a notch. Tuned as tightly as they could be to me, their minds seemed to be drawing energy from some different level of consciousness…almost like a Zen Theta state. Typically, people didn't hit Theta-level brain waves until they were deeply unconscious, but these warriors remained wide awake. Despite their thug-like, almost military bearing, now that I was focusing on them, they seemed remarkably chill.

Hopefully, they'd stay that way.

I'd advanced into the field midway when Conal hopped off his platform and walked toward me, Niall and a few others following behind. We were approaching each other like two duelists on a polite field of battle, but I didn't miss the crowds that were growing.

"Simon," I muttered.

"Traditional transmissions are all blocked, and we're working on the arcane web," he murmured back, looking like any millennial tapping on his phone. "That should be locked down in five minutes if you can keep him talking without going all fancy and shit."

"You sure about that? What about the Internet being forever and all that?"

He snorted. "Not this time. Conal's followers can see him, yeah, but there's nothing being stored. If something does go down here, it'll be like the Snapchat revolution."

"It needs to be more like the *Men in Black* revolution," I said, taking in the completely obvious plants of plainclothed Garda in the crowd. So far, there weren't any uniformed police who'd joined the fray, but I had no doubt they were close. And there was only so long you could keep a Dublin law enforcement officer on the hook before he decided to see what the potential fuss was all about. "If this gets ugly, I don't want a bunch of people comparing notes, even without video evidence."

"We live in a video-evidence world," Simon countered, not looking up from his device. "If it wasn't recorded by all these people? It didn't happen. Groupthink, opt-in hallucination, you can call it whatever you want. It's not actionable." He dropped to muttering for a few seconds, then grunted with frustration. "Yo, I need more time."

"Then don't move." Focusing intently, I created an illusion that I was not one person, but two—and the second me looked like Simon standing tall and fierce. Masked by that illusion, the real Simon kept typing furiously. It would hopefully buy us the time that we needed.

Either way, I didn't agree fully with Simon's assessment of the threat here. The power of memory was a deep and dangerous thing. If an entire group thought they'd seen something, but was told they hadn't, it was a breeding ground for conspiracy. If things went south here, the St. Stephen's Green incident could live on with the same ferocity as JFK and the grassy knoll, and that wouldn't help anyone.

Another figure moved in the crowd as my gaze raked across it, instantly recognizable to me, but still catching me off guard. I furrowed my brow. What the devil was the Devil doing here?

"Justice Wilde." Conal, Niall, and his little retinue of guards stopped in front of me, forcing me to focus on the issue at hand. "The time for the Council to protect the Connecteds of the world is past. We thank you for your service, but it is time for you to step aside."

"What is it you truly want, Conal?" I countered, and once again, I felt Kreios's presence in the throng of Neo-Celts and tourists. I didn't have his ability to force Conal to speak his truth, but when the man spoke again, his voice rang with an undeniable fervency.

"I want what humans have wanted since they first stretched upright on this earth and strode forth — self-dominion. Freedom. The right to evolve and grow and use the power that surges up within them," he declared. "For too long have the Connecteds of the world bowed beneath the fears of the many. For too long have they cowered and scraped, hiding themselves in the shadows while the many walked in the light. But now, we are the many. We are mighty and strong. Now we are being called to use the gifts of our strength for the good of all, not just for the amusement or wealth or power of the few."

Conal lifted his arms, and the arms of his small retinue lifted as well, the field suddenly going electric. Projections appeared one after the other around the park, dancing above the ground with a precision that had less to do with magic and more with badass tech.

"*Simon,*" I hissed, not moving my lips, but the Fool only glanced around, taking in the images.

"Projections only, nothing recorded. All part of the show."

Still, my stomach rolled as I took in Conal's projections. There were easily a dozen violent images being played out on the green, each worse than the last. The Salem witch hunts, the Spanish Inquisition. The Holocaust's atrocities. The Troubles. Stonings, beheadings, and fire—so much fire. The parade of injustice against those who were believed to be witches or men and women of magic, the forced servitude of alchemists and oracles, the debasement and blinding of those who only ever wanted to look toward the light.

"These are the atrocities we can lay at the feet of the Council, as much as we can lay them at the feet of the mob and the weak and venal governments and religious orders who looked the other way. You all stood by and watched, allowing the blood of the Connecteds to run like rivers, skin to scorch and blacken, families and communities to be torn apart, priceless lore to be ripped from the pages of history and set to flame. You."

My conscience pricked at me, but the words surging up within me, demanding to be spoken, would do no good—not yet. Not when I still needed to understand Conal's endgame. I hadn't been a part of his original plan, I was sure of it, even if he was using my convenient presence to create the conflict he so craved. Like any good political agitator, he had a call to action in mind, and I needed to let him creep toward it—especially since

Simon was still typing like mad beside me, for all that he gave the appearance now of standing straight and tall, his eyes on one of the projections.

Finally, one of them flickered. Simon chortled, but his fingers never stopped moving.

Conal narrowed his eyes on Simon and then snapped them back to me. "But the time for dwelling on the past is over, as is the time for Connecteds to bind themselves with the chains of the past. We seek a new beginning, honoring Mother Earth and all who would care for her!"

He waved his hand dramatically, and one by one, the images around the green winked out to be replaced by new images. People marching in the streets of major cities all over the world, carrying branches, flowers, and enormous depictions of the Tree of Life—some carved in wood, some flowing as long cloth banners, some catching in the sunlight as metal shields.

It's just a parade, I told myself. Parades happen all the time. Parades are allowed, are encouraged, give people the opportunity to express themselves nonviolently. I could see what Conal made sure I saw as well. Not in every city, but in enough, there were men and women in the crowd watching the chanting and singing Neo-Celts, men and women who watched them with hard eyes and an air of expectation. The spectral opposition warriors, my unwanted deputies, ready to make sure those with the power didn't wield it to the detriment of others. It would have been easier to be on the side of the people with flowers in their hair, frankly.

My eyes leapt from scene to scene as Conal's exhortations grew more impassioned. "Look hard and well, Justice Wilde. These are the people your Council has not helped all these long years. These are the people who now no longer need your help. We are the Connecteds of the world, and we can help ourselves."

Another shift in the crowd showed me the High Priestess, looking bored — because that was her look. But she was here. And the Devil was here, and the Magician as well, I knew, ranged around the Green Knight in a triangle, keeping him in the center. I didn't know exactly how you could force a person to ascend, but the odds were not looking good for Conal to escape their net.

Only, I didn't want this asshat to ascend. "You idiot," I seethed. "You think that because you weren't a part of any psychic community other than your own, you're all that's out there? The houses of cards have worked with Connecteds for hundreds of years. The Council didn't need to help mortals find their magic. They found it themselves. You do your magic, your way, in accordance with your druidic upbringing. But the other Connecteds of the world deserve to find their way too."

"In the dark?" he demanded. "In the shadows?"

"In their own time," I countered. "Not yours. You with your grand robes and your privilege and your safety don't get to choose for the rest of the world."

"And I say you are wrong!" He gestured to the displays of the dozen cities flickering around the green.

And then, of course, it happened. It happened so quickly that it was hard to say if it was orchestrated by Conal or simply if the first action was the catalyst for all the rest, but in each of the cities being shown in the projections, a horrifying chain reaction began. A shove. A curse. A thrown rock. A woman going sprawling, a man struck —

A battle joined.

Only this was a battle of magic.

Multicolored fire leapt in the streets of LA, the Neo-Celts of Rio de Janeiro suddenly bristled with weapons, and the lilting Irish chants in Paris rose in force and weight to become a screaming torrent of sound, driving everyone to their knees. The spectral opposition warriors leapt instantly into the fray, of course, and their own Connected abilities were brought to bear, to suppress, to stop, to quell—

I lifted my hands and swept them out, sharp and wide, issuing my orders with abrupt, unflinching intensity, touching their minds as they quivered on the brink of manifestation, shimmering in theta state. *"Protect!"*

In every projection, in every image...my spectral opposition warriors stopped. And were immediately overwhelmed, of course, because there were too many striking at them. But even as they were buried, crouched and cowering, their minds shifted, their energy grew, their protective power building and building—

While the mob only grew more frenzied.

"Conal!" I shouted. *"You* are starting this. You will end it."

Because it all came down to him. He was the nexus point. He was the threat. The time for me to act was now.

"I will not stop," he said, turning to me, his face swathed in glee. He wasn't paying attention to the Council members who now stepped out of the throng, and he certainly wasn't paying attention to the police officers moving more quickly through the people, people who'd begun chanting excitedly and gathering around the projections with eager delight. There was chaos in Amsterdam, a full-on riot in Moscow, and Cairo—

"I said, *enough*." Now it was my turn to lift my arms, and all over the world, plain for anyone to watch, my warriors — unwanted, unbidden, untrained, untried, but mine nonetheless, their desperate attempts to follow me barely walking the line between panic and protection, but nevertheless walking that line, seeking the balance — lifted their arms too. The energy crackling in their minds coalesced into physical form, serving as both my vessel and my fuel. Blue fire leapt from man to woman and back again, crisscrossing the parade routes, stretching out over the larger city, while overtop it, red murky smoke steamed and danced. The fighting stopped, the raging and rioting stopped — everything stopped, for at least a moment.

Conal, however, didn't stop.

"You *dare*," he raged, and he turned in a quick circle, his arms flinging wide as his entourage fell to their knees — everyone except for Conal's brother, who appeared turned to stone as he stared, wide-eyed, at his brother. Suddenly, new images appeared all around the green — doorways shimmering with silver carvings. My local band of spectral opposition warriors sprang into position, their hands crackling with my own shared blue and red fire, but horror transfixed their faces.

I could relate.

Conal's mouth opened, but his voice was strangely garbled. "Too long has the tyranny of the foul and debased taken over this world, ruining it and defiling it. The time to step into the light is come!"

He spoke in a language that I suspected only I could hear…because I had heard it once before. The chittering, rumbling hissing of a company of shadows.

The doors that led to the In Between sprang open, and chaos poured forth.

CHAPTER TWENTY-SEVEN

The dozens of different creatures that hurtled out of the twenty-one doors of the In Between swept through the green so quickly, I barely got my hands down in time to set up a protective barrier to protect the throng of onlookers and Garda officers. Unfortunately, that meant I'd trapped most of Conal's followers in with us, along with my brave band of fighters.

"Simon," I yelled as I turned, then turned again, trying to make sense of what I was seeing. "The Neo-Celts!"

"Got 'em!" Simon surged forward, breaking the illusory image I'd built around him and rushing straight for Conal's band.

Meanwhile, the first wave of beasts hit me, a flurry of hissing wraiths with bright blue eyes, grasping claws, and hulking shoulders. I reacted a little too slowly, my mind fractured in a million different places. First I focused on the efforts of the spectral opposition warriors both here and working to contain the angry crowds on both sides of the fight in the streets of the major cities of the world. Then I skipped to the question of how in the hell Conal could have summoned the power to animate the sacred doors of the In Between. And finally, I realized my protective barrier was being breached despite my best efforts. Far too many of the throng of people surging forward to join the fray and not enough running for their lives the way they should be.

The first attacker from the In Between, a neon-red wraith, brought me fully back into the present moment as it reached out and raked me with a long, sicklelike claw. Its touch was as cold as loneliness, and I staggered back, reeling with the sudden wash of understanding that swept over me.

Hallowed, Hallowed, Hallowed, Hallowed...

I could hear them. I could see them. And, unlike the first time we'd met in the shadows of the In Between, I could understand the language they were speaking, the hissing excitement of what was to come.

Horror iced me to my bones. *No.*

Then another one hit. And another, opening up my skin with each swipe, while I struggled to keep my brain from exploding. Because these wraiths weren't the only trespassers here; they were arguably not even the worst.

I scrabbled away, barely avoiding a face plant into the turf, but my precarious windmilling brought me face to snout with another clutch of creatures, fat, hideous monkey-like imps, with long arms and longer claws, each swipe of their paws sending an electric jolt through me.

Suddenly, the sound of pounding boots rattled across my senses, and a fire-headed phoenix in flowing green robes and clinking chakra jewelry, wielding the staff of Gandalf in one hand and Harry Potter's wand in the other, exploded in front of me.

"Back *off!*" Nikki shouted, and the screaming imps fled back.

Fury suddenly clicked in, and I roared, bringing my hands around and exploding the imps back beyond the veil for good — or at least back into the In Between, where the bastards belonged.

I swung around, searching for Conal. He stood with his arms outstretched, his face bathed in a brilliant smile as he surveyed the carnage around him, never mind that his own people were getting trampled by what looked like a swarm of angry bees in one quadrant of the green, their clothes catching on fire in another as writhing, coiling serpents belched fire, some even having long, sinuous feet. I immediately thought of the illuminated manuscript pages in the Book of Kells and shuddered at the other horrors that might await us if I didn't get those doors closed.

Lurching forward, I realized that something had latched on to my ankle, and I looked down to see a tiny beast that looked like it was all mouth and wings hanging on to me for dear life, its teeth sinking into the tender flesh of my calf. This was another creature of magic, and I had to fight a wave of nausea as I desperately tried to kick it off. It wouldn't drop, and when the next monkey raced up to me, I whirled with a tight sweeping kick, knocking the imp away while dislodging the biting ball of feathers.

By then, I'd almost reached Conal, and I allowed my momentum to keep driving me forward, tackling him to the ground. To my shock, he didn't fight my physical onslaught with the burst of magic I'd expected and braced for. He struck me with his fists, rolling over on top of me, and driving punishing blows against my face and chest as if he could pound my heart right into the ground.

I recovered quickly, pain having that effect on me, and thrust him off my body with a surge of blue fire. He screamed and fell back, but once again, he didn't send out a return surge of angry energy, though his entire body crackled with a web of sparking circuitry. I fixed my gaze on him, glaring with fury—and blinked. He *was* surrounded by a net, I realized. A web. A shroud of ultimate and extreme power, but one that served as nothing more than a cloak of protection, one not even driven by Conal's own energy...but by another's.

"Get *away* from him!"

A bolt of power with the force of an angry bull gored through my side and sent me flying, and as I twisted around, I saw Niall crouching over Conal, the latter's power flaring brighter, stronger—but suddenly dwarfed by Niall's white hot corona of flame.

Oh...*no*.

Suddenly, all the details converged at once. The fight between brothers that had no resolution other than driving a powerful, tradition-bound parent away. Niall's aw-shucks aversion to being involved in his brother's ministry, yet he was always there, standing just out of reach of the camera and the crowds, watching with careful eyes. Even the gift of Ireland's own precious soil to me—the act of a true believer whose faith was all the more formidable because he *understood* true power. Because he wasn't the Green Knight, he was the Hallowed Knight.

Niall McCarthy, the Hallowed Knight of the ages, sent by the gods to lead them back to Earth.

So strong, he'd managed to hide his true powers from his father, his brother, his people...even from me.

The Connected ability that smoked and crackled in Niall outshone, for the moment, even my own, temporarily drained as I was by the attack. He positively glowed with energy and excitement, rage and fear, a potent combination made all the worse by the fact that

Conal was now back on his feet, eager to continue the fight. Given Conal's manic smile, I wondered if he even knew the truth.

I didn't understand the dynamic between these two, but I couldn't stop Niall by myself. Not and deal with the raging creatures from the In Between—

A shot rang out across the clearing, and I whirled. In my distraction, I'd allowed the force field surrounding the green to falter. Four Garda officers, their Connected abilities making them shine like beacons among the crowd, had forced their way through. And they'd brought their guns. Unfortunately, their gunfire was simply absorbed by the enormous, bearlike creature that loomed in front of them, the added force of their ammunition making wings burst from the back of the creature and turning it into a monster straight out of high fantasy nightmares—a Balrog on steroids. It suddenly occurred to me how many of these creatures looked like snatches and bits of creatures of myth and story, cobbled together into real and frightening life. How many authors had stumbled unwittingly into the In Between and, quite literally, lived to tell the tale?

I lurched toward the officers, then realized that Kreios was there, standing in front of the humans and facing off against the Balrog, who roared in fury at being denied its meal. Suddenly, instead of one Devil, there were six, then twelve, and I turned to other problems.

Conal was shouting again.

"Behold the glory of a world returned to its most ancient and primal form, where the survival of the fittest depends not on who holds the guns, but who holds the magic within their hands." He raised his own hands, and now fire did glow at the end of his fingertips, but I wasn't fooled. Niall was the power behind the throne.

Niall was the Connected the Council should have feared all along.

I raced toward him, and I wasn't alone. The Magician fell into step with me, only the moment he did, a surge of panic so blindingly real nearly drove me to my knees. "No!" I tried to gasp, only it was too late. A wall of green fire erupted all around us, and a new round of creatures sprang up from portals in the very ground to wrap us in their fury.

I burst through the line of them first, which I'd both known and feared I would as Armaeus distracted them in battle, and found myself in front of Conal and Niall. The former still preened with delight at the chaos he assumed he'd wrought, but the latter stared at me with a flat, intractable fury that took my breath away.

"Why?" I demanded. I felt if I could understand that, I could understand all this.

"Because you and your Council have *ruined* this world," Niall said, his voice vibrating at a level I couldn't understand. "How many centuries, how many millennia were you given to set the course of humanity along a more sustainable path? By allowing humans the right of self-dominion—*all* humans, not merely those who were tied to the very core of Earth's power, but those who had long since turned their back on such grace—you condemned her to a slow and steady death. A death that has become all the closer for the rash acts of humanity that you have allowed to continue unabated."

"It is a *world* of humans," I protested. "It's not anyone's place to stop them from their own destruction or their own recreation, should they find it."

"And I say you are wrong. If they would rule this earth, they must earn it—and only the Connecteds of true strength will have the right to try." Niall didn't raise his arms high the way his brother did, and in that moment, I wondered how these two could even be brothers, as different as their energy was. But they both shouted their next command with gusto.

"Come forth, come forth!"

The doors of the In Between blasted open again, and through them now trooped the long, sinuous forms of the Fomorians, ancient rulers of Ireland, condemned to their forms as creatures of the dark and deep when they lost their battle to keep dominion over the other ancient powers vying for control. The moment they stepped foot upon the green, the humans staggered, dropping like flies — but not all of them. Only the ones who had no spark within them, or such a faint spark that it would have to be nurtured into full flower with long and careful tending.

"The era of allowing non-Connected humans to rule this earth is at an end," Niall proclaimed. "We will take, but there are too many in our way, too many who would destroy. Who do not know how to live off the land but continually rape and defile it for their own purposes. And so the ancient terror will flow over the mountains and the seas, destroying all who live like parasites upon this earth, to be defeated only by those with the power within them to set the world to rights again."

"Are you *insane*?" I demanded, even as the full contingent of the Council flickered into place around the green. The inference was clear. They would as soon destroy everything within this net than allow the Fomorians to escape. There would be no balance of magic if two-thirds of the planet had been wiped out by it, and those who were left were then flattened by an international war against creatures from the primeval past. "You can't let these things out!" I lashed out with magic along with the Devil and the Magician, restraining the Fomorians.

"They're already out," Niall sneered. "And your puny Council can't hold this newest wave of ancient gods for long. The rage of Earth against its human invaders can already be seen. The soil and rock of this planet is capable of healing and it is capable of destroying, each in equal measure. Some of the blows are with a blunt instrument, some are with a razor's edge, but they are happening all the same. They are simply not happening fast enough."

"Behold!" Conal's sudden exultation drew our attention. Both brothers practically radiated excitement, their eyes on the doors to the In Between, and I flinched back as a sudden new burst of ice-white light beamed out from that space, piercing the green to converge on a central figure…a central figure who collapsed to the ground.

I froze in horror. "Armaeus!"

Niall and Conal dropped to one knee, their faces suffused with awe as they stared at the doorways to the In Between.

"Gods of our fathers, rule us," Conal said with abject reverence. "Destroy your ancient enemies and protect the children of this earth."

I turned to the doors, my mouth going slack.

Radiant beings stepped out of the light and onto St. Stephen's Green, each new figure bringing with it melodies of the same song, swelling to an unbearable chorus of beauty. The Tuatha dé Danann. They were too bright for me to fully see, bathed in a corona of the same white light that was pinning Armaeus to the ground, and they moved toward him like an inexorable tide.

Their power and his power could not coexist in this world, I knew in an instant. Their power and his power could never coexist.

Their power and his power would break the world in two.

And Armaeus had already been weakened—fatally weakened—protecting me.

"Sara." The Magician's soft call ripped through me, and I battled forward, the white light now turning on me, lashing at my shields like a hurricane crashing against a crumbling shore. I staggered, nearly falling, then pushed on again, desperate to reach Armaeus.

The Magician spoke again, but his words were thready, barely whispered in my mind, garbled and indistinct. *"Know this — remember!"*

"Armaeus!" I screamed. I didn't want to remember anything he told me. I wanted him. Only him.

But his words came anyway, frighteningly brittle and wan. *"Remember…that I — I will love you, ever…more."*

The Fomorians I had trapped, turned and writhed, caught in my bands of power, but I knew I wouldn't be able to hold them for long. Soon they would break free, the battle would start anew, my shields would falter, and the world would be ripped apart. I knew it as surely as I knew I was losing Armaeus, the Armaeus I had finally claimed and loved with every fiber of my being, who had stayed in the center of the green not only to fight the creatures who'd beset us, but because the center of the green was where the ultimate power of the ancients would be directed…because he was protecting me.

Once again.

Exactly as he said he would.

Horror speared through me, enormous wings of fire burst open from my back, arcing over me with furious heat. I whirled, bringing my hands together to release an entirely new magic, born of my grief, fury, and terror. Blending the red and blue of my separate infernal infernos, a geyser of purple fire erupted from my palms. I would *not* break the barrier holding the ancient terrors of the Celts within it. I would *not* allow any of these creatures — these infernal *gods* — to escape, I would *not* —

"*You won't,*" murmured Death's harshly beautiful voice in my head. An entire network of galvanizing pain laced around my arms, turning and churning, as the ink Death had inscribed on me tightened its hold. "You were made for this. Call me to the battle, Sara Wilde. Bring us both, to do what must be done."

I shuddered, but I had seen, I knew. All the beginnings, all the ends and everything —

In Between.

My wings suffused in roiling flame, I blew the purple fire out of my hands and onto the ground in front of me, where it shot out in four directions, then rounded on itself, two bars constrained and supported by the circle of the sun. A Celtic Cross.

The figure of Death crystalized in its center, her eyes wild and fierce, her body wrapped in a long dark cloak, flapping in the gales of wind and power that swept across St. Stephen's Green, her cropped white hair swept up defiantly atop her head.

And in her arms, she held a silver harp.

CHAPTER TWENTY-EIGHT

A strangled voice at the far end of the green cried out, "No!"

Moving more quickly than I would ever have given him credit for, Conal leapt up, pushing his brother out of the way and racing ahead. But instead of running for Death, who calmly settled the harp against her body, the purple flame coalescing into solid form to provide her with both a stand for the instrument and a perch to sit upon, he raced toward Armaeus's still form. The power emanating from the Magician rocked the green in waves, his body writhing, and I sensed more than saw Conal's desperate lunge as he yanked an athame out of his cloak and lurched toward Armaeus.

I didn't even blink. In one moment, I was struggling toward Armaeus, in the next I was standing over his body, wings of fire outstretched, flame licking off my skin as I reformed and brought my hands together sharply. A sound like a thunderclap rocked the green, and Conal stopped midflight and crumpled to the ground with a shattering of bones, his scream rising above the chaos.

And then, the cool, clear note of a single plucked string filled the whole world.

The Fomorians stopped, frozen as they reached and stretched and strained. The non-Connected humans who had crumpled to the ground jolted where they lay, lost to the moment but not to the world, their hearts once more pumping blood, their lungs once more billowing to pull in the thick, lush air of life. The Connected souls reacted even more forcefully, their faces turned up to the sky as tears rushed down their faces.

Not only in the green either. The flickering images still projected against the tree line of the green showed a world gone still with wonder. Death might be placing her hand upon her instrument here in the heart of Dublin, but the shining, plaintive tone she drew from it was heard around the world.

At my feet, Armaeus shifted, and I nearly collapsed with relief. He was alive! He sighed out a rush of syllables, then sang a low and resonant, mournful tone, ancient in its timbre, which started as little more than a whisper. It quickly swelled to meet the second tone of Death's harp, then the third.

And then, in concert with Armaeus's murmured invocation, Death played her fingers along the shining strings and bent into her song.

The music that filled the green this time had an even more striking effect. The members of the Council turned, their faces caught up in various shades of wonder and shock. Tears stood in the eyes of even the most cynical—Tesla, the Emperor, and, with a sudden rush of wings, I realized the archangel stood beside me now as well, his face rapt as he listened to Death's ethereal harmony. While Michael had always appeared pale to the point of translucent, drained of all color, as I watched, a rush of pigmentation swept through him, darkening his skin and filling out his slender form into a magnificent being of strength, setting every feather of his enormous wings into glorious, radiant color. I gaped, emitting the tiniest gasp, and he turned and looked at me—truly looked at me in a way I wasn't certain I'd ever seen him do before. I stepped back from the weight, the terror, and the desperate loneliness of that gaze, the staggering burden of a secret that must never be spoken.

And then the moment was past, and it was only the cool, pale form of the Archangel regarding me, his lips twitching with private amusement.

He nodded to the green beyond me. "Behold an age of ancients come to life, Justice Wilde."

I turned and followed his gaze, and realized that it was not merely the Fomorians who were caught in the thrall of Death's harp. Their glamour fallen away enough for me to see the other gods' forms more clearly. Nearly thirty figures stood at attention, their hands outstretched, fingers splayed wide, as if they could grasp the meter and measure of Death's mournful song and twist it in their hands, a living thing. And in truth, with every new chord she played, a pressure built throughout the green, pressing in on my mind and my heart, compressing my very bones. While I rocked beneath this pressure, the Fomorians crumpled to the ground, wailing with despairing, impotent fury, their bodies becoming slowly—so slowly—less distinct, more fluid. As if all the tears of earth were being shed to wash them full away.

And still the other figures watched, their own blinding light evening out around them, their faces becoming more distinct as the Fomorians lost detail. Smooth, fair skin, pale eyes and paler hair, tall, elegant bodies dressed in pristine robes of all the richest colors of the earth and sky. Many wore gleaming crowns of interworked gold and silver in their hair, and their feet were shod in leather slippers that also glinted of gold. They looked as if they would speak, they looked as if they wanted to speak, but no words fell from their lips, not even so much as a sigh escaping, as their lips parted on the hope of a whisper that never came to life.

And slowly, oh so slowly, they took a step back.

Outside the canopy of my barrier, the earth suddenly came to life with a furious, frightened rebuke. Storm clouds built in the space of two breaths and broke with a tumultuous rage, rain pelting the areas of the green not protected by my fire. Trees erupted into white flames, crackling and spitting, while the wind howled and moaned. I couldn't do anything else but hold the line—the cross that bore Death's form with one hand, the barrier above us with another. At my feet, Armaeus's eyes remained closed, but still the ancient song was pulled from him, as if he was merely another instrument carefully and skillfully played by Death.

The ancient gods of Ireland took another step back.

More storms broke throughout the world, lashing at the mobs and driving them asunder, both Neo-Celts and spectral opposition warriors alike scrambling away from the onslaught. The earth cried out for the Tuath Dé not to abandon it a second time, but the Tuath Dé had no choice. This was no longer their world. This would never be their world again.

They took another step back toward the glowing doorways of the In Between.

The cadence and energy of Death's music picked up then, the impact swift and harsh. The creatures of the In Between went first, tumbling and rumbling and screaming with fright and rage, flying back into the doors from which they'd been disgorged. One by one, those doors disappeared, until only one remained. But it wasn't the door the Tuath Dé had come through, and they seemed to realize it. They turned as one and regarded that gateway, even as it seemed to grow larger and draw them closer. One door, shimmering with ancient runes and symbols, the magic of a people long since dead, the music of a priestess long since turned to other horizons.

"You will go." Death spoke above the strains of her harp, her words as low and melodic as Armaeus's, a higher counterpoint to his low and steady chant. "Back to the lands of your people, to the emerald hills and the shining shore. The call of this world a whisper fading evermore. Your time is over here. Your path is now the stars."

The first of the golden people stepped back through the gate.

"*No.*" This time it wasn't Conal who spoke, but Niall. I turned, feeling the crimson smoke spilling off me, snaking across the ground toward him through the high grass. I didn't know if I had anything else to give him, but apparently, he brought out the best in me.

His words had a galvanizing effect on the golden Tuath Dé, though. They stopped and turned toward him, and Niall pointed at me—no. Not at me, the miserable sexist fuck.

At Armaeus.

"He is your enemy, the enemy of earth, the breeder of insurrection and doubt. He is who keeps you from your doors. He, not a priestess overreaching her station or a usurper challenging your power, he. You kill him, you break them all."

A sudden move from the Tuath Dé was all it took. As I sensed them turning and directing their focus to where Armaeus still lay defenseless on the ground, I expanded once more.

My wings exploded with crimson fire, smoky flame that somehow was both liquid and fire at once, but they swept over Conal and Niall, consuming them both in a conflagration intended not to kill, but to contain. Though I really wanted to kill something, and I felt that rage burn clear through me, scorching the earth at my feet. I danced back from Armaeus, desperate not to cause him any more pain, but he seemed oblivious to the world around him, so deep inside his mind that I suddenly wondered if he would come out again. Shoving that thought away, I turned back to the Tuath Dé—

And realized they were staring now at me—me, not Armaeus. Not even Death. Their eyes shone with surprise and recognition, and I heard once more the chittering of the darkness. Not the language of the Tuath Dé, but the language of the watchers in the In Between. Only now it was clearer, truer. I still couldn't quite make out the words, but the panic resurfaced again, so strong it almost buckled my control. I glanced down more sharply at Armaeus, and realized he'd stopped chanting. Which in and of itself wasn't a bad thing—but then I realized he wasn't breathing either.

Armaeus!

Death's song rose again, covering my words while the cadence of her playing changed a second time. But my resolve was breaking as fear leapt within me, and suddenly, Kreios was on one side of me, Eshe on the other, both of them holding my arms locked in position. Death's music grew and spun around us, and as I stared out at the Tuath Dé, willing them to leave, I couldn't stop the tears from falling. They hit the ground with a shuddering hiss, and I realized I was completely surrounded by a sea of crimson, smoking fire. Conal and Niall were nowhere to be seen.

The last of the Tuath Dé disappeared through the door, and it shimmered out of sight.

I yanked myself out of Kreios's and Eshe's arms and lunged for Armaeus.

"Sara—" Kreios pulled me back before I could reach him, and lifted me easily off the ground, my legs kicking fruitlessly in the air. "Your fire, Sara! The barrier!"

I realized instantly what he meant. With the shattering of my focus, the barriers that had blocked the green from outside entry had completely disintegrated. Though the storm that had broken over the city of Dublin had done a fair job of driving people away, there was still a throng hunkered down beneath the trees. When I dropped the barrier, they spilled out onto the green and started racing forward, only to stop abruptly when there was nothing to rush toward. Conal and Niall were gone. Death was gone. The Council members other than Eshe, Simon, and Kreios were gone. Dozens of agents, police officers, and the Neo-Celts were sprawled on the ground as if they'd been leveled by a sonic boom. So, as the last people standing, we suddenly became the eye of a hurricane, and I whirled on Kreios.

"What's happened to him?" I demanded. "What were they saying, that what was lost can now be found? What does that even *mean*?"

Kreios looked at me as if I had three heads, pushing past me to reach Armaeus. He knelt over the Magician's fallen, broken body, and gathered him up in his arms. Then looked at me again, his face tortured and his eyes panicked. "This isn't right. But we'll make it right."

And they vanished.

I gasped, lurching forward as if I could follow them wherever they'd gone, but now it was Eshe and Simon's turn to lock their hands on me. "Your work isn't done here, Sara. You know that," Eshe hissed.

"What's going to happen to him?" I demanded of her. "What can you see?"

"It doesn't work like that."

"It damn well *can*, Eshe. You know that as well as I do!"

She looked at me sharply, blinking in shock, then her eyes turned milk white for the barest second. She jerked as if she'd been electrocuted, her hands lifting to her face—and she disappeared too.

"No!"

I whirled around, my hands breaking free of Simon's hold, looking for someone to incinerate, but the first person I connected with was a whirling dervish of flying emerald robes and bright red hair.

"Dollface!" Nikki said, tumbling with me to the ground and then bringing me right back up again, her face next to mine. "You need to keep your head in the game. The Garda wants to arrest you, and ain't nobody got time for that. But if you're here, you're arrestable, so you need to make like you're two people and have one of you run off and the other one—poof.

I stared at her. "I can't…" But of course, I could, and Nikki more than anyone knew I could. She'd been there in the In Between with me. She'd seen me do the impossible six times over.

I twisted away from Nikki and started running, barely acknowledging that Garda officers were running toward *me* as I burst in flames. For just a second, I hung in the cosmos, not knowing where Kreios had taken Armaeus, not knowing where I was going. The result was me hanging in space, watching the illusion I had created.

I was running across the green, immediately drawing the attention of the authorities. Nikki had been right, and several Garda took off after me with decided intent. Even as I started to fade, the chaos reached Simon and Eshe, everyone seeming to realize at the same time that the Wonder Twin brothers, Conal and Niall, had disappeared.

I searched the grounds for Death, hoping, praying that she was all right. If not...

Tears sprang to my eyes as my rabbiting brain bounded back to Armaeus. The price here had been too great—too great!

Then I pictured Dr. Sells's clinic as clearly as if it'd been telegraphed to me, and I hurtled through space, desperate to reach Armaeus. He had stepped in front of the firing squad one too many times for me, and that crap had to stop right now.

It *had* to. And he needed to be alive for me to yell at him about it.

I stifled the sob building in my throat.

He had to.

CHAPTER TWENTY-NINE

I reappeared in the lobby of Dr. Sells's clinic, instantly recognizing the surroundings, from the bustling staff and the high-tech equipment at the intake station to two familiar figures huddled together in the reception area. There was something universally familiar about frightened souls in a clinic, but my eyes snapped straight to the figure in front of me, clearly there to greet me. Kreios.

"What is it, what's happening, where did he go, what?" I demanded as the Devil lifted his arms as if to fend off my verbal attack.

"He's not here. But he told Dr. Sells you would most likely return here."

"He did?" I pulled up short. "So he's okay enough to be communicating. That's good." I scanned Kreios's face. "That's good, right?"

Kreios grimaced. "It is what it is. Armaeus is stable. You can go to him, but first you have another problem to address."

Something in Kreios's voice made my stomach cramp. "What are you talking about?"

He gestured to the reception area. "Go and find out yourself. When you're finished, Armaeus is in his conference room at Prime Luxe."

"Conference room." I straightened, feeling inordinately better. You didn't put trauma victims in a conference room. That would be like double jeopardy. "Okay. I'll see—"

But Kreios was already gone. Rolling my eyes at the fact that every single member of the Council who'd mastered teleportation seemed inordinately fond of disappearing midsentence, I turned and trudged toward the reception area, straightening with a sad smile as the smaller of the two figures, the German shepherd Night, turned his muzzle toward me.

"Lainie," I said.

She turned as well. "You came," she murmured, sounding so much like Seamus McCarthy when he'd first seen me, I drew up short. "I didn't know if you would."

"Of course I came." I moved toward her and settled on the seat beside her, taking her hands in mine. "Why? What's happened?"

"It was something I saw," she said, her voice halting. "You, and those you work with, all of you such bright lights. But you're being tracked by shadows. Like you, but not you. I didn't understand, but I knew this wasn't right. I knew I had to tell you."

"Shadows," I echoed.

She nodded. "Like your seconds, or your doubles, but not quite that close. Still, they were very strong. And wherever they went..." She looked away, swallowed. "There was so much death."

I blew out a long breath, my mind scrambling through all the possibilities. I knew about Connected syndicates, of course. I'd been briefly part of one of them as head of the House of Swords, and the history of organized crime stretched deep into Connected history. It was only natural for people with unusual gifts to figure out a way to profit from those unusual gifts. Humans were nothing so much as human, and power...what had Death said? Something about power in the wrong hands being dangerous? Especially power that makes you feel like a god.

"You were right to come," I said. "And to warn me. We'll find these others and stop them. I promise. But right now, we're going to have to protect you too, Lainie. You and your family."

She nodded, dropping her hand to Night's back. "Mr. Kreios said the same thing. He said there would be a limo to take me...somewhere. At least for a few days. Until we can sort everything out."

"Good." I looked up, and sure enough, there was a sharply dressed chauffeur now standing at the entryway to the clinic's waiting room. He wasn't as fabulous as Nikki had been when she'd been pulling chauffeur duty, but then again, who would be?

Speaking of Nikki, I realized that in my shock and fear for Armaeus, she was still halfway around the world. And that...simply wouldn't do. I'd spent far too long these past few days without her by my side. I was done with that.

I helped Lainie to her feet, and the moment she was safely bundled into the limo, destined for Prime Luxe, I poofed back to St. Stephen's Green and found Nikki. Death was still MIA, and Simon had left the green, but I'd locate both of them later. For now, I returned with Nikki to Armaeus's conference room via fireball express.

The smile of relief and excitement I'd been busily composing on my face as I thought about reuniting with

Armaeus, however, was wiped clean away the moment I stepped into the room.

Nikki's arms immediately wrapped around me, holding me upright when my knees buckled. "What's this?" I gasped, recovering quickly to stride to the sickbed set up in the middle of the room, a sickbed clearly constructed for some kind of alien life form.

Or the Magician, in this case.

Kreios and Eshe stood at either end of the hospital bed, their eyes locked on one another, their hands outstretched. Electricity arced between them while Dr. Sells stood off to the side, her hands racing over a keyboard as data streamed across a portable monitor. Armaeus lay on the bed, or what I assumed was Armaeus, but skin no longer draped his body, and neither bones nor muscles nor veins made up his form. He was a pure mass of energy in an only vaguely humanoid form.

"What the hell?" I tried again.

"You need to tap into the vagus nerve," Dr. Sells snapped at me, her tone causing me to whip my head around. Naked fear rang in her voice. "You can see it, even in his current form. It's a nerve that stretches from the brain to the abdomen, contributing to all human function in a way we have not completely figured out. It's—it's the part glowing crimson."

"Okay," I said as I stepped forward again. "What'd he do to the nerve? Why is it so bright?"

"We don't exactly know. The Magician didn't make his intentions clear when he advised me this procedure he's directed me to perform had a success rate of 98.3% with 84.7% likelihood of unexpected complications that may result in a variance to the successful outcome that was, in short, unpredictable though with a greater likelihood of a positive than a negative result. He declined to give me exact numbers on that final percentage."

I blinked at her, my head spinning. "Of course he did. When was this?"

Kreios cut in. "When he told me you would be arriving at Dr. Sells's clinic and I should be there to greet you. That was two weeks ago."

"Two weeks ago?" None of this made any sense, but none of it mattered either. I could see the vagus nerve pulsing with crimson heat, and I lifted my arms, my hands igniting with my own combination of blue and red flame. "What is it exactly that I'm doing?"

"Vagus nerve stimulation," Dr. Sells said flatly. "This is completely uncharted territory in someone with the Magician's unique bodily makeup, so —"

So she had no better idea than I did, in short.

I didn't wait to hear more. I plunged my hands into the medical cocoon that Kreios and Eshe were maintaining, and reached through the faux body form of the Magician. Operating purely on instinct, I wrapped my hands around the vagus nerve and held on tight —

As I was electrocuted.

The explosion that racked my brain and body felt like every one of my molecules was being blasted into the stratosphere. I thought I heard screaming, I definitely smelled burning, but the overwhelming sensation I had was of the Magician flicking open his eyes, connecting to me with a wild untrammeled joy that I'd never seen in his face before. And I realized I was looking at a...fuller version of the Magician, a Magician who was *complete*, who was true and powerful and mighty and *complete*.

Agony ripped through me, an entire section of my body being torn away, sundered from the whole as a sense of deep and powerful loss and loneliness rocked me, the sensation so profound, I jerked my hands off Armaeus's vagus nerve and immediately slumped to the floor.

"Dollface," Nikki gasped. She rushed to my side, hauling me upright again, but my eyes were only for Armaeus. With her help, I staggered back to the bed, but Armaeus was there, he was *there* with a body and a face and hair and eyes. He looked up at Kreios and Eshe and at Dr. Sells, his brow furrowing only when he swung his gorgeous golden gaze to me. I sagged to Nikki's side, tears welling in my own eyes, so damned grateful that he was alive, that he was here, that he was back, that I could help him —

And then the Magician opened his mouth, his focus fully on me. When he spoke, his words were elegant, rich, and harrowingly succinct.

"Do I know you?"

CHAPTER THIRTY

I roused myself from the pane of glass, straightening as the door opened behind me. In the room beyond, nothing had changed. Armaeus still lay in a hospital bed, an entire fleet of monitors and machines whirring around him, a perfect symphony of data trackers and energy modulators and systems analyzers. According to Dr. Sells, Armaeus had ordered this suite custom-made for him…five years earlier. Long before he'd even met me.

Much longer still before he'd forgotten me.

No sooner had he recovered from the jolt back to a sort of awareness I'd made possible than he'd passed out again, his body shutting down everything but the most vital processes. Dr. Sells had ordered him moved to this suite, which Kreios and I had facilitated. Once connected up to every monitor known to man, technology I couldn't even hope to understand, he'd dropped even deeper into a coma. Kreios had departed immediately to brief the Council, but I'd remained here, sequestering myself in this dark observation room, my head against the glass.

Armaeus had left me. Completely.

The demigod lying in the room beyond me hadn't been completely unconscious, not the entire time he'd been transported and hooked up and processed and tested. He'd slipped in and out of awareness, long enough to speak with Kreios, Dr. Sells, whom he clearly still knew — and to turn his oddly golden eyes on me, questing and intrigued, but without a flicker of recognition. He'd asked Kreios a series of long and convoluted questions, he'd bossed Dr. Sells around as she'd hurriedly refined the room configuration, and he'd watched me like a bug. No one told him who I was, and I certainly didn't. How can you compress years of your life and entire lifetimes of your heart into a sound bite sandwiched between tersely ordered computer tutorials and logistical scanning? Eventually, I'd wandered off, more tired than I'd ever been in my life, until Dr. Sells had found me and shown me this room.

I didn't know how long I'd been here. Not days, certainly. Probably hours. Yet time seemed to flicker and jump, the same minute reliving itself over and over and over again, like it had in that room in Dublin, when I'd held Armaeus in my arms and imagined our lives together forever. How could everything have fallen apart so quickly?

"Sara."

The voice was a familiar and welcome one, but it still took me several long moments to drag my gaze away from the glass. Kreios stood in front of me, wearing a dark, official-looking suit, with a white shirt open at the collar, revealing his deeply bronzed skin. I blinked quickly, trying to make sense of what I was seeing. "You're looking…very stylish," I allowed.

"The Magician had arranged a particular protocol in the event of his temporary absence from the Council, a protocol that was invoked at the moment of his collapse."

"Good, good…" My gaze drifted back to Armaeus. "Has Death returned?"

Kreios shook his head. "No. But according to Simon and Tesla, both of whom are tracking the electrical currents circling the globe, there has been no great disruption to the earth's energy systems. So she's either hiding, or fighting something we can't track, or recovering somewhere."

"In Between?" I asked, not liking the sound of that.

"We simply don't know. Jimmy's gone too."

"Dammit…" I sighed. Jimmy would have told me if Death had been killed, I was certain. But him not being here made everything more complicated. "So now what?"

"For the foreseeable future, the Council will be led by myself and the Emperor."

I blinked. "You had me right up until the end there. Since when is the Emperor equipped to lead the Council?"

Kreios grimaced. "Since power broke along the lines of those interested in using the Council to guide the acts of humans and those members of the Council who still believe in the course of balance."

"Yeah, we weren't exactly balanced during what just went down in Dublin."

"And yet we were more balanced than what the Emperor has even now called for. We have Conal and Niall in custody, awaiting delivery to the proper authorities. Viktor is of the mind that the proper authorities is the Council itself, from which the two would be returned to the rightful place at the head of their cult."

"What? No," I protested, a spurt of adrenaline waking up my nerve endings. "That's a terrible idea. The exact same thing would happen just as soon as they regrouped. The Neo-Celts didn't learn anything from their little pre-Beltane demonstration. Most of them were knocked flat by the end of it and probably don't remember much at all."

"Exactly so. Another likely option is to return the brothers to the local authorities, who have no doubt assembled a list of indictments as long as their arms to level against them."

I pursed my lips. "That would be fine for Conal, but Niall is no shrinking violet. He'll be out of custody within twenty-four hours, and then we're back to where we started again."

"Option three is for Justice to do her job and bring the brothers to Judgment."

Narrowing my eyes, I glowered at him. "Was this entire little speech just a redirect to get me to go collect those asshats? Because I am *not* in the mood, Kreios."

"Not at all," he said, not bothering to hide his smile. "They are already at Gamon's door. But she cannot let them in without you there. So—"

Not wanting to miss my chance to play the hip new Council game, I disintegrated into a fiery poof before the Devil could finish his sentence.

I reappeared on an all too familiar ledge, a stark space open to the elements that looked like an entry bay to a Norwegian airplane hangar—if such a hangar were etched into the face of an icebound mountain. The wind was cold and bracing, which, along with the fact that I wasn't alone in this space, woke me up further.

Three figures stood waiting for me. Niall, Conal, and Gamon.

The brothers looked slightly worse for wear. Conal, I realized, was not completely awake. Instead, he was held up by some force of magic versus any ability of his own. Beside him, Niall stared at me with a curious peace in his eyes. Not defeat, peace. Gamon, for her part, looked her usual fierce self, her long black hair braided down her back, her attire the usual darkly hued combat gear and shit-kicker boots. Her hands were gloved and her expression unrelenting.

"Took you long enough," she muttered.

"You know, I was a little busy." I jerked my head toward Conal. "You do that to him?"

"No, I did." It was Niall who spoke, his voice tinged with sadness. "His entire life, Conal wanted nothing more than to be the knight errant. To lead the world into a more ordered, gracious, and chivalrous experience. To give people something worth fighting for with the return of reverence for the earth that has long since bled away."

"But he wasn't a Connected," I said.

"He was not, not at first. There was a spark of ability in him, to be sure, the nascent flame that exists in all of us. And perhaps that was even more fitting in the end. He was the champion of those who sought to reach beyond their station, drawing forth an ability they themselves could never claim without his aid. I was the Hallowed Knight, but never wanted the job, even after it became clear that it was mine to claim. Conal did. He always did. How could I not assist him?"

"People died, Niall," I said sharply.

"They died in the pursuit of a lofty ideal. Is that so wrong?"

I wasn't about to touch that one. "But he was a fraud. You were the one with the ability. You were the one who held the Connected skill that he promoted as his own."

"It was his, after a fashion." Niall shrugged. "I didn't have one-tenth of my brother's magnetic charm, nor his looks, nor arguably his youth when he first expressed magical ability."

"You mean when he first siphoned it off you."

He shrugged. "I didn't realize that was in the nature of my abilities until it happened, and Conal was so elated, so beside himself with joy, I had no interest in popping that balloon. As a younger child, he was given to great bouts of depression at the state of the world, and so giving him the gift of hope was something any brother would've done."

"And your falling-out?"

"Necessary to establish his place of primacy," Niall said, as if this was the most logical thing in the world.

"You called the ancient gods back to Earth," I said, speaking as slowly and succinctly as possible. "You both did. That's not the mark of sane men."

"It was my charge to do so, instilled in my very bones by the ancient gods. Conal only wanted to help people grasp the power within themselves, much as I wanted to help him nurture the tiny flame that he was born with. My power was so much greater than his, but his vision was well beyond anything I could have conceived. And so he taught the people to believe, and, being Irish as we are, he turned to the old ways to find the stories that would help them believe. And the very land responded. People came bearing gifts, symbols of the old ways, stories he could not discount. Genuine miracles of faith and healing."

"The Fermanagh dirt." I couldn't deny the fact that Niall had helped save Nikki's life. That didn't excuse his other behavior, but...it complicated matters.

"A perfect example. That soil has been there for thousands of years, and it is only now that science is willing to believe enough to test it and see that yes, in fact, it has healing properties. The people who live on that land have never needed scientific tests to know that it was true. They needed only to use it and believe in it."

I grimaced. "That's a very dangerous line. You could say the same about any religious icon or even Tinker Bell. Without the scientific test to back it up, it's just a fairy tale."

"But fairy tales so often have their roots in truth, do they not?" He hesitated. "One thing I'm sure you figured out that I did not realize. Why I had to step in with that Fermanagh soil…"

"I got it," I said, holding up a hand. "Conal was behind the poisoning. I just don't understand how. That kid with the card…?"

"Was no mere child, Justice Wilde. Nor the lasses with their bubbles. They were the wee people, the fairies. Loaned to Conal for the express purpose of paving the way of the Tuatha dé Danann back to the world of light. Conal wanted to be sure the poison took, though he'd no idea what its longer-range effects would be. He took every step he could."

"He used the fairy folk?"

"I would've counseled against it if I'd known his plans. But he was already secretly in contact with the Tuath Dé by then, and well…" Another shrug. "You know what they say. Any man can lose his hat in a fairy wind."

"But why Nikki? Why did Conal attack her, not simply me? She was no threat to him."

Niall sighed. "That's not true, I'm afraid. Nikki Dawes represents the one non-Council member still alive for whom you would lay down your life—your life and your cause and the Council itself, if it came to it. Conal intended Nikki Dawes to be a vessel for the

Fomorian, eventually. They were supposed to find her in the In Between, which the fairies opened for her, singing her into the shadows. He intended to be able to control her, knowing you would never kill her if you thought she could be saved, not even to destroy the gods within her. I...in the end, that was not something I could allow." His smile was soft, even sad. "Love and life are such precious things, you see, in this world or any other."

I could only gape at him as he turned to Judgment, who'd been watching silently this whole time. "So it is up to you to judge us, I see. The Morrígan herself."

Gamon studied him with her flat gaze. "I would've pushed you off a ledge a long time ago, buddy. But there are protocols to follow, and my job is to put you through those protocols. How you and your little brother do is much more up to you than anything to do with me. I just have the ability to make your stay ever so slightly more pleasant, or not so much."

Niall had the grace to pale slightly, but said nothing. He knew what he'd done, and he wasn't apologizing for it. He wasn't apologizing for his brother, either.

"Niall, you have to understand, your way is not the right way," I pressed, locking up his revelation about the poison in a box of crazy to be reopened...never.

"And the Council's is?" he shot back.

I winced, thinking of the Council being run even in part by Viktor Dal. "Not always. But there must be a way for all of us to coexist, or none of us will survive. This isn't a matter of pushing the old gods out and keeping them that way, this is a matter of reconciling all the new gods we've created and finding a way for us all to live together. Your way, Conal's way, would have caused bloodshed. You know it would. And it would've been the innocents who died in the end."

Niall nodded, something shifting in his face. "Coexistence. I will think on that during Judgment Gamon's...protocols. Which I have richly earned."

A scraping noise sounded behind us, and we all turned, the gates of Gamon's own personal Valhalla finally opening. She cracked a mirthless smile as she nodded toward Niall. "Congratulations, your stay might not be quite as miserable as I'd hoped. Scoop up your brother and follow me."

As tenderly as any older brother, Niall did as he was told, folding Conal's body up in his arms. Before he turned to follow Gamon, though, he glanced back at me, his face alight with awe. Awe...and something perhaps even stronger.

"She is the Morrígan, the queen of warriors," he murmured, his words enraptured. "That makes her my fated mate."

I glanced between him and Gamon, a sudden and completely incongruous spurt of laughter struggling to escape. I managed to hold it in until the door slammed shut behind them, then sighed.

"Well done, Sara Wilde."

"Were you here that whole time?"

Kreios stepped out of the shadows. "There were some truths that needed to be spoken, some desires that needed to be shared. I live to serve."

I glanced back at him, going still as I noticed the envelope in Kreios's hands.

"What's that?"

"This is an envelope that was lying on Armaeus's desk when I returned from the Council briefing. It contained a letter addressed to you."

"Oh." I reached for it, absurdly relieved. "So he knew this was going to happen to him. Like he knew where to tell you to find me when I arrived from Dublin."

Kreios lifted the envelope out of reach. "He did, yes. But he wrote this letter in 1478."

My hand froze as Kreios continued. "The envelope also contained a second letter, addressed to me, though of course, I also was not alive at the time of its writing. I've had Simon analyze the paper and the ink, and it's authentic. The envelope itself was an illusion, a package alone, spelled into reality by, presumably, the events of this day."

"So the letters weren't addressed to us, specifically, but to whom? Justice and the Devil?" I spoke the words woodenly, hope dwindling within me. There was too much about the Magician I didn't understand. I had known that all along, but I'd always assumed that there would be time for that discovery.

Now, I was no longer sure.

Kreios nodded. "These writings are more than five hundred years old, and the penmanship is definitely Armaeus's, for all that the phrasings are archaic. I took the liberty of Simon deciphering both pieces. I hope you don't mind."

"Of course not," I murmured. I wasn't sure I would have been able to temper my frustration if I'd opened up a letter written in Old English. I would've been able to translate, but there were too many words and phrases that would have confused and obfuscated Armaeus's original intentions, and I had no time for that.

I had no time.

"The notes were short but surprisingly clear once they were broken down to the core information. Armaeus made a decision in 1478 to break apart his psyche and stuff a series of memories down a very dark hole. He did this to ensure the safety of the balance of magic in the world during a very bleak time in human history."

"I can't imagine the 1400s had much to recommend them."

"No," Kreios agreed, "but the Magician, being the Magician, left a codicil. If he ever needed to recover those memories, he would put in place a finder of consummate skill and speed, who would not only recover that which had been lost but who could make him whole."

"He said that," I deadpanned. "In 1478."

"He did."

The chill of Gamon's frozen aerie disintegrated around us, and once more we were in the shadowy observation room, overlooking Armaeus's inert body. Even without the benefit of my third eye, I could tell he was so deep down in his own psyche that there would be no pulling him back out. He'd prepared for all this. He'd worked and conjured and prepared.

"But why did you forget me?" I whispered, looking out over Armaeus's still form. "What could possibly have led you to do that?"

Kreios stepped up next to me, laying a light hand on my shoulder, reassuring and certain at once.

"I don't know, Sara Wilde," he said softly, his richly accented words a balm to my ragged nerves. "But after all the years I've known him, I can tell you this. The Magician always has a plan."

~~~

Thank you so much for reading THE HALLOWED KNIGHT! If you enjoyed this book, reviews are the life's blood of an author, and I would sincerely appreciate yours wherever you bought this book!

ALSO: Interested in learning more about the Tarot, upcoming book releases, and other bits of arcana and mayhem? Get Connected (heh) and sign up for my mailing list at www.jennstark.com/newsletter!

~~~

A Note From Jenn

The Knight of Pentacles isn't generally the kind of guy who will bring about the destruction of the world, honestly! Turn the page for an interpretation about the Knight of Pentacles that will ensure you welcome his arrival to your reading!

The Knight of Pentacles

As I've shared before, court cards are generally about people—the ones you know, the ones you'll meet, or possibly even yourself. The Knight of Pentacles, however, has some unique characteristics beyond his suit. Knights specifically are cards of action, from slow and steady (Pentacles!) to racing ahead at full throttle (Swords). So this Knight in your reading is all about the reassurance that your world is going to move forward at a pace you can manage, and that you will be rewarded financially if you take things slow and smart, versus moving forward at full throttle. When a person, the Knight of Pentacles is often a quiet, stable younger man, sometimes with very strong opinions, very much the epitome of "still waters move deep." You won't want to rush this person, but you'll know they will be there for you through thick and thin! (And, bonus, they'll be good with money!) So if you draw the Knight of Swords in your next reading, ease up on the gas, take a deep breath, and know that money, safety, and good health is rolling toward you, slowly but surely!

Acknowledgments

Writing THE HALLOWED KNIGHT has been one of my favorite adventures, as I have a soft spot in my heart for Ireland (and I hope you do, too!) Thank you to all my readers for continuing to read my books, which allows me to spin these tales for you. I remain truly grateful to Elizabeth Bemis for her beautiful work on my books and my site—especially my gorgeous series covers. My editorial team of Linda Ingmanson and Toni Lee continue their tireless efforts on my behalf as well. Any mistakes in the manuscript are most definitely my own. Thank you to Edeena Cross and Sabra Harp for their brilliant beta reads, and to Kristine Krantz, who once again survived my early drafts. And, of course, thank you, Geoffrey, forever and always. It's been a *Wilde* ride.

ABOUT JENN STARK

Jenn Stark is an award-winning author of paranormal romance and urban fantasy. She lives and writes in Ohio. . . and she definitely loves to write. In addition to her Immortal Vegas and Wilde Justice urban fantasy series and Demon Enforcers paranormal romance series, she is also author Jennifer McGowan, whose Maids of Honor series of Young Adult Elizabethan spy romances are published by Simon & Schuster, and author Jennifer Chance, whose Rule Breakers series of New Adult contemporary romances are published by Random House/LoveSwept and whose modern royals series, Gowns & Crowns, is now available.

You can find her online at jennstark.com, follow her on Twitter @jennstark, and visit her on Facebook at facebook.com/authorjennstark.